THE AUTHORS

Caryl Brahms (Doris Caroline Abrahams) was born in Surrey in 1901, into a colourful, Sephardic Jewish family who had come from Turkey a generation earlier. She was educated privately before studying at the Royal Academy of Music. She began to write for the *Evening Standard*, then the *Daily Telegraph*, where she was ballet correspondent. Her first book, *Footnotes to the Ballet*, appeared in 1936, and her long partnership with S. J. Simon, fellow lodger in London, started in 1937. After his death she continued to write and then, in the late 1950s, began a second remarkable partnership, with Ned Sherrin, who edited her posthumously published memoirs, *Too dirty for the Windmill*. A governor of the National Theatre, Caryl Brahms remained a forceful figure in the theatrical world until her death in 1982.

S. J. Simon (Seca Jascha Skidelsky) was born in 1904 in Harbin, Manchuria, into an equally idiosyncratic White Russian Jewish family. During his lifetime he was famous as a bridge player – representative of Great Britain in numerous championships, joint inventor of the Acol System, and author of the classic *Why You Lose at Bridge*. His wife, Carmel Withers, was also an international bridge player. He died in London in 1948.

Brahms and Simon published their first book together, *A Bullet in the Ballet*, in 1937 and followed this hit with a series of comic ballet thrillers, including *Casino for Sale* (1938). During the war they turned to 'backstairs history', producing hilarious versions of the past in books like *Don't, Mr Disraeli!* (1940) and *No Bed for Bacon* (1941). The close, if occasionally turbulent, partnership of these 'Lunatics of Genius', with their bubbling wit and fantastic invention, is unique in British comic writing.

The Hogarth Press also publishes *A Bullet in the Ballet* and *No Bed for Bacon*.

CASINO FOR SALE

Caryl Brahms & S. J. Simon

'The Provinces exceed anything that could be put into
a novel. Never will a novelist invent the incident
of the wife of a Major of *Gendarmerie* putting into verses
the Vicar's sermons.'
The Goncourt Journals

*New Introduction by
Ned Sherrin*

THE HOGARTH PRESS
LONDON

Published in 1987 by
The Hogarth Press
Chatto & Windus Ltd
30 Bedford Square, London WCIB 3RP

First published in Great Britain by Michael Joseph Ltd 1938
Hogarth edition offset from Michael Joseph 1952 edition
Copyright Caryl Brahms and S. J. Simon 1938
Introduction copyright © Ned Sherrin 1987

British Library Cataloguing in Publication Data

Brahms, Caryl
Casino for Sale
I. Title   II. Simon, S.J.
823'.912[F]   PR6001.B6

ISBN 0 7012 0771 X

Printed in Great Britain by
Cox & Wyman Ltd
Reading, Berkshire

INTRODUCTION

Casino for Sale, known in America as *Murder à la Stroganoff*, was the second novel on which Caryl Brahms and S. J. Simon collaborated. They had met a few years before when they were both living in a student's home run by a friend of Caryl's mother in the Finchley Road, London. She had finished her studies at the Royal Academy of Music (failed L.R.A.M.) and was beginning to make a surreptitious career as a journalist, critic and light versifier for *Time and Tide* and the *Evening Standard*. Unwilling to risk parental disapproval, particularly her mother's, she adopted Caryl Brahms as her pseudonym – also useful because, in an age when women journalists felt that there might be prejudice against them, it had a more androgynous aspect than Doris Caroline Abrahams.

S. J. Simon, her fellow lodger, was a White Russian who had been born in Harbin, Manchuria, in 1904. He was working part-time as a host at a bridge club (not the Acol, where he was frequently to be found) and, in Caryl's words in her memoir, *Too dirty for the Windmill* (published by Constable in 1986), 'like all Russians he was studying forestry'. She devised the appropriate pen-name for him. Sacha (or Simon) Jascha Skidelsky – known as 'Skid' – metamorphosed into the more manageable S. J. Simon. In the middle of the thirties the Home Page of the *Standard* found an extra chore for Brahms to add to the light verse she was already contributing. The paper owned the rights to some drawings by David Low of a dog whom he had created 'to scamper among the manic Hitlers and frog-like Mussolinis'. Caryl was detailed to write captions to go with them. 'At first we called the dog Mussolini, but then the Italian Embassy complained to our editor, so we changed it to "Musso": "Musso the Home-Page Dog". After a while I found it impossible to think of something new for Musso each day, so I roped in Skid.'

From this collaboration they moved on to their first novel, *A Bullet in the Ballet* (published in 1937), which, having been received guardedly by their publisher as 'dangerously two-stoolish', was welcomed enthusiastically by the press. Caryl remembered its reception as mixed, but Howard Spring in the *Evening Standard* found it 'a better murder mystery than nine novels out of ten of its sort because it is packed with humour, because it pulls the leg of solemnity both in "detection" and in ballet-mongering'. The *News Chronicle* judged it, 'one of the funniest stories I have ever read' and for the *Times Literary Supplement*, 'the book stands out for shockingness and merriment'. With a cast of ready-made characters to hand, Brahms and Simon immediately looked around for a new background against which to set them. They had become attached to Stroganoff, the impresario, Arenskaya, the star dancer dwindling into a teacher, Nevajno, the choreographer of the future, Ernest Smithsky, the English dancer who, in another of their memorable phrases was 'no Nijinsky', and Inspector Adam Quill, who leads the reader into the exotic, hot-house ballet world. The events of *A Bullet in the Ballet* took place during a London Ballet Season. For *Casino for Sale* the Ballet Stroganoff are transplanted to the south of France and the faded resort of La Bazouche, A.M., where an advertisement offering 'CASINO À VENDRE. *Occasion Unique*' proves irresistible to Stroganoff.

The setting was familiar to both authors. The casino scenes delighted Simon who was a keen gambler and was even more interested in the tricks and systems of those who played the tables. (Apart from bridge he was also devoted to dog racing, permanently optimistic that his *new* system, which could be as simplistic as averting his eyes from the track while the race was being run, was infallible.) For Caryl, the south of France was a home from home. Her mother was an invalid and spent a good deal of time there. 'We moved like pampered gypsies, surrounded by servants, from Villefranche to Monte Carlo and back.' Here as a child she had seen early ballet companies playing in the sort of casino theatres she and Simon later used in *Casino for Sale*, but they were something of a let-down after her dancing classes in Masonic rooms in Essex. She wrote:

Music became my world's foundation – the extended line of the dancer was the poetry in this pilgrim's unpredicted progress. When the Diaghilev Ballet left London at the end of six or eight weeks' season, I grieved; but each winter my parents went to the south of France in search of sunshine to lessen my mother's asthma, where I would join them for the hols. It had been here that my mother first took me to see the Diaghilev Ballet at the Casino. Someone with a difficult Russian name was appearing in a ballet called by a difficult French name. I was terribly disappointed. It wasn't at all like my dancing class. Fortunately, they were dancing *Les Sylphides* on my next visit, which did much to restore Diaghilev to my favour. I felt that this ballet of tulle-clad dancers floating in the moonlight was a bit more like the Masonic rooms – and in the shades I see the pale faces of the great Diaghilev and the genius Fokine wince.

In spite of the success of *A Bullet in the Ballet* the partners had not been entirely happy about their method.

In *Bullet* the Brahms-Simon mix was all too apparent. Skid took over the detection and the love scenes, and I did the ballet bits. Together we wrote the narrative. Thereafter we were to write all of our novels together save for the occasional descriptive passage which I would write. The work progressed bumpily, punctuated by Woodbine cigarettes and frequent cups of tea amid storms of wild laughter. Inevitably, Skid being Skid, it started late. It was like a long, laughing, wrangling conversation with both of us jumping in on one another. We would speak lines to each other and laugh at our own jokes until one of us stopped and said 'out'.

There were hiccoughs on the way. When they first presented the book to their publisher he spotted the murderer a few pages after he had opened it so they had to invent another killer and go back and re-distribute clues and red herrings appropriately. Once again, Caryl considered the press reaction to be mixed but the *Observer* called the book 'funnier than their richly funny *A Bullet in the Ballet*'. *Punch* congratulated them on having 'created a really comical figure' in Stroganoff. The *Daily Telegraph* found it 'far funnier than life', and for the

News Chronicle it was 'funny enough to make a professional critic break from time to time into yelps of laughter'.

Of the ten other novels which they wrote together only *Six Curtains for Stroganova* was entirely concerned with the Ballet Stroganoff but in 1980, thirty-two years after Simon's sudden death in 1948, Caryl Brahms published four short stories in her collection of *Stroganoff in Company*, one of which she had written with Simon in the mid-forties. The others were her own, written in the seventies. 'A Contract in the Ballet' covers a disastrous Stroganoff season in New York. In 'A Bishop in the Ballet' the company are innocently involved in a drug-smuggling plot. In 'A Brabble in the Ballet' they are at Monte Carlo. ('A Brabble', according to Dr. Johnson's Dictionary, is 'a clamorous contest. A squabble. A broil'. A perfect word for the Ballet Stroganoff.) For 'A Kidnap in the Ballet' they are back at La Bazouche, the scene of *Casino for Sale*.

La Bazouche is by no means Cannes. It is not even Menton or Monte Carlo, being smaller than either. but it can boast a Casino Municipal. Moreover it can rely upon its alert and energetic Sûreté.

'Ballet Company,' the officer was saying, 'called after some Rousski dish.'

'Piroshki?' suggested the new man, keen as French mustard.

'Stroganoff,' his superior remembered. 'Last time he was here there was trouble . . .'

It is this trouble which Inspector Quill investigates in *Casino for Sale*.

Ned Sherrin, London 1986

CHAPTER I

CASINO À VENDRE. Occasion Unique.

CASINO FOR SALE. Original Opportunity.

Apply at once

Baron Sam de Rabinovitch,

89 Boulevard Sens Unique,

La Bazouche, A.M.

TIENS!' said Vladimir Stroganoff, slapping his bald dome with an inspired hand. 'Ça c'est une idée.'

A casino, he explained to the startled stranger in the *Club des Imprésarios*, was a certain source of wealth. With the fabulous profits that would roll in from the roulette and baccarat he would at last be able to endow the Ballet Stroganoff with the magnificence that had always been his dream. He was off to buy it at once, before somebody forestalled him. Had the stranger by chance a time-table to lend him?

* * *

'Sign here,' said Baron Sam de Rabinovitch with a strong sense of astonished frustration. Delighted as he was to get rid of his old Casino so easily, he could not avoid an undercurrent of bitterness that it had been achieved without the aid of the convincing sales talk he had spent so many hours in preparing. But the bald-headed gentleman who had rushed into his office without knocking had given him no chance to get going.

'You received my telegram—no?' he panted.

The Baron had indeed received a rather breathless telegram that morning. It read:

'DO NOTHING TILL I COME. WAIT. STROGANOFF.'

'You are M'sieur Stroganoff?'

The bald dome nodded happily. 'It is I. You have heard of me—no?'

'No.'

'You have not heard of the Ballet Stroganoff?'

The bald dome shook off an obvious bewilderment. 'Poof,' he said, 'it matters nothing, for now I buy the Casino. My lawyer he come to-morrow but we do not wait. How mooch?'

Baron de Rabinovitch had not yet grasped the full possibilities of the situation but he had grasped them sufficiently to approve the last sentence. Taking a lightning decision he passed over his best cigars. Stroganoff absently stuffed one in his pocket.

'This I smoke later,' he announced. 'But now I buy the Casino. How mooch?'

Cautiously the Count named his first figure.

'It is cheap,' said Stroganoff to his horror, 'but I buy just the same.'

Ten minutes later he was signing document after document with lightning speed. Baron de Rabinovitch watched him broodingly. He could not decide whether he was elated or depressed.

*   *   *

'Voilà!' said Stroganoff with a last triumphant flourish of his pen. 'The Casino it is mine. I go to look at it immediate.'

And leaving the Baron de Rabinovitch suspended between two breaths, he strode from the room, darted across the boulevard and halted in rapture before a pendulum of workmen dangling in front of a festoon of windows. Gloatingly he advanced upon the chromium plated door and grasped the handle only to ricochet into the arms of the Baron who had followed him out,

'The key,' said Stroganoff eagerly.

The Baron was slightly anxious, but the feel of Stroganoff's pink slip in his pocket gave him courage.

'This,' he said, 'is the Casino Buttonhooke.'

Stroganoff goggled at him. Somewhere he had heard that name before. Suddenly he remembered. It was the man who borrowed his ballerinas. A grim foreboding began to steal over him.

'But where,' he asked weakly, 'is my Casino?'

'Taxi,' said Baron de Rabinovitch triumphantly.

CHAPTER II

THE collection of pained-looking palms, tiled turrets, and *Lotissements à Vendre* notices known as La Bazouche A.M. might have served for the décor of a ballet—Plage Fleurie. A *décor*, set by an absentminded *Régisseur*, who had forgotten to send out for the flowers, and was making do with property orange trees.

Designed as a background for loitering fashion, Le Bazouche hopefully borders a stretch of the Mediterranean, as blue, as rock-threaded, and as inaccessible as any other Edwardian fashion resort. But the laggard call-boy must have forgotten to round up the more exclusive players, for only egg-faced walkers-on, in guise of the petite bourgeoisie, are to be seen trailing stoically about the bijou harbour and the promenade[1] obviously wishing that the sun would come out. That *Régisseur* again! For though each night he was at pains to cover the cyclorama with as neat a design in pin-point stars as is to be found anywhere between San Remo and Hyères, he frequently appears to mislay the warm amber orb beneath which the visitor to the French Riviera expensively browns. In addition to the stark promenade, the tiny port, and the orgy of effer-vescent architecture which is the *Ville*—tram-riddled and narrowly paved—there is the *paysage*. Those stairs-for-giants, by means of which thrifty peasants have cultivated the sur-rounding mountains. These are mostly given over to grey-green carnations, still in the leaf, or green-grey olive trees.

Add to these natural advantages the *Hôtel Moins-Magnifique* —500 *chambres en face de la mer*.

On a sunny day the terrace bears a luxuriant crop of multi-

[1] *des Anglais*, of course.

10

coloured mushrooms, beneath which the star players in this fascinating production are wont to sit and wait for their drinks. This afternoon it was not raining.

The Beard on the hotel terrace looked sympathetic. Not that it would have mattered if it had looked formidable, for Stroganoff was in no mood to notice shades of expression. He flung himself furiously into the chair opposite.

'I have been swindle,' he announced.

'Assurément,' agreed the Beard courteously.

'I buy a Casino and—poof!—it is the wrong one.'

Somewhat miraculously the Beard seemed to follow this sketchy scenario.

'You mean that Baron de Rabinovitch has sold you his Casino by the sea.'

'I do not believe that he is Baron,' said Stroganoff violently. 'But I buy the Casino—yes. I am the innocent. I do not know that Buttonhooke have the Casino here already. I do not discover until I sign everything.'

'But you must have noticed the new Casino as you drove from the station?' said the Beard. 'You can't avoid noticing it.'

'I notice it,' agreed Stroganoff, 'but, naturellement, I think it is this Casino that I buy. And the price seem so little that I sign at once before the Baron he ask more.'

It took a few minutes more for the Beard to digest this tale of high finance while the author of it waved his hands furiously at an oblivious waiter. 'Pourcentage' Citrolo, journalist, ballet critic, cynic, blackmailer, and potential corpse, was used to dealing with fools and eccentrics. This one seemed to be both. Furthermore his face was familiar.

'This,' exploded the familiar face, 'is insupportable. First there is the slow journey. Then the stationmaster who do not believe I lose my ticket. Then I am swindle. And now the waiter he take no notice. Never, since Arenskaya decide she want to dance "Giselle," has there been such a day.'

The card index which served as Citrolo's memory clicked over and stopped at the right place.

'You are then Vladimir Stroganoff?' it indicated.

Stroganoff was pleased. 'You know my ballet?'

'Of course.'

'You attended my season in London?' asked Stroganoff hopefully.

'Alas, no!'

'It was superb,' said Stroganoff. 'You were in Paris maybe?'

'Unfortunately, no.'

'In Vienna, Belgrade, Sofia?'

'I was in Marseilles last week.'

'Oh,' said Stroganoff, dimmed. 'You realize,' he explained hastily, 'that we were not at the strength complete?'

'I realize,' said Citrolo tactfully, 'that you have a dancer there of great promise.'

'The little Ostorojño? She is my discovery. It was,' said Stroganoff, 'the flaire magnificent. When first I see her, she is in class in Holland Park. No fouetté—no développé—only a mother. I interest myself in the child. I send her to Paris. I get her best teachers. I even listen while the mother she talks. And how that child develop. Blum he is astonished. De Basil enchanted. Even Massine remark her. But it is I who have the contract.' A shade of gloom crossed his face. 'But her mother she now say that she break because in Marseilles the press it is not sympathetic. Maybe,' said the broadminded Stroganoff, 'it is possible that our performance there left a little to be desired, but is that, I demand you, a reason why the critics they write as though my ballet it always dance like that?'

But to Stroganoff's surprise Citrolo did not appear to agree.

'A critic,' he said, 'is concerned only with that performance which is taking place before his eyes.'

'Poof,' said Stroganoff, 'the critics write what the owner of the paper tell them.'

'But not Citrolo,' said the critic majestically. 'It is well known that Pavlo Citrolo has never written a line that was not his sincere opinion.'

The name seemed to impress Stroganoff more than the credo. He delved into his pocket to produce a newspaper cutting.

'It is you, then, the criminal who has written this?'

Citrolo bowed.

Stroganoff did not bow back. Instead he drew himself to his full height and tried to quell Citrolo with a look. Unfortunately, Citrolo wasn't playing. His eyes had wandered down the terrace where a neat ankle, a jaunty hat, and a portable typewriter were hurrying towards him. Coming closer, the ingredients consolidated into anxious blue eyes under a froth of curls. Stroganoff looked at them in some annoyance.

'Go away, Galybchik,'[1] he said.

Galybchik took no notice. After three months as Stroganoff's secretary, August Greene was used to being told to go away.

'Am I in time?' she asked eagerly.

'Too early,' said Stroganoff, 'much!'

'We mustn't buy the Casino,' said Galybchik. 'That beastly Buttonhooke has built a better one almost next to it.'

Stroganoff glared. 'Why do you not tell me this before I buy?'

'You've bought it?' wailed Galybchik.

'Naturellement, I bought it,' said Stroganoff, 'it is the ruin absolute. Unless,' he added, always hopeful, 'I find someone to take it from me.' He looked at Citrolo. Citrolo shook his head.

'Oh, dear,' said Galybchik, and sat down suddenly. She was crying. Citrolo, loath to miss an opportunity, patted her sympathetically—not quite on the shoulder. Absently she tried to slap his face, missed by a mile, and went on crying.

Stroganoff watched the scene in some confusion. He did not quite know what to do next.

Down the vista came Nicolas Nevajno, choreographer of the future, wrapt in his latest creation. He saw the group, brooded his way to their table, sat down, gulped Stroganoff's Cinzano and continued his meditations.

'Garçon,' said Stroganoff urgently.

'Ssssh,' pleaded Galybchik, 'Nicolas is thinking.'

'Stop him,' said Stroganoff, 'else he will have the idea superb

[1] Russian for 'Little Darling.'

for new ballet, and whenever Nicolas he have the idea superb it cost money.'

But it was too late. Genius was visibly working.

'This place,' he said, 'fills me with a depression profound. The tasteless building. The little stifling streets, the sea that is like a picture postcard—it is worse than a Golovin. There is no rhythm, no Gesamtkunstwerk. It is not symbolic of anything.'

'But it has two Casinos,' said Stroganoff, 'and I have bought the wrong one.'

Nevajno brushed this trifle aside.

'Never has dejection grasped me so firmly. But I suffer it gladly. It is in my depressions that I work best. It was from just such a womb that "Boutique Infame" was born. Who knows but out of this morass of gloom will be born an even greater masterpiece.' He paused for his effect. ' "Plage Bourgeoise." '

'Wonderful,' cried Galybchik.

'It will be the success superb and make for Stroganoff much money. So,' said Nevajno, suddenly practical, 'you schange me small scheque?'

'No,' said Stroganoff.

'Per'aps,' said Nevajno, noticing Citrolo for the first time, 'you do me this favour?'

Citrolo did not trouble to reply.

'Do I not tell you,' said Stroganoff, 'that we are the ruin? We buy the Casino, and Buttonhooke he have a better.'

'Then why we buy it?' asked Nevajno, rather confused.

Galybchik explained the situation patiently but Nevajno was still puzzled. In what way, he enquired, was the Casino Buttonhooke superior to the other? He had passed by both and didn't like either.

Citrolo went into some practical details which in their cumulative effect reduced Stroganoff to the verge of tears, but the genius was not even listening.

'You forget,' he said, 'that there is one asset Stroganoff possess that Buttonhooke has not.'

'What?' asked Galybchik agog.

'Me,' said Nevajno.

With a clatter the table fell to the floor. Stroganoff was on his feet, his eyes shining, all his depression forgotten.

'But you are right,' he cried, 'I am stupid. What matters it to me that Buttonhooke has the buildings, the publicity, the millions? It is I who have the Ballet Stroganoff.'

'So what?' said Citrolo.

'It is not the millions that make the success. It is the artistic directions. Buttonhooke—poof! Casino Buttonhooke—poof!'

He paused on the eve of a portentous announcement.

'I bring to Bazouchka my ballet!'

'Bravo!' cried Galybchik.

CHAPTER III

THREE months have sped energetically on their way since the waiter cleared the empty glasses that had been confidently raised to the new management.

Though it must be admitted that during this period of intense activity the Casino Buttonhooke prospered, it can also be claimed that the Casino Stroganoff has not yet failed.

For every six sables that sweep their accompanied path through the portals of Casino Buttonhooke, a dyed squirrel finds its way to the Casino by the sea. Stakes at the Casino Stroganoff are smaller than those wagered '*au Cercle Button'ooke*,' but they were just as passionately pledged. Buttonhooke, it is true, has the world of fashion reclining about his roulette wheel—a soupçon of royalty suspended above the flick of a card. But the Casino by the sea opened out a number of fascinating vistas for Stroganoff to play with.

His pet innovation was his school for Croupiers. Every morning at half-past eleven, while Arenskaya was giving his Ballerinas hell at her classe de perfectionnement, a waxed moustache surmounted by a glassy eye gave languid lessons in throwing and raking to a prentice personnel. This proved to be quite a good scheme until Buttonhooke meanly riposted with a glib manual 'POINTS FOR PUNTERS' and immediately the attendance fell off.

As a slogan: 'TOUT LE MONDE GAGNE CHEZ STROGANOFF' was hard put to it to compete with the calculated propaganda emanating from the Buttonhooke Press with its tentacles spreading to Paris, New York and Berlin.

Each night the horizon blushed under the cherry-coloured

Neon assertions of the Direction Buttonhooke, while the single ejaculation 'NEVAJNO' flashing defiantly from the Casino by the sea kept only the ballet-lover away.

Each morning saw a notice posted back stage on the board of the Stroganoff theatre. *Casino Call* 15 *heures.*

Members of the company, who could be snatched from whatever rehearsal was furiously being waged at the hour in question, were pressed into service as walkers-on during the slack session in the rooms, and though this involved the management in some elaborate book-keeping, the net effect was good.

Kurt Kukumber, as befitted a methodical gambler, always arrived at the rooms early. He would take up his seat within easy vision of the wheel, open his notebook, and pass the next forty minutes in annotating and recording, until, statistics collected, he was ready to start his infallible system. At five o'clock he would leave—broke—and wander off in search of a prospect to supply him with funds for to-morrow.

To-day his luck was rather better. It was already a quarter past five and he still had ten francs left. Hopefully he pushed a *jeton* on twenty-five. A lean hand reached over and removed it.

'It is foolish what you do,' said Nevajno to the switched round glare, 'I cannot bear to see you lose your money any longer on a method so devoid of line. The roulette wheel it has a rhythm dynamic: the numbers they like to emerge in the plasticity irrevocable. Never would fate be so unbalanced in design as to allow twenty-five to follow fourteen.'

'Vingt cinq,' said the croupier.

'Excuse me,' said Nevajno, 'an appointment.'

Twenty-five had brought luck to Stroganoff's star dancer, Olga Ostorojno. She gathered in her counters, and turned her sleek dark head to flash a grateful smile at that dubious rake, Citrolo, standing behind her. She even thought for a moment what a nice man he was.

Citrolo, who had been thinking for quite a long time what a nice girl she was, smiled back at her and suggested a cocktail. Experience should have made him wary of ballerinas; he had

known many and actually married one, the famous Dyra
Dyrakova, who had divorced him even before he had had time
to be unfaithful. But ballerinas still fascinated him, and this
one, so young, so eager, and probably so easy, attracted him
strongly. Besides he had not yet met her mother. He was,
however, destined to meet her very shortly.

No sooner had Ostorojno accepted his invitation to a glass
of champagne than the fat woman beside her turned round and
forbade it. Olga did not argue. Neither, after one look, did
Citrolo. Obstinacy was visible in every feature of Madame
Ostorojno. It showed, too, in her gambling. Relentlessly she
had been backing her daughter's age until even the kindhearted
Dutchman next to her was moved to plead with her.

'Please, madame, try another number.'

Madame Ostorojno glared and pushed a further *jeton* on
eighteen.

The croupier regarded her wonderingly. Almost he felt
tempted to put the lady's stake in his pocket and stand the loss
himself if a miracle occurred. Dino Vanilla had a contempt for
all punters. He had a contempt for everybody who was willing
to gamble the wrong side of a percentage, and more especially
for the system-mongers who tried to cajole the laws of mathe-
matics into getting the sum wrong. He himself had no objection
to an investment with the market rigged, the horse doped, or
the pack stacked; but until somebody invented a method of
regulating a roulette wheel, the game held no appeal for him.
In happier days, before an incautious description of Mussolini
as a Socialist had run him out of Italy, he had served his
apprenticeship under that Prince of Manipulators, 'Banco'
Dacarpo, and though he had not had time to finish the course,
he was efficient enough at any rate for the clientele of La
Bazouche, unsuspicious souls who attached no special signific-
ance to the angle at which the tie tilted at an accomplice, and
did not even comment on his elaborate shuffling of the packs
that were placed in the Baccarat Shoe. How they amused him—
the suckers!

'Dix-huit,' he said evilly. 'Pardon—trente cinq.'

'Let us,' said Citrolo, 'escape to the bar while your maman is engaged in the discourse so amiable with the croupier?'

Olga Ostorojno nodded. They crept unobserved through the gamblers, round the table and reached the door only to find the way blocked by a small but commanding figure in vivid red. It was Arenskaya, Ballet Mistress to the company.

'I am very angry,' she announced, waving an accusing finger, in time with the famous red feather in her hat. 'I who have had Pavlova, Kchesinska, Spessitsiva and Karsavina, all come to me that I might give them hell—I, Arenskaya, have to tramp through the rooms that I may give hell to a little nobody. Do you not know, my precious one, that your batterie is of the most revolting, that your turns they would not pass in a cabaret, and that your fouetté, it practically does not exist? It is half an hour since you should be in class. Transfer yourself.'

'As for you, M'sieur,' she looked at Citrolo, 'you will come with me. I am thirsty.'

She beckoned, and Citrolo followed obediently. People always followed when Arenskaya beckoned—except possibly Stroganoff. He was used to her. They went into the American Bar.

'Blue Whizzbang?' asked Hank, the barman, hopefully. It was his specialty.

'Champagne,' said Arenskaya. 'You charge it to the Direction.'

'Now,' said Arenskaya, as they settled in their chairs, 'I tell you why I devote to you my time. It is for two reasons. The first—you must cease to be unkind to my friend Stroganoff in your writings.'

Citrolo was annoyed. Criticism of his work always annoyed him.

'My notice was quite fair.'

'Bien sûr—it was fair. But why you write it?'

'Madame,' said Citrolo in tones of a refrigerator salesman referring to a rival make, 'it is as well that we should understand each other on this subject. I am a critic.'

'Entendu!'

'I do not aspire to be called an honest man.'

'Ça c'est évident.'

'I have done many things in my life of which other men might be ashamed. I expect to do many more. Of decency— what the English call le public school—I have, thank God, not a trace. I will cheat when there is a reasonable certainty that I will not be caught. I will steal provided it is safe. I will seduce any attractive wife whose husband possesses neither a revolver nor a solicitor. I will blackmail anyone foolish enough to pay. There is only one thing in the world of which I am proud. It is my artistic integrity. There is no money in the world that could make me write one word I do not believe.'

'Mais, c'est pas logique, ça,' protested Arenskaya, 'if you would be a villain you must be a villain toujours.'

Citrolo nodded. 'I agree. But there it is. Often this conscience of mine has annoyed me extremely—it has spoiled for me many opportunities that I might have turned to profit either in bank or bed. Sometimes I've tried to be nice to some young artist who might be nice to me, but it was always useless. The moment I sit down to write, my pen is steeped in vitriol. Au fond, I would not have it otherwise. You complain that I have given the Ballet Stroganoff a bad notice. Have I given the Buttonhooke Ballet a better?'

'Non.'

'If the Stroganoff Ballet wants a good notice from me it must give me a good performance—croyez-moi, madame, there is no other way.'

Realizing that she was fighting a losing battle, Arenskaya changed the subject.

'The second reason I bring you here is more simple. It is to tell you that you shall not sleep with the little Ostorojno.'

'Why?' asked Citrolo, puzzled.

'I do not consider you good influence. Ostorojno is still vierge and her lover he should play a part in the artistic development. I have for her already a mate. His elevation it is wonderful. I perceive him when he lift her in class and I see them at once together in *Sylphides*.'

Citrolo was genuinely shocked.

'You can't mean the Englishman who danced with her yesterday. Madame, I am ashamed of you.'

'Mais, non—it is not Ernest Smithsky,' said Arenskaya, 'he is fairy anyway. Me, I talk of D. Dovolno—he is with Button-hooke. So now you understand why it is essential that they sleep together. Not only will Ostorojno be contented, but it will bring Dovolno back to us.'

Citrolo bowed. 'Your scheme is admirable. My one regret is that I cannot connive at it. The girl appeals to me. I have always had a weakness for ballerinas.'

'You have slept with many?' asked Arenskaya, interested.

'I have had my successes.'

'That is enough then,' declared Arenskaya. 'Now you oblige me and live on your memories.'

'It is just my memories that trouble,' said Citrolo. 'When I watched her in *Lac des Cygnes*, I was reminded of another dancer—a greater dancer.'

'Dyrakova,' said Arenskaya. 'Bien sûr, there is a resemblance. She is a great artist that one. But a silly woman. It is well known. And her taste in men—'orrible.'

'Thank you,' said Citrolo, 'she was my wife once.'

'Sans blague?' enquired Arenskaya dumbfounded. 'But she leave you, of course?'

'Of course. But not before she had taught me all I know of the technique of dancing.'

'What does she know of technique that one?' snapped Arenskaya.

Galybchik trailed in, looking round vaguely.

'Go away,' said Arenskaya.

Galybchik was furious. Only Stroganoff was allowed to tell her to go away.

'I am looking for Nicolas,' she told the barman.

'No use looking for him here,' said Hank. 'I schanged him a scheque yesterday.'

Galybchik nodded sadly and trailed away to the gaming rooms. But Nevajno was not there either. He was sitting on the beach, watching a bather who had got into difficulties, and meditating a new symbolic work to be called *Défense de Nager*.

*   *   *

In London ex-Inspector Detective Adam Quill was startled to receive the following letter:

Casino de La Bazouche.

Monsieur

   The three suits you make for me are a disgust. I am glad you remind me I have not paid you. Whistle.

Stroganoff
Directeur du Casino de La Bazouche.

Quill sent the letter back to La Bazouche and three days later the right one arrived:

Mon cher M'sieur Quill (it read)

   I invite you urgently to come and pass your vacances at my Casino. Casino—you exclaim in surprise! Mais, oui— c'est vrai! I, Vladimir Stroganoff, have bought a Casino here in La Bazouche. It was the bargain immense.

   You have doubtless read of La Bazouche in the paper of my enemy, Lord Buttonhooke. Buttonhooke he has the Casino too, so he make the publicity enormous that will bring the visitors hot hand to Bazouchka. He is mean man— all the space he devotes to his Casino which is large and ugly. Never by chance does he mention the cosy maison that is mine. But, poof, it matters nothing. It is but the inartistic that will go to Buttonhooke—the connoisseur he will come to me. I have for him the attraction irresistible.

   You demand what it is? Can you not guess? You are right, mon cher. It is the Ballet Stroganoff. I have transported here all my company. Arenskaya, Nevajno, Ernest Smithsky and a new dancer of great promise whom you will glow to meet. The little Olga Ostorojno, though her mother you will not like too much. Our opening night it was the succès fou. The theatre it was nearly full, and the critics in the ecstasy of delight. All save one, but him I will deal with soon.

Buttonhooke he have the ballet at his Casino too. It is so bad that to improve he must always try to steal from me my dancers. But my children they are loyal. Save for Dovolno, Shasslyk, Cashcavar, and Yaghout, no one has listened to his blandishments. And anyways I have the plan that will reduce him to drink the dust.

You have doubtless heard of the great Dyra Dyrakova— the most enchanting Sugar Plum since Trefilova. She is coming to us. It is practically arranged. Already I have find her address and written the letter eloquent. She has not danced in France for two years—ever since Anton Palook he drop her in Aurore. *Never, she swear, will she appear in France again—it is to her not lucky. So she take a studio in Paris, and les petites Anglaises from your so draughty Sadler's Wells, they flee to her for lesson. But time it soften the memory—even that the accident happen in my company— and it is with confidence that I predict she will not resist the magnificent offer that I make her. The sensation of her appearance will be immense, and all le monde will desire to see and come to me. Buttonhooke will be broken man.*

So you see M. Quill, it is the holiday intéressant that I offer you. You will find the Casino irresistible. We have the American Bar, the restaurant, and the Baccarat. Our clientele it is regular. They are becoming to me a second family. Often I desire to restrain them when they play too heavy but my croupier principal, the good Vanilla, he reason with me. The more they lose, he point out, the quicker we shall be rich, and I realize that he is right. He is a man remarkable that one, and loyal. Already he refuse to go to the Casino Buttonhooke. A man with vision.

Nevajno he is working on new ballet. The première is in two weeks. So hasten to us, M. Quill, that you may arrive in good time. I send you fare, for I am rich since my London Season when my Petroushkas so sensationally perish. Though already my stockbroker, he make the demands exorbitant, and my Casino it borrow from time to time. Bring with you your good friend, the Sergeant Banner, and any other policemen that you may love. We give them all the welcome royal.

    Amicalement.

Stroganoff
Directeur du Casino Stroganoff

    P.S. Last night a gambler in temper suicide—my Casino it is now complete.

Quill spent the rest of the morning trying to visualize Stroganoff running a Casino. His imagination not being up to it, he decided to go and see for himself. He had the leisure. A legacy from an aunt, who had never seen *Petroushka* either,[1] had enabled him to retire from Scotland Yard, and the Detective Agency that he had started on the strength of it did not as yet take up much of his time. So far he had had only one client—a fascinating lady of fashion with a mislaid husband and a lover whom she suspected of trying to find him.

Quill caught the Blue Train, was made to alight from it in the middle of the night at Toulon, waited four hours for the local, and eventually arrived at La Bazouche in time for lunch at the *Hôtel Moins-Magnifique*. It was revolting.

The restaurant was crowded and he was forced to share a table with a bow tie, detachable cuffs, and a hopeful expression. Kurt Kukumber welcomed Quill with the enthusiasm of a Montmartre guide sighting an American tourist, praised the climate, expatiated on the view, and recommended the hors d'œuvres. Quill thanked him.

'De rien,' said Kukumber and proceeded to further courtesies. In spite of frequent disappointment, Kukumber still clung to a child-like faith that such pleasantries could never fail to promote unfaltering confidence in the recipient and turn the trick that followed into a mere matter of routine. What trick he would use on Quill, he had not yet decided.

Neither had Quill, though by this time he was quite certain that one was about to break. He waited for it, but it gradually became apparent that Kukumber did not believe in hurrying

---

[1] Special joke for readers of *A Bullet in the Ballet,*

his victim and that this lunch was due to terminate with no mention of the gold brick, the fabulous legacy, or even the Spanish prisoner. Quill found himself looking forward to the moment when they would certainly make their appearance, and got quite a kick out of allowing the insistent Kukumber to pay for his lunch. But he began to feel mildly irritated when Kukumber followed him out of the hotel, hailed a *fiacre*, justled Quill into it and drove furiously to the Casino, not even slowing down as they passed a fascinating glimpse of Stroganoff watering the geraniums. At the Casino, Kurt alighted hurriedly, leaving Quill to pay the cabman. He could not stop, he shouted over his shoulder. He must be there for the start. His system demanded it.

An avuncular commissionnaire directed Quill to Stroganoff's office. 'Do not hope for too much,' he advised, 'Monsieur le Directeur he rarely buy from travellers.'

Quill plodded his way up a faded carpet, past a yellowing statue, through dingy curtains, along a threadbare oilcloth and came to a sudden stop outside a newly painted door. The inscription in chromium letters stood out:

VLADIMIR STROGANOFF
Défense d'entrer.

Quill knocked and went in.

Galybchik was sitting at the typewriter attacking in a spirited manner a letter to the *Conseil Municipal*, which complained bitterly of the noise made by clients leaving the Casino Button-hooke. It purported to come from a body of sleepless rate-payers who, somewhat unaccountably, had elected Stroganoff as their spokesman. Just an item in the Stroganoff campaign against Buttonhooke, as Galybchik in a burst of confidence explained to Quill.

'He's full of plans,' she said, admiringly, 'though, of course, not all of them are practical. But to-night we are playing our ace.' She paused. 'Nicolas,' she said.

But Quill, it seemed, had never heard of Nicolas.

'Nevajno,' explained Galybchik.

Quill remembered. 'Schange small scheque,' he said reminiscently.

The major part of the instinctive liking that Galybchik had taken to the handsome profile that had walked into her life, dwindled away.

'Geniuses are different,' she said firmly. 'Ordinary people have no right to grudge the little extra it costs to support them. Nicolas says so.'

Quill changed the subject. 'So Nevajno is going to save the day?'

'It's a wonderful ballet,' breathed Galybchik, 'Nicolas has never done anything better. I can hardly understand it myself,' she added in awe.

Stroganoff bustled in, proudly deposited a solitary tulip in a large vase, stood before it, gloated, caught sight of Quill, turned round, and before the ex-detective could do anything about it, kissed him warmly on both cheeks.

'And the good Sergeant Banner?' he enquired, clearly prepared to greet him in like fashion.

Quill explained that he had come alone.

'No matter,' said Stroganoff, 'I introduce you to my new secretary. Her name I forget, so you shall call her "Galybchik" like everybody else.'

'We have already met,' said Galybchik, smiling brightly.

'She is as stupid as Stanley, explained Stroganoff, 'but somehow she annoy me less.'

The smile died.

'But why we linger here?' demanded Stroganoff of himself. 'You have not yet seen my Casino. Come.'

Along the frayed oilcloth, through the dingy curtains, past the yellowing statue, down the threadbare carpet, went the bald dome and the profile. An amateur photographer eyed them lovingly as they passed. A picture of the pair, he felt, would easily sell to *Esquire* under the caption, ' . . . so she ran off with my best friend.'

In the restaurant they were preparing for the seven o'clock rush. To them, Emilio—Prince of Waiters. Sacked from the

Ritz, the Carlton and the Buttonhooke Casino, he was hopeful of holding down his present job for at least six weeks.

But Stroganoff waved him away. Emilio had been engaged on the strength of his assurance that most of the customers of the Casino Buttonhooke would follow his napkin, but already a succession of soup-stained clients had shaken much of Stroganoff's confidence in this statement.

'Plus tard,' he said, and hurried Quill into the American Bar.

'Wiskyansoda?' he suggested.

But Hank was already busy with a couple of Blue Whizz-bangs.

Citrolo came hopefully up but Stroganoff bowed coldly.

'He's a critic,' he explained to Quill. 'One without taste.' And Quill made the correct deduction without difficulty.

*   *   *

'This,' said Stroganoff, with the pride of an Archbishop officiating at a Royal wedding, 'IS MY ROULETTE. Let us approach.'

Advancing to the edge of the crowd Stroganoff balanced himself precariously on tiptoe. Quill's superior height enabled him to see more easily.

'Everybody seems to be backing five,' he said to the over-balanced Stroganoff.

'Poof,' said Stroganoff, picking himself up. 'At roulette the direction it cannot lose. There is the pourcentage,' he explained.

'Cinq,' said the croupier. A hum went round the table. It was the third time in succession that the number had come up. The croupiers distributed lavishly.

'Do not fret yourself for me,' said Stroganoff, who had managed to edge nearer the table. 'One losing coup it is nothing. See they are backing five again and we get it all back.'

'Cinq,' said the croupier.

As always when the bank is losing, a wave of excitement went through the crowd. It was a miracle, but miracles have a knack of repeating themselves. An avalanche of counters fell on five.

Stroganoff came to a decision. 'Stop,' he said to Vanilla, 'you are not in the vein to throw. I myself will do it.'

He pushed Vanilla off and mounted the rostrum. Acting on impulse, Quill staked fifty francs on number five.

Stroganoff beamed avuncularly at his audience.

'Rien ne va plus, mes enfants,' he announced and threw.

'Cinq,' he said, despairingly, a moment later.

Into the night strode a disconsolate figure. It was Kurt Kukumber. He was the only player who had lost that afternoon.

*   *   *

It was a beautiful evening. The *Régisseur* in charge of the ballet, *Soirée en Bazouche*, had let himself go in the matter of sunsets. The sky was a picture postcard labelled 'Evening with the Fishing Fleet.' The trees were dark, squat silhouettes against the streaked crimson and gold. The Casino Buttonhooke had been pleasantly reduced to a square shadow dotted with lights, while the sea was a soft and distant shimmer. In the bay, Lord Buttonhooke's yacht, *Ziegfeld Girlie*, rode the shimmer. She had a lovely line. Almost the *Régisseur* felt tempted to turn the moon on her, but remembering that the cast must have time to change for dinner, he concentrated on the sunset. You felt that it would never rain again.

It was a beautiful evening, but for once 'Pourcentage' Citrolo was unresponsive to the perfumed breeze. He, who always prided himself on avoiding show-downs, had been trapped into one. Grateful that for once he could reconcile conscience with his desires, he had praised the dancing of Olga Ostorojno, but had added incautiously that it would never blossom to full maturity until it had escaped the *bourgeois* tentacles that were encircling it. The reference to Madame Ostorojno was unmistakable and Madame had made no mistake about it.

Energetic darting from room to room had enabled Citrolo to avoid her for two days. But that careless cocktail hour stroll in the garden had proved his undoing. With a suddenness that suggested she had been crouching there, Madame Ostorojno

materialized from behind a rose bush and attached herself
firmly to his arm.

'Why do you dislike me, M'sieur?' she began.

There were a number of reasons but it did not seem politic
to dwell on them. Citrolo contented himself with a polite
disclaimer.

'Then why,' demanded Madame Ostorojno, 'do you call me
an octopus?'

Citrolo winced and tried to shake himself free. The resemblance was striking.

'You misunderstood me,' he pleaded. 'What I meant was
that young art should be given a chance to develop on its own
lines. I do not approve of stifling the impulse.'

'Neither do I,' agreed Madame Ostorojno. 'You must not
think of me like you do of other mothers in the ballet. I am
not like them. I never attempt to interfere with Olga. I advise
her, of course, and guide her, and push her a little sometimes—
but influence her? Never!'

'You wish to tell me,' said the sarcastic Citrolo, 'that you
are not like mother and daughter.'

'How right you are,' cooed Madame Ostorojno. 'Olga looks
on me as a friend. Her best friend.'

They were in sight of the terrace where Citrolo observed
with some annoyance that Olga Ostorojno was sharing a far
too intimate cocktail with a far too good-looking young man.
Madame Ostorojno saw them too.

'I'll soon put a stop to that,' she said, with a comforting
assurance, and taking a firmer clutch of Citrolo's arm led him
away again.

'I'm glad,' she said, 'that our little chat is helping us to
understand one another.'

'Completely, Madame,' Citrolo assured her, 'but I must
hasten to dress.'

'Just one little matter,' the octopus pressed. 'Should Lord
Buttonhooke ask your views on Olga you will recommend
her—of course.'

Citrolo was fast losing patience.

'On the contrary,' he snapped, 'I shall tell him that she is as yet too young.' It did not suit him at all to have this bud transplanted to a company where she would be in constant proximity to the handsome young sprig on the terrace.

* * *

The young sprig in question was at the moment warmly pressing Olga's hand under the table.

Olga looked at him in mock reproach. 'I do not believe that you love me. No man who loved me could stand idly by, while Ernest Smithsky partnered me in Swan Lake.'

Dovolno laughed. 'Do not let us go all over that again. What future was there for me with Stroganoff?'

'As much as with Buttonhooke. More—for with Stroganoff you could have danced with me!'

'You should have come to Buttonhooke too.'

'But I don't want to go to Buttonhooke,' sighed the little Ostorojno. * * *

'But I don't want to go to Buttonhooke,' sighed the tearful Galybchik a few tables away.

'My art demands that you should come,' said Nevajno grandly. 'You are necessary to my concentration.'

Flattered, Galybchik sighed again.

'But can't I help you to concentrate with Stroganoff?'

'Stroganoff is limited,' explained Nevajno. 'He lacks the capital. Par example—my name outside it is not in the neon—only in the electric light.'

'I'll speak to Stroganoff,' promised Galybchik weakly.

* * *

'I'll speak to mother,' promised Ostorojno. 'But it will not be any use. Mother does not permit me to go out after the theatre.'

'She was quite willing for you to have supper with that rake Citrolo.'

'That's different. He's a critic. Besides I never told mother.'

Dovolno sulked. 'That sounds as if you wanted to go out with him.'

'I did. I had to. I mean,' said Ostorojno, 'there were reasons.'

'Reasons of publicity.'

'And others. He's a beast,' added Ostorojno violently, and Dovolno was instantly mollified. He was a placid person and now that it was established that the reason was not the obvious one that could matter to him, he was utterly incurious about its actual origin.

'If you went out with Citrolo without telling mother, you can go out with me the same way.'

'She'd find out. Just as she found out about Citrolo.'

'Buttonhooke,' said Dovolno approvingly, 'stands no nonsense from mothers. You'd be much better off with him.'

'Shut up,' said Ostorojno. 'Anyway, he hasn't asked me yet.'

*   *   *

'Anyway,' said Galybchik, 'he hasn't asked you yet.'

Nevajno looked his contempt at this quibble.

'Nevajno does not wait for things to happen. He plans them in advance. When Buttonhooke has seen my *Sleeping Princess* it is certain he will clamour for my services.'

'Perhaps he won't like it,' suggested Galybchik and was instantly repentant.

But it was too late. Deeply offended Nevajno had already stalked away.

With a sigh Galybchik paid the waiter.

*   *   *

On his yacht Lord Buttonhooke was gazing indulgently at a yard or so of tulle helped out with a few expensive spangles. Of all his hobbies, Sadie Souse easily cost him most. One could generally forecast the running expenses of a yacht while one could never quite guess what whim might seize Sadie next.

At the moment she was being comparatively reasonable. All she wanted was some refined adornment for the tulle—say a

large diamond tiara—somep'n that Prince Alexis Artishok
would admire.

'I'm nuts about that guy,' she added with a dazzling smile.

Lord Buttonhooke had noticed this already. It did not worry
him unduly. Like so many exiled Russians, Prince Alexis had
more charm than money, so Lord Buttonhooke, with more
money than charm, quite liked the fellow. The man was a
sportsman, even if he was a foreigner. Anyone who could win
at pinochle so seldom and laugh at his jokes so often must be
a sportsman. Together he felt they made a good team. And
even if his Japanese valet did spend hours over the Prince's
trousers, that was merely a trifle.

'The Prince,' said Sadie, clamping a spray of orchids to her
corsage, 'has been telling me about the snow-white stallions he
used to keep in Russia. I think I'd like a snow-white stallion—
only a little one.'

Lord Buttonhooke agreed peevishly, making a mental note
to have a word with the Prince. If the fellow was to remain a
guest on his yacht he must really be warned to make his
reminiscences less expensive.

The Expensive Memoirs just then made their appearance.
Prince Alexis Artishok looked uncannily like exiled Russian
Royalty is expected to look. Making way for him on the
Promenade des Anglais one searched instinctively for the lines
of resigned suffering under his eyes. They were there. As he
passed on his way it was almost impossible to refrain from
some comment on the horrors of the Russian revolution.

The Prince came forward and buried his bearded dignity in
Sadie's hand.

'So,' he said, 'we all go to see the new ballet by Nevajno?'

'Not me,' said Sadie quickly. She had started life with
Ziegfeld, and wished to be allowed to forget it.

'You are right, Madame,' declared the Prince. 'I myself am
not overfond of the Ballet Moderne. Give me the Maryinsky
with its spacious spectacle and the glamour of the great
ballerinas. Would that there were to-day some vast theatre
where illusion might be permitted to reign as then it did.'

'Say, that's an idea,' said Sadie.

'Oie,' said Lord Buttonhooke, forgetting his refinement.

Sadie and the Prince exchanged a mutual shudder.

*   *   *

'Good-bye, Madame,' Citrolo made his exit from the terrace with deep relief.

'Good-bye,' said Madame Ostorojno. 'See you to-night at the performance. Your seat is next to mine.'

CHAPTER IV

In its inessentials the first night of a new ballet is the same the whole world over, whether this event happens to be taking place at Covent Garden or in Kansas City.

Or even at La Bazouche.

Expectancy is in the air, not unmixed with a certain amount of dread. There is sure to be something to look forward to in the casting—something to regret. Some ballerina is certain to have hurt her foot, another is equally certain to have remained obstinately healthy. There will be the usual strong rumour that the dress-rehearsal was a flop, that the ballerina loathes her *variations*, and that the costumes have not yet all arrived. The novelty digested, it will be discovered that the first ballet—probably by Fokine—is to serve the purpose of a sort of public limbering up, and the last work, a divertissement ballet—*amende honorable* to those of the company with no rôle in the new work—through which the company will trundle with a formal, switched-on radiance.

There will be a number of hurt balletomanes who feel entitled to free seats and have not got them; and a number of hard-pressed Philistines with free seats thrust upon them by their persuading wives and sisters-in-law. There will be a sprinkling of ecstatic intellectuals and a churning of dancers from some other company. And, of course, the usual whiskered foam of Russian generals. In this case many of them have sat up in the train all night in order to get here.

The amateur photographer enthusiastically focussed his camera on Lord Buttonhooke's astrakhan collar, which had just come striding through the entrance, and pressed a flash-light.

'Blast!' he said. Somebody had jogged his elbow and all he got was a picture of Arenskaya talking to Quill.

Lord Buttonhooke strode to the vestibule. Behind him, a rather plumper, a rather shorter shadow, in a slightly smaller astrakhan collar, bounced. A little late in life, the Baron Sam de Rabinovitch had developed a violent bout of hero-worship. Lord Buttonhooke had contrived to be in a big way all those things that the Baron had always aimed at in a small way. A Brain! A Colossus among men!

The Colossus, at the moment, was getting distinctly the worst of it with an usher who was adamant that the seventeenth row side was the right seat. Horrified, the attendant Baron fought his way back to a bustling Stroganoff and launched his protest. Stroganoff shared his horror.

'My box it is at your disposal,' he said courteously. 'It is almost empty.'

It was, in fact, occupied by Arenskaya, her pianist,[1] Galybchik, Quill, and a fidgety Nevajno.

'To-night,' Arenskaya was prophesying comfortably, 'will be the flop terrifique.'

'Hush,' said Galybchik, 'Nicolas is nervous.'

'I am not nervous,' flared Nevajno, 'only high strung.'

'Me, I suffer badly with nerves always,' announced Arenskaya firmly. 'To me the ballet it is an ordeal. I suffer double—first I suffer for my children and then I suffer for myself when I was young and danced the rôle. Always I remember the moment when I was first to dance *Raimonda* before the Tsar—and also the night I dance *La Péri* privately for Rasputin, who had eye on me.'

At the mere recollection the lights modestly went out. The curtain rose on *Carnaval*. One look at Florestan, and Citrolo went out, too.

*   *   *

Save for Vanilla, moodily stacking a pack of cards, the Baccarat room was empty. He did not appear to welcome Citrolo with any particular enthusiasm.

[1] Their permanent feud temporarily in abeyance.

'Bon soir,' said Citrolo, 'I have been reflecting, and it seems to me that you are cheating a little on your returns, n'est-ce-pas?'

Vanilla glowered.

'That, mon cher,' said Citrolo, 'is not prudent. I have been very reasonable with you. Many blackmailers of my acquaintance would not have been content with a mere twelve and a half per cent of the profits you make from your so skilful manipulations of the cards. It is my principle never to be greedy nor to press my collaborators too hard. But really, mon ami, I have to insist that you must, as our English so elegantly put it, play fair.'

A torrent of words broke from Vanilla's outraged mouth. It was evident that he did not regard Citrolo's twelve and a half per cent as reasonable. He pointed out that 'Banco' Dacarpo, who had taught him his trade, took only five per cent—and this by courtesy. Not under compulsion.

'Dacarpo taught you,' Citrolo said smoothly, 'but I found you out. That is always more expensive.'

Vanilla looked at him in grudging admiration, and changed his tactics.

'Business has been bad,' he pleaded, 'one of my pupils mistook a signal and went Banco at the wrong time. My returns are accurate—only the profits are small.'

'It was on those small profits that you present Arenskaya with a bracelet?'

'It was stolen, that one,' Vanilla said defiantly.

Citrolo nodded. 'Eh, bien, mon ami—this time I will overlook it. But only this time. Should your profits be small again, our friend Stroganoff will have a shock coming to him.'

'It would give me much pleasure,' said Vanilla lovingly, 'to put poison in your fish.'

'Assuredly,' agreed Citrolo.

'I often ask myself how it is I have not done this thing before.'

'I will explain,' Citrolo was kindness itself. 'I select my collaborators with much forethought. Blackmailees are divided into many classes—of which only two are dangerous. The very desperate and the very clever. With these I do not collaborate. You, my friend, are neither.'

Vanilla's vanity was wounded. He seethed with rage.

'That I am not desperate is not your fault. But that I am clever, everybody admits. Dacarpo himself has always claimed me as his best pupil. There is only one reason why I do not kill you.'

'Precisely,' said Citrolo, 'C'est question de courage. You are frightened of the guillotine.'

'It is not true.'

'But emphatically it is true. You might have the courage to knife me on an impulse—in the back—and against that I can protect myself. But you would never commit a premeditated murder—you would see the shadow of the knife hanging over you, even as you planned. So you see, mon ami, I am quite, quite safe.' He put out his cigarette and turned towards the door. 'Au revoir,' he said, and don't forget, 'twelve and a half per cent to the last centime.'

He went.

Vanilla seized a pack of cards and relieved his feelings by tearing them across.

'Wish I could do that,' said a wistful monocle, materializing at his elbow. 'But,' it added, 'I know an awfully good trick with a couple of goldfish. I'd like to show it to you.' It looked round helplessly.

*   *   *

In leaving the auditorium so early Citrolo had been even wiser than he guessed. No sooner was he clear than Ernest Smithsky came on breathing heavily as Eusebius.

'Who's that?' said Lord Buttonhooke, startled.

'He is a dancer superb,' said Arenskya, with a certain low cunning. 'Your company it need him badly. Why you not bribe him to go?'

But Buttonhooke, though no balletomane, knew better than that. He took refuge behind his inscrutable smile, a sheer waste of concealment, for by this time Arenskaya's eyes were fixed in some horror on the fat girl—half a beat behind the rest of the corps de ballet. Presently she began to express herself freely on this subject. From force of habit, the pianist looked affronted.

The ballet straggled on. The only person who seemed to enjoy it at all was Galybchik. She gasped her pleasure as Ostorojno tapped her pointed way across the stage as Columbine. In her cherry-sprigged flounces, with cherry-coloured flowers in her hair, Olga Ostorojno took her audience as surely as she took her stage. Her dark beauty warmed the wan little rôle, and suddenly, with her entrance, a period came to life.

'That's the girl I want,' said Buttonhooke.

'You try and I scratch your eyes out,' announced Arenskaya affably.

Nevajno was sulking. Even the fact that Harlequin was at this moment energetically muffing his *brisés*, failed to mollify him. He had always thought of Buttonhooke as the patron— almost the father—of Progress, and here he was, enjoying Fokine.

Gazing at the poke bonnets, the mittens, the crinolines, Quill found himself homesick for the Tiller girls.

At last *Carnaval* came to a crowded end. Arenskaya dismissed it in a sentence. 'Pas d'une gaieté folle,' she pronounced.

Nevajno got up. 'At last,' he said, and hustled importantly out, Galybchik at his heels.

*   *   *

Backstage all was confusion. A vital piece of scenery—the aluminium escalator—had not arrived. Nevajno was protesting that on no account would he allow the curtain to go up on a property staircase left over from last season's performance of *La Bohème*.

*   *   *

To the born balletomane, the most important part of any ballet is its interval. Here he is free to describe his emotions to an audience far too busy describing its own to contradict.

Buttonhooke, though officially established as a patron of the art, never felt himself a really happy bubble in this artistic kettle. Particularly as this was the moment when mothers and others with ambushed ambitions bore down upon him to establish contact with a view to contract.

To escape the onrush he wandered into the roulette-room and threw the maximum on seventeen. Seventeen duly turned up.

'We celebrate,' said Arenskaya behind him.

*　　*　　*

'It is a very generous offer that Lord Buttonhooke has empowered me to make you,' said the Baron de Rabinovitch for the eleventh time.

'Non,' said Stroganoff firmly.

The Baron wiped his brow. While not exactly a menace, the Casino Stroganoff was still a thorn in the side of the Buttonhooke policy, and the Baron had been told off to buy out the impresario. He was still trying. His arguments were eloquent and irrefutable. Even a child could grasp that behind Lord Buttonhooke's offer lay only the desire to do his old friend Stroganoff a good turn.

'Non,' said Stroganoff, again, 'I will not be the swindle twice.'

'But you don't understand,' began the Baron all over again. . . .

'Mon cher,' said Stroganoff, 'I follow everything that you say. Your arguments they are superb. But me, I argue to myself like this: the good Baron—he is the swindle. The good lord—he is the swindle even bigger. If they desire that I sell my Casino, then it is clear that I must keep.'

'You do not trust us,' said the Baron, hurt.

'Assurément non,' agreed Stroganoff blandly, 'I would not trust you with the pole of a barge.' He turned suddenly, delved into a drawer and produced an opulent-looking box of cigars, which he held out to the Baron. 'But we have not the hard feelings—no?'

'No.' The Baron, mollified, stretched out his hand.

But the box was empty.

'Big joke,' explained Stroganoff, laughing consumedly, 'I catch everybody.'

The Baron controlled himself. 'About the Casino. . . .'

'But I have tell you already,' said Stroganoff, still slightly puzzled that the Baron did not seem amused, 'I do not sell. That you wish to buy assures me that my Casino will soon be the success immense. The prestige of my ballet it will resound round the world and millions will rush to congratulate me. Tiens—here is one already,' he added, as a wrathful figure pushed its way towards their corner of the foyer.

The Balleto-Medico had not seen Stroganoff for several weeks, but he was in no mood for polite greetings. It was evident at once that his all-night journey with the whiskered foam of Russian generals had done little to mellow his judgment.

'Your *Carnaval*,' he opened, 'should be taken down, dusted and not put back again. It is the worst since last season at the Wells.'

'Impossible,' said Stroganoff, horrified.

'Never,' said the Balleto-Medico with some justification, 'have I seen a Eusebius like Smithsky.'

'It was in his contract that he dance the rôle,' groaned Stroganoff.

'Console yourself, my unknown friend.' Ambassador de Rabinovitch, wishing to stand well with the foreign power to which he had been sent, attempted to pour oil on the troubled waters. 'Your all night vigil is soon to be rewarded with the new ballet by the genius Nevajno. . . .'

'Nevajno!' said the Balleto-Medico scornfully.

'Nevajno,' said Stroganoff royally, 'and that reminds me,' he asked, 'how you get in?'

'Press,' said the Balleto-Medico, not without pride, 'I am covering this for *Rhythm To-morrow*.'

Instantly Stroganoff was affability itself. 'You will write glowingly—n'est ce pas?'

'I hope to give it hell,' said the Balleto-Medico.

The affability vanished. 'You are the ingrate. The son prodigal. After all the seats I have given you in Opera Houses the world over.'

'Behind pillars,' put in the Balleto-Medico.

'That was the coincidence regrettable. To bear the malice, it is not kind. Recollect the many favours that I have done you. Who taught you first to love the ballet?'

'Diaghilev,' said the Balleto-Medico.

'Who made clear to you the inner beauty of *Le Cotillon?*'

'De Basil.'

'Who was it allowed you the acquaintance of my so beautiful ballerinas?'

'Arenskaya,' said the Balleto-Medico.

'Poof,' said Stroganoff, avoiding defeat. 'Nobody read your paper anyway.' He turned to resume his skirmish with Rabinovitch, but the Baron, his mission a failure, had departed to make his report to Lord Buttonhooke.

Buttonhooke was at the bar with Arenskaya drinking champagne. Rabinovitch whispered in his ear while Arenskaya finished the bottle.

'Stroganoff cannot hold out much longer,' he surmised. 'If we can only fix a really good scandal it would finish him.'

' 'Ank,' ordered Arenskaya, 'Encore de champagne.'

*   *   *

Citrolo had wandered backstage through the pass door, and into Ostorojno's dressing-room. Assuring himself that her mother was not present, he walked in, planted himself on the arm of her chair and teased her gently.

'I have been talking to Buttonhooke,' he said, untruthfully.

Olga swung round. 'Did he like my *Carnaval?* Was it good?'

'He adored it,' said Citrolo glibly. 'He wanted to offer you a contract, but remembering how unkind you were to me last night I managed to persuade him that you were as yet too young.'

'Oh—you didn't!'

'But I assure you, Mademoiselle,' said Citrolo, 'I did this thing. And I assure you I shall continue to do it until . . .'

Olga applied heated wax smoothly to her eyelashes. 'But this is old-fashioned melodrama,' she said, unwilling to believe that Citrolo could be serious.

'I am the old-fashioned villain,' said Citrolo, rolling his eyes horribly.

'Old-fashioned villains are always killed in the end,' laughed Olga.

'And who shall kill me?' demanded Citrolo, grabbing her hand while he had the chance. 'Not that little wrist.'

'This little wrist has a mother, and a boy friend. Either will kill you quite cheerfully.'

But the mother who bustled in did not seem to be meditating murder at the moment.

'Your shoes?' she said. 'Are they comfortable? Is your hair secure? Your shoulder-straps—let me test them. How do you feel? Where's your shawl?'

Citrolo fled.

*   *   *

'So I give her hell,' Arenskaya was saying, 'and the next time she dance perfect.'

A bemused Buttonhooke looked at her.

'There is no doubt I am the greatest teacher of all time.'

Champagne had lent a sparkle to the lights, a richness to the dim plush hangings, and a glamour about Arenskaya's services. Art, thought Lord Buttonhooke with a clarity of perception that belongs to the slightly drunk alone, is art. His class, he decided, could do with discipline.

'I will give you a contract,' he said jovially.

Arenskaya drew herself up to her full height. She was still not very tall. 'Is it,' she cooed, 'that you are making me an offer for my services?'

'Why not?'

'I will tell you why not,' screamed Arenskaya suddenly. 'You are the serpent—the serpent in the bosom—not mine!

You creep here, you crawl there, you force me to drink the champagne, and then when you think I am sou you try to rob poor Stroganoff of me, though you are well aware that without me the Ballet Stroganoff it could not go on one day.'

'Hush,' pleaded Lord Buttonhooke.

'I will not 'ush,' Arenskaya assured the relieved spectators. 'He is a crétin, a crook, a robber. He rob us of Dovolno—that poor boy who is too young to know what he does—and leaves us Smithsky to dance with Ostorojno. You who have seen Smithsky to-night will understand the crime he has committed.'

A murmur of approval ran through the audience. Inspired, Arenskaya rose to greater heights of oratory. Lord Buttonhooke felt himself becoming unpopular. Slightly red behind the ears he turned to the bar.

Hank took this opportunity to present him with the bill.

* * *

In the baccarat-room the Baron de Rabinovitch, oblivious of Vanilla's tilted tie, incautiously went banco. He did not win.

'You are reckless, my friend,' said Citrolo, who had the knack of appearing at awkward moments.

'A trifle,' said the Baron airily, 'a mere two thousand francs.'

'Business is good chez Buttonhooke.'

Champagne had rendered the Baron foolhardy. 'Wonderful,' he said. 'A gold-mine.'

'I thought so,' Citrolo mused, 'I have been thinking so for some time. It is beginning to appear to me, that the small sum you pay me monthly for the collaboration of my silence concerning a certain incident at Avignon in your so adventurous life is no longer sufficient.'

'My overheads,' began the Baron much too late.

'My friend,' said Citrolo, 'I am not one to turn the screw. Many blackmailers of my acquaintance would seize on your prosperity to double or treble their demands. I am content with a modest increase of fifty per cent. This you can afford easily especially if you refrain from going banco when Vanilla is croupier.'

A deflated Baron nodded meekly and dwindled away towards the bar. Citrolo edged towards the table. Almost he felt like a small flutter himself, but after one glance at the angle of Vanilla's tie he changed his mind.

'Banco,' said Prince Alexis Artishok, beside him.

Citrolo studied with interest the long elegant fingers that reached out for the cards and flicked them carelessly over on the table to expose a Queen and a Nine. He looked at the Prince again and sighed both his recognition and regret.

Vanilla had evidently been taken by surprise. He shovelled over the counters in a daze, his eyes glued on the magician who had achieved the impossible with a stacked pack. The magician smiled—very slightly. Into Vanilla's eyes crept a look of reverence.

'Maître,' he muttered under his breath.

* * *

'And so,' said the pianist, 'I told Arenskaya exactly what I thought of her.'

'Did she listen?' asked Quill.

'No,' said the pianist.

* * *

Kurt Kukumber, elegant in a tight-waisted dinner-jacket and a ready-made tie, looked at Citrolo pleadingly:

'Business has been bad,' he explained. 'The public to-day reads too much. Every time I begin a story my prospect has read it already.'

Citrolo was merciless. Annoyance with himself at his caution in not tackling the higher game had made him impatient with the smaller fry.

'You must alter your methods.'

'I will do so,' said Kurt eagerly. 'Always I am studying my trade, learning all the latest tricks. It is unfortunate that all the good swindles I discover need capital, and my system it is for the moment unlucky.'

Citrolo yawned. 'It is hardly worth collaborating with you my friend. Almost would it be of more profit to myself to collect the small reward that the police at Nantes still offer.'

'Give me time,' pleaded Kukumber. 'I have to-day found a prospect very promising. An Englishman of the most gullible. We met at lunch and already I have him interested. . . .'

* * *

The Promising Prospect and the pianist wandered wearily down the corridor that led to the auditorium. She was telling Quill how she had nearly won the Premier Prix au Concervatoire de Bruxelles.

* * *

'Nicolas,' gasped Galybchik, 'is being temperamental.'

There was only one solution.

'Send him here,' said Stroganoff resigned, 'and I schange him small scheque.'

* * *

The sonnette went off like a fire-alarm. Slowly, almost reluctantly, the players left their tables and drifted back to the auditorium. Stroganoff entered his box, found no vacant chair, and wandered off to lean sulkily against a pillar. From his comfortable seat in the stalls the Balleto-Medico waved to him.

With a smirk the conductor took his bow. The spotlight focused maliciously on the double bass and unwaveringly held its ground. The conductor gave up and swung his baton.

The Balleto-Medico leant back and closed his eyes as a fitting prelude to the strains of Tschaikovsky. He opened them indignantly a moment later. Tschaikovsky had certainly not written this. The curtain rose to reveal a chromium-plated palace.

In the box Quill determined to be intelligent. A diligent re-reading of the argument in the programme had enabled him to grasp that this amazing mass of metal was the scene of the christening of the Princess Aurora.

King Impecunious has invited six fairies to stand God-mother to the Infant Princess: They are:

> Fairy Film-face
> Fairy Yumph
> Fairy Stock-Exchange
> Fairy Gold-digger
> Fairy Sugar-Daddy
> and
> Fairy Malthusia.

Each arrives at the party to bestow her own particular quality on the Princess. There is also a Fairy Godfather, but the poor wretch is far too busy partnering the ballerinas to have time to deliver his present.

Relentlessly the fairies dance. In turn they are supported, relinquished, regained, and lifted—but not dropped.

The guests—in spun glass and zip-fasteners—circle the royal cradle, obviously checking up on the window space accorded to their gifts. The cradle bears a distinct resemblance to a model battleship, while the baby looks exactly like Winston Churchill.

Suddenly a perfectly furious fairy comes shooting down the escalator. King Impecunious has carelessly omitted to invite the Most Important Fairy of All—her name is Publicity. Piqued, she looks round and dances a hideous curse: 'Never shall any one of you make the Front Page until . . .'

With a final furious series of pas de chats she vanishes. Queen Impecunious takes up the pas de chats. She is telling her husband what she thinks of him.

Tableau 2. Dawn. The gaiety is at its height. Several of the guests have remembered to bring their toe shoes, and several others are showing every sign of breaking into a traditional Russian dance—traditional, that is, to the Ballet Nevajno. Mercifully, the early editions arrive before they get started.

Not a headline. Not a photograph. Not a gossip item.

Furious, the guests turn on King Impecunious.

* * *

Furious the Balleto-Medico turned on Stroganoff.

* * *

Tableau 3. King Impecunious goes to war. Nobody believes his intentions are peaceful, and he's got to convince them some way. He is unable to mobilize an army as he cannot obtain publicity for his recruiting campaign.

Tableau 4. Peace Celebrations. The Princess Aurora, a well-equipped eighteen-year-old, sends to the chemist for a sleeping draught. All her natural qualities have led inevitably to a certain lassitude. 'I should like,' she says, turning a yawn into an *arabesque*, 'to sleep for a hundred years.'

Tableau 5. She does so.

Tableau 6. The awakening. Prince Foie-gras enters to awaken the Princess with a kiss. In his hand he carries a detonator. (This, Quill was given to understand, was Symbolic.)

Tableau 7. The wedding of the Princess Aurora. A quiet affair almost without Bridesmaids and practically without a Prince.[1] Vulgarity is out of fashion. Everybody is tremendously refined.

Suddenly the Fairy Publicity, swearing horribly, comes shooting down a light ray. She brandishes a newspaper placard at the well-bred guests. It reads:

IMPECUNIOUS PRINCESS MARRIES MONIED
MONARCH

* * *

The curtain came down but before the audience had time to recover it went up again. The company bowed their acknowledgments to a stunned silence.

A shock of black hair strode furiously on to the stage.

'Speech,' called the pianist, taking her cue.

[1] Prince Foie-gras is being danced by Ernest Smithsky, which may account for this.

Oblivious to the fact that it prevailed already, Nevajno raised a majestic hand for silence.

'Imbéciles,' he began, 'why you not boo?'

'Boo,' said the Balleto-Medico obligingly.

'That you like my ballet I do not expect. But that you should not greet it with turbulence I cannot understand. Almost might I be Petipa. Where are the whistles, the hisses, the hoots that the Nevajno tradition demands on its first night?'

This time the house responded. Nevajno stood beaming amid the cat-calls. Now he was in his element.

Buttonhooke, an unaccustomed pang of sympathy reaching his heart, hurried over to Stroganoff. Calamity had made them brothers.

'C'est terrible,' shouted Stroganoff above the din. 'Worse even than the première of *Gare du Nord*.'

Citrolo, passing by, stopped to hurl a casual thunderbolt.

'How many "r's," ' he enquired smoothly, 'in horrible?'

'Gag him,' advised Buttonhooke earnestly. 'Gag him before he gets his notice off to the papers.'

'Oui,' said Stroganoff mournfully, 'mais comment?'

He pondered, stroking his bald dome. Inspiration came suddenly. 'I have the idea magnificent,' he confided, and bustled off.

*   *   *

Prince Alexis Artishok had not bothered to watch the performance. He had remained in the baccarat-room to the growing indignation of Vanilla. It was nice and social of the Master to come here to demonstrate his skill, but there was no need for him to win quite so much money doing it. And it was almost unethical on his part to lend his aid to the assortment of tulle and sequins playing beside him.

Sadie Souse on the other hand, was delighted. She never lost at baccarat while Lord Buttonhooke was within call, but she seldom won.

'If I was always as lucky as this,' she confided to the Prince, 'I could lose the old walrus altogether.'

The Prince took a look at Vanilla's scowl and decided that he had tormented the croupier enough for one evening. He helped Sadie scoop in her winnings and led her, protesting slightly, away from the table.

'That is the feed for the chickens, Madame,' he reproved her. 'One of your accomplishments should not be interested in a few milles.'

'No?' said Sadie.

They settled at a table and the Prince passed his cigarette-case.

'Just now,' said the Prince, making play with his mongrammed onyx lighter, 'you spoke of your dependence on a walrus. Almost you seemed to imply that you were not in love with our good host.'

'Cheese it,' said Sadie.

Prince Artishok smiled. 'In that case you will permit me the liberty of suggesting, Madame, that you are not making the most of your opportunity.'

Sadie was hurt. 'I'm not doing so badly.'

'You are content with trifles,' contradicted the Prince. 'Furs, bagatelles of jewelry, nothing of real value. Should Button-hooke cease to admire you, you would be forced to find another protector almost at once.'

This was a new viewpoint to Sadie. It had never occurred to her that her demands were too small.

'You mean I should soak him for something really big?'

'Imperatively,' said the Prince.

'A settlement?'

'If you can manage it.'

Sadie shook her head. 'I couldn't. Not now. Not a really handsome settlement that is.'

'Exactly,' the Prince nodded. 'It is both too late to discuss settlements and too early. A Protector may be induced to make a settlement before—when he is eager—or later—when he has tired—but not during.'

'I was a mutt,' Sadie sighed.

'We all make mistakes,' the Prince comforted. 'Besides, there is still time. You may not be able to persuade Buttonhooke to give you large sums of money for there is in that, to him, no glory—only disbursement. But you can still persuade him to spend it for your benefit.'

'You mean some really expensive present?'

'I mean an exceptional present,' said the Prince. 'A sensational present. Something that Buttonhooke could boast of giving.'

'The Kohinoor,' said Sadie inspired.

The Prince was amused. 'Alas, it is not on the market. Neither for the moment is any other notorious jewel.'

'Oh.'

'However there is still the famous Otchi-Chernia diamonds. They are not on the market officially, but I might persuade them to become so.'

'How much are they worth?' demanded Sadie the practical.

'Five million francs perhaps.'

'And you can get them?'

'Possibly. They are in the possession of the famous Russian dancer, Dyra Dyrakova.'

Sadie was interested. 'The same that Percy was talking about getting to dance for his company?'

'The same. It was my suggestion,' said the Prince, smoothly, 'that he should engage her.'

Sadie looked at him in admiration. 'Got it all planned—haven't you?'

'Almost,' the Prince agreed. 'With Dyrakova here I think I can persuade her to sell. She has always declared that the necklace is her most valued possession, it was given her by the Grand Duke and made a lovely scandal at the time—but, well, I happen to know that she has not so much money now. But she's as proud as the devil, and it will need great tact.'

'You got that!'

'I've got that. Anyway, I think that I can persuade her to sell. But,' the Prince asked, 'can you persuade Buttonhooke that he wishes to buy?'

'Leave it to me,' said Sadie, with assurance.

CHAPTER V

'M<small>AIS</small>, mon cher,' said Stroganoff. 'Soyez raisonnable. You ruin me.'

'You exaggerate the power of my pen,' said Citrolo, dryly.

'Mais non,' said Stroganoff. 'It is well known that for the *Ballet Sérieux* there is only one critic.'

'Haskell!' suggested Citrolo.

'Haskell—poof!' said Stroganoff. 'Everybody they read Haskell. But for the real criticism, for the seasoned judgment, for the higher understanding and for that kindliness of vision that warms the heart of the balletomane, there is none that can approach Pavlo Citrolo. Whenever there is a new ballet, the connoisseur he rushes for your column in *Paris Soir*.'

'*Le Matin Populaire*,' corrected Citrolo, not at all pleased. 'You are not logical, my friend. You praise my work and at the same time ask me to betray it.'

'Not betray,' urged Stroganoff, 'just disguise a little.'

'For Nicolas' sake,' put in Galybchik, pleadingly.

There was a knock at the office door. Vanilla entered.

'Chips,' he said abruptly.

'Encore,' said Stroganoff, appalled.

Vanilla nodded. Stroganoff opened a box and counted elaborately, while Galybchik made complicated entries in two ledgers.

'My system—it is perfect,' explained Stroganoff with pride as Vanilla took his departure. 'Every franc we lose, I can find him.'

'Admirable,' Citrolo agreed. 'I wish you good night.' He rose.

Stroganoff pushed him playfully back into his chair.

51

'Mais non,' he protested. 'We are not agreed. We have not yet had the little talk, the little smoke.' Hurriedly he reached for the opulent box on the table and passed it to Citrolo. 'Cigar?'

The box was empty.

'Big joke,' explained Stroganoff into the silence. 'Galybchik, les cigares véritables.'

Citrolo lit a cigarette.

'My friend, there is nothing for us to discuss.'

There was a knock at the door.

'Go away,' said Stroganoff.

But it was Madame Ostorojno. Clearly she was finding it difficult to decide whether to bawl out Stroganoff or beam at Citrolo. Stroganoff settled the question by attacking first.

'What you want?' he snapped. 'I cannot do it.'

Madame Ostorojno glared. 'I've come to tell you we're leaving. After to-night's fiasco we cannot stay any longer. We have our future to consider.'

Stroganoff winked at Citrolo. 'Big bluff,' he explained in an audible aside, 'to raise the salary.'

'Oh, no it isn't,' said Madame Ostorojno. 'To-morrow we go to Buttonhooke.'

'I have your contract,' said Stroganoff comfortably.

Like a tank, Madame Ostorojno buffeted her way to the desk, rummaged in the drawers and emerged triumphantly brandishing a document. The resourceful Galybchik pounced and snatched it from her. Stroganoff in turn snatched it from Galybchik and walked to the safe.

'This,' he said, twiddling furiously, 'I put in here where only I know the combination.' He muttered, 'S. Y. L. P. H. . . .' He straightened himself and rubbed his hands. 'Now you may depart to Buttonhooke and my advocate he get me big damages.'

Undaunted Madame Ostorojno swept to the doorway. 'You've not heard the last of this,' she snapped. 'Come, Mr. Citrolo.'

But Citrolo settled himself more comfortably in his arm-chair. Of the two he preferred the frying-pan.

'You realize now,' said Stroganoff, as the door slammed,

'the trouble that I have to overcome. I have to think for my whole family and prevent them when they would be foolish. They look on me as father—it is on me they depend in everything. That is why I plead with you so hard not to write unkind. You would not have it on your conscience that you took their mouths away from the bread.'

Citrolo shrugged.

'Would you condemn the little Ostorojno on the threshold of her career?'

'She danced efficiently,' said Citrolo, 'I shall say so. The blame lies with the choreographer.'

'You do not understand Nicolas,' said Galybchik hotly. 'His conception is above your head. He is a genius.'

There was a knock at the door. Genius strode in. Ignoring Stroganoff he went straight over to Galybchik.

'We celebrate,' he said, 'Come.'

'Celebrate what?' asked Citrolo puzzled.

Stroganoff explained. 'It is a system. Nevajno he always celebrate the reception disastrous.'

'I suppose he books a table in advance,' said Citrolo.

Galybchik stepped into the breach. 'Leave us, Nicolas. We are talking business.'

'Business!' said Nevajno disdainfully, 'Ollright—I wait for you in the cabaret.' He went.

'You weaken, no?' Stroganoff asked Citrolo hopefully.

Citrolo stood up. 'I'm sorry,' he said with finality. 'You are wasting your time. Nothing can induce me to write what I do not feel.'

'The conscience artistic,' said Stroganoff despairingly. He had met with this before.

'I regret.'

'Maybe,' suggested Stroganoff brightening, 'if I should write it for you? I am the writer eloquent. Already I begin my memoirs.'

There was a knock at the door. It was Lord Buttonhooke and the Baron de Rabinovitch. Oozing tact the Colossus and his shadow advanced on Citrolo.

'We have come to congratulate Stroganoff,' said Button-hooke, 'but we see that you are before us.'

'He has not congratulated us yet,' said Galybchik meaningly.

'Nor has he any such intention,' put in Citrolo.

'Tut-tut,' Lord Buttonhooke reproved. 'Surely among men of the world such matters can be adjusted.' Instinctively his hand stole to his pocket.

Light dawned on Stroganoff. He beckoned Buttonhooke to a corner and started to whisper frantically. The words ' 'Ow mooch?' floated clearly across the room, causing Galybchik to blush and bang her typewriter. Citrolo smoked on imperturbably.

'Five thousand,' whispered Buttonhooke.

'C'est terrible,' whispered Stroganoff. 'Never have I paid more than two.'

'Five thousand,' whispered Buttonhooke firmly.

'Three,' whispered Stroganoff.

The whispering became bitter and impassioned and ended only when the Baron joined in to point out that Stroganoff was bargaining with the wrong person.

'You are right,' said Stroganoff, escorting them to the door. 'It is foolish,' he said cryptically, 'to spoil the liner for a pennyworth of paint,' and turned to face his Cunarder.

'M'sieur,' he said coldly, 'you will not listen to my pleadings—you will not listen to my heart. I must recourse to the only thing that you appreciate. 'Ow mooch?'

Somewhat surprisingly Citrolo put back his head and laughed.

'You appeal to me,' he said, 'you do really. I'm almost sorry to have to refuse you.'

'Two thousand francs,' said Stroganoff the tempter.

'Not enough.'

'Three thousand,' said Stroganoff. 'We have the little drink and we seal the bargain. Galybchik—the glasses.'

'I'll have the drink,' agreed Citrolo, 'but not the bargain. And then really I must say good night. I go to press in forty-five minutes.'

'Five thousand,' said Stroganoff.

'No.'

'Six,' said Stroganoff despairingly.

'No.'

This was unbelievable. Possibly, reflected Stroganoff, the sight of ready money might influence this sea-green incorruptible. He had not, of course, anything like the ready money available but perhaps a cheque? His hand went to his cheque-book pocket but encountered instead a small glass bottle. His sleeping draught. Instantly an entirely new train of thought began to bubble in that fertile dome. He glanced at the whisky bottle and the glasses that Galybchik had produced and got busy.

'We drink first,' he said, 'and we talk more business later.'

The unsuspicious Citrolo drank.

*　　*　　*

'. . . impossible to contradict that the new Nevajno choreography bears the signs of the genius irrefutable.' Stroganoff was saying: 'Full stop.'

Galybchik's pencil flew.

'The faultless technique of Ernest Smithsky,' he resumed, shuddering slightly at the memory, 'once again awoke the acclaim of the immense audience enthusiastic. Full stop. Of the corps de ballet, it can be exclaimed: "Never has a band of artistes so on-the-beat been seen!" They truly proved themselves to be the pupils of their famous teacher—Arenskaya.'[1]

Galybchik scribbled conscientiously. In his armchair, the august critic of the *Matin Populaire* slept blissfully on. Four tablets from a bottle sternly marked 'ONE ONLY—*to be taken at bedtime*'—had been sufficient to safeguard his complacency for some hours to come. His subconscious must have been pretty indignant over the eulogies his self-appointed literary ghost was hacking out for him, but it was in no position to do anything about it.

'A décor,' Stroganoff was fervently dictating, 'both costly and modern. . . .'

---

[1] 'It is kind to give the old one the poof.'—VLADIMIR STROGANOFF.

'And symbolic,' suggested Galybchik.

'And symbolic,' Stroganoff agreed. 'A Tchaikovsky-Stravinsky score, added to, and orchestrated by the brilliant young composer, Polyshumedshedshi. Dancing of a virtuosity unrivalled in a conception of the most ravishing—all combined to make the evening memorable for the ballet-goer. The work was rapturously received. Full stop.'

'Had we better?' asked Galybchik nervously.

'Certainement,' said Stroganoff, 'I myself heard a voice cry "bis!" '

'That was me,' said Galybchik.

The door opened. A wisp of tulle came quickly into the room. It was followed by a beard.

'Pardon me,' fluted Sadie Souse, 'is Percy anywhere around?'

'Lord Buttonhooke,' explained Prince Alexis Artishok.

'He is gone,' said Stroganoff shortly. 'You go too, no?'

But Sadie was examining the sleeping Citrolo with some interest.

'Passed out?' she enquired. Here was a condition that aroused her sympathy.

'Oui, oui,' Stroganoff nodded energetically. 'The good Citrolo he has drink too much. We leave him here to sleep it off.'

The Prince obligingly collected the tulle, apologized smoothly for the derangement, and departed.

'We ought to have locked that door,' said Galybchik.

'Why you not think of it?' Stroganoff snapped. He crossed to the door just in time to push out the Balleto-Medico.

Soberly they went back to work. But soon Stroganoff was himself again.

'And what,' he was demanding, 'shall we write of the Man Behind the Ballet? Of the heart that found the courage to present, the brain that had the vision to perceive, and the patience that withstood the many shocks of the artistic impasses that are part and parcel of a conception so immense—What, in short, shall we say of Vladimir Stroganoff?'

'What?' asked Galybchik.

CHAPTER VI

Ex-Detective-Inspector Adam Quill woke thankfully from a dream in which Arenskaya—in a scarlet nightgown—was gazing at him with much the kind of expression Marlene Dietrich had turned on Herbert Marshall in a Lubitsch film, and with about as much success. He stretched out his hand and reassured himself about the empty pillow beside him. A luxurious yawn linked him to the present. He was on holiday. He was in the South of France. He was in the sunshine. He was in the company of easily the most amusing people in the world, and this time he had no corpse to worry him.

He stretched out his other hand to throw back the shutters. The room was small but it had its comforts. Rain slanted in. Quill shut the window and rang the bell.

Some twenty minutes later an old man came trundling in with a tray. Beamingly he removed the lid to reveal a few greasy strands of bacon and the hard fried remains of a very small egg.

'Voilà!' he said triumphantly, 'Le h'english breakfast.'

Quill was not impressed. 'Bring me some tea and toast.'

'Café,' said the waiter reproachfully.

'Tea,' said Quill firmly.[1]

The waiter shrugged and shuffled out.

The telephone rang. A cascade of words burst into Quill's eardrums. It was Stroganoff burbling about bodies and police.

'Please,' pleaded Quill. 'A little slower and a little softer.'

But slowness, it appeared, was out of the question.

'Mais mon cher, do you not understand? The body it is in my office, it is dead entirely, and me I am almost in the prison.

[1] On subsequent mornings he drank coffee.

57

So you come at once and tell the gendarme that it is not I who kill him.'

'Kill who?' asked Quill, struggling hard to find some handle to this slippery stick.

'Absolument,' agreed Stroganoff. 'He is dead. So you come at once.'

Quill gave it up and started to dress. Presently the 'phone rang again.

It was Galybchik.

'Mr. Quill,' she gasped. 'Something terrible has happened. They have arrested Stroganoff.'

Quill groaned. It seemed hard that this thing had to happen to him on the first day of his holiday.

'Hurry,' begged Galybchik. 'Don't bother to shave.'

Quill promised to go right over. 'Don't touch anything,' he added entirely through force of habit.

As he was leaving the 'phone rang for the third time. Guessing correctly that this would be Arenskaya he did not trouble to answer.

*   *   *

'Bonjour,' said the Commissionaire, hailing Quill as an old friend. 'Useless to call to-day. The director has been arrested.'

'Why?' Possibly, thought Quill, this man might know something.

The commissionaire shrugged. 'Sais-pas. It is easy to get arrested in Bazouche. Our Gustave is very excitable. All his life he has arrested first and asked the questions after.'

'Really?' said Quill.

'But do not mistake me,' said the commissionaire, worried that Quill might think he was casting aspersions on Bazouche's Chief of Police. 'Gustave is the man honourable. Never will he take a bribe—practically. He respects and honours the profession that is his, as every man should. He is not,' he said with unexpected indignation, 'like the critic Citrolo, who was doubtless well paid to write this.' He picked up a copy of *Le Matin Populaire* and pointed with a quivering hand to a column. 'It is infamous that anyone should stoop to write this. Read it, M'sieur, and you will share my indignation. I love the ballet,' said Anatole, the Commissionaire, with deep emotion, 'I have loved it all my life. But last night I did not love. I would, if I could, warn every balletomane in the land of this outrage on beauty. But, alas, I have no paper. Citrolo has the paper and always till now I have respected him for his judgment and fairness. But now I see that he is like the others—only worse. Balletomanes have learnt to trust Citrolo—to believe what he writes. In writing this,' he pointed to the column again, 'he has betrayed their trust.'

As Quill was glancing incredulously on the glowing eulogies Stroganoff had dictated last night, Galybchik came rushing out and grasped him urgently by the arm.

'Police,' gasped Galybchik. 'They're up in the office. Hurry or they'll move the body.'

'Whose body?' asked Quill petulantly. 'Won't anybody tell me who's dead?'

Galybchik considered the request and appeared to find it reasonable.

'Citrolo,' she said.

Quill remembered a vague meeting in the cocktail bar yesterday.

'The critic?'

Galybchik nodded.

'Bon,' said the commissionaire with deep satisfaction.

*   *   *

Up in Stroganoff's office, the scene might have been taken direct from a sleuth's nightmare. There was the body, lolling against the armchair, its features horribly contorted. Beside it lay a revolver, an empty bottle of iodine marked 'poison,' and a glass of milk—untouched. There was a bullet hole. It was not in the corpse. It was, in fact, as Quill was to note later, on the wall opposite. There was a noose dangling from the ceiling. There was an armchair, overturned as though for luck, a half-smoked cigar on the mantelpiece and some promising-looking ash on the carpet. The safe was open. The bureau had obviously been ransacked. On the desk lay the prospectus of an appetizing gold mine.

A plump little man in a soiled blue uniform was sitting at the desk studying what was obviously a clue-riddled letter, It read:

All is discovered, so—poof—I kill myself. Pavlo Citrolo.

He scowled forbiddingly at Quill and Galybchik.

Quill introduced himself. Instantly the little man was all smiles.

'It is an honour to meet you, M'sieur. I read about you in the case of the dead Petroushkas. You permit me to present myself. I am Gustave Clemenceau. No relation. Always I have been the admirer of your Scotland Yard. It will be an honour, cher collègue, to work with you.'

Quill made suitable noises.

'It is a pity, of course,' said Gustave, 'that the case is so simple. Already I have arrested one murderer and I hope soon to have the second.'

Quill examined this high-speed worker with a certain amount of grudging admiration. He himself would never have the confidence to make an arrest within two seconds of seeing the victim. Of course, Gustave had mistaken his suspect. Inevitably he found himself wondering if, when the mistake was discovered, the comments of the Sûreté to Gustave would, in their essentials, equal the comments made to him by Scotland Yard when, after some three weeks of hesitation, he had arrested the wrong man. But, of course, it was possible that the Sûreté encouraged Gustave to work on the inverted principle of arresting everybody in sight, arguing mathematically that the greater the number of arrests, the better the chance of the murderer being among them.

'This morning,' began Gustave. 'I am in my garden with my marrows. They are beautiful. Madame Bonfemme arrives to tell me the telephone rings in the police-station. I do not expect a call this morning, so I know at once something unusual has happened. I hurry. It is the director of the Casino. There is a dead man in his office. A famous dead man—a figure well known to us all. The critic Citrolo. He is dead—suicided I am led to believe. But Gustave believes nothing. Only his trained eye sees, his trained brain notes.'

'You've had a lot of experience,' said Quill.

'Of big crime—no,' said Gustave candidly. 'It is my first murder. But I have read and I assure M'sieur that I am capable.'

'Evidently,' said Quill.

'I tell the director to touch nothing till I come. I cover my marrows and I hurry to the scene.'

With the narrative approaching its climax Gustave paused for effect. With studied casualness he passed over an opulent box of cigars.

It was empty.

'Big joke,' said Galybchik tearfully.

Quill passed his cigarette-case.

'So,' resumed Gustave only slightly disconcerted, 'I arrive, and what is the scene that greets my eye? This!' He stretched out an accusing hand. 'And in the middle of it a large bald man. It is Stroganoff. He talks all the time. He tells me Citrolo is suicided. But I wave him aside and I look for myself.'

'I examine the body. It is clear at once that the man Stroganoff lies. It is not suicide. The victim has been strangled. See the bruises are on his throat.

'I question the man Stroganoff. I ask him how comes the body into the office? And, believe it or not, M'sieur, he confesses that he leaves it here last night. He admits, if you please, that Citrolo was with him till a late hour drinking. Then he drank too much and fell asleep. And then, if you please, the man Stroganoff tried to make me believe that, with his victim reduced to insensibility, he went home and left him to sleep it off.'

'So he did,' said Galybchik defiantly.

'You are still here,' said Gustave coldly. 'You go.'

Galybchik remained rooted. Only Stroganoff could tell her to go away.

'Next,' said Gustave complacently, 'I examine the room. At

once I see that the suicide theory is not logical. Citrolo has chosen for himself too many ways of death.' He counted them over on his chubby fingers. 'The poison, the pistol and the armchair overturned, which is the most foolish of all. For your suicide,' he pointed out, 'does not tussle with himself. Neither does he strangle himself with his own hands.'

'Relentlessly I reason. This scene has been arranged to deceive me. Me—Gustave Clemenceau. No relation. Who, I ask myself, has set this trap? The answer is easy. It is the man Stroganoff.'

Quill ran a perturbed hand through his hair. The exuberance of the props fitted in only too well with his knowledge of the Stroganoff mentality. He was reasonably certain that Stroganoff had not committed the murder but there seemed no doubt that the old boy was deeply involved.

'I pounce on the man Stroganoff,' cried Gustave, 'I riddle him with questions. He turns, he twists, he telephones, but like the bullets of a machine-gun my logic it pursues him. It is the test of endurance. Which will exhaust the other first?'

Quill found himself wondering. It must have been a great battle.

'But the trained mind wins,' said Gustave triumphantly. 'At last the man Stroganoff ceases to struggle and admits all.'

'All?' said Quill.

'Almost all,' amended Gustave. 'He denies only that he killed Citrolo.'

Quill suppressed a smile.

'He admits that he set the scene, and arranged the many ways of suicide. But he still swears that Citrolo was asleep when he left last night and that he arrived this morning to find him dead. It was the fright, he says, that turned him *Régisseur*. So I arrest him. As you see, cher collègue, it is a case peu compliquè.'

'You are making a big mistake,' said Galybchik loyally.

'Taisez-vous,' snapped Gustave, 'or I arrest you too.'

Quill remembered something. 'Talking of arrests, you spoke of a second murderer.'

Gustave nodded wisely. 'That is so. It is a murderer that one would hardly suspect.' He paused. 'It is the man Lord Button-hooke.'

Galybchik gasped while a tremor of unholy glee ran through Quill. This last sounded much too good to be true.

'You are astonished,' said Gustave, 'I am astonished too that a lord so prosperous should be so debased. But there is little doubt. In his terror of arrest the man Stroganoff try to save himself by exposing his accomplice.'

A shock of black hair strode into the room. It looked for Stroganoff, failed to find him, looked blandly round, failed to notice anything unusual, saw Quill, recognized him, assumed its most amiable expression and made straight for him.

'You schange me small scheque,' said Nevajno winningly.

In her corner Galybchik quietly fainted.

*   *   *

'Mais, mon cher,' said Stroganoff, 'soyez raisonnable. Could I foretell that the good Citrolo would make for himself the bump-off?'

The gaol at La Bazouche had not kept pace with modern ideas and Stroganoff's cell lacked many of the amenities to which the comfort-loving impresario was accustomed. There was no roll-top desk, no easy chair, no opulent box of cigars and no carpet to spill ashes on. Instead there was a truckle bed, a bench, and an iron grille that gave out on an empty cell opposite. Stroganoff was stretched on the first, cosily sipping an inexplicably produced glass of Russian tea, while Quill, uncomfortable on the second, was manfully trying to extract from him the salient facts of the case.

Not for the first time that morning Quill found himself sighing for one of those retentive-minded witnesses, so obligingly doled out to other detectives, who could be relied on to relate the circumstances in chronological order, leaving out no detail however small. Gustave, who had insisted on accompanying him in his study of the scene of the crime, had been far too busy audibly fitting clues to his own theory to be of much use. Galybchik, recovered from her faint, obviously knew something but stubbornly refused to divulge it. While Nevajno, having at last been made to realize what had occurred, was concerned only with a new idea for a ballet to be called *'Vacances Sanguinaires.'* The corpse had been removed for an autopsy and the contents of its pockets collared by Gustave and put under seal. So Quill was reduced to relying on Stroganoff.

The latter, at first, had persisted in sticking to the version he had supplied to Gustave, and it was only after much pressure that Quill could induce him to admit that he and Citrolo were not sufficiently buddies to get drunk together. From there it was but a step to obtain from him a confession of the enthusiastic notice he had written for himself.

'It was good—no?' asked Stroganoff, pulling out a cutting and lingering gloatingly over the best phrases.

Quill was gloomy. 'It seems to me that you are in a bad jam. You admit that you drugged Citrolo—that you wrote the notice. . . .'

'Mais non,' said Stroganoff quickly. 'I do not admit that. It is big secret and I tell only to you.'

'A secret anyone who reads the notice can discover.'

The journalist was hurt. 'Pensez-vous! But it is very efficient.'

'It contains the Stroganoff signature in every sentence.'

'I forget that.' Stroganoff nodded pontifically. 'My style it is distinctive.'

'Exactly.'

'But why you worry?' Stroganoff demanded. 'Since I tell you that it is not I who do the bump-off it is then some other. So cease to pester me, mon cher, and hurry to find this criminal, for I am eager to be at my Casino to-night.'

Patiently Quill explained for the third time that before he could reasonably be expected to find the criminal he must know more about the victim and the curious scene of his death. He would like to know how much of the mischief in the study Stroganoff was responsible for and how much had been contributed by others.

'Try and remember,' he pleaded, 'and tell me exactly what you did this morning.'

Stroganoff's brow puckered in a tremendous frown of concentration.

'First,' he said brilliantly, 'I awake. At once I send a boy for *Le Maton Populaire*. My notice it is there. My best sentence—the one that concerns myself—it has been cut. Then I am furious. Almost I telephone the paper to reason with them, but I remember in time that it is not I who is suppose to have write it. So instead I ring for my breakfast. I shave, I dress, I go to the Casino. I reach my door. I unlock it.'

'You always keep the door locked?'

'Certainement,' said Stroganoff with dignity, 'except when I forget. You must understand, mon cher, that in the room are many things of the most valuable.'

'Such as?'

'First, there are the records of the Ballet Stroganoff. Then there are the contracts. There are the chips for the Casino and the account books for the losses. It is curious,' he mused, 'why there is always more chips in the book than in the drawer.'

'Never mind that,' said Quill.

'But I mind enormous,' said Stroganoff. 'Comme ça my roulette it is the ruin. That is why I am glad when you write that you come here for your holiday. M'sieur Quill, I say, will assurément solve for me this little mystery.'

'Is that why you asked me?'

'Mais non,' said Stroganoff quickly and changed the subject. 'Also in my office there are the two chapters of my autobiography. They are very valuable; there are many who would give much to look at them. So you understand it is essential that the door it is locked so that nobody can get into.'

It did not seem to Quill that so much emphasis on the impregnability of the room was at all wise in Stroganoff's predicament.

'You are certain that the door was locked?'

'Certainement.'

'Is there any other entrance to your office?'

'Non. The window it is locked and the wall it is sheer.'

Quill sighed. Here he was at last presented with one of those cases with all doors and windows locked which every hard-pushed author resorts to sooner or later. Of course, it had to come on his holiday.

'Is there more than one key to the door?'

'Si,' Stroganoff nodded. 'Galybchik—she have one.'

'Anyone else?'

'Non. But certainly,' Stroganoff argued, 'a little lock it is not difficult for the cunning assassin.'

'Of course anyone who had wanted to could have had an impression made.'

Stroganoff nodded. 'So you see you have the many clues and . . .'

'I shall want the many more,' finished Quill. 'Let us continue. You unlocked the door. . . .'

'I unlock the door,' resumed Stroganoff resigned. 'I enter. You understand that I am prepare to find Citrolo much awake and cross so I am ready with the speech tactful. But Citrolo he is still sleeping. I am worried. Maybe I give him too many tablets. I approach closer and I see that he is bump-off. Strangle.'

'Now,' said Stroganoff, 'I am much upset. I realize I am in the danger. I have fall from the fire into the soup. The circumstances they are of a suspicion formidable. I too have read the detective stories. So I reason with myself. To call the police tout de suite it is not wise. They will ask the question, they will learn that it is I who see Citrolo last and then I will be in prison. At all costs, I say, I must prevent that. The Ballet Stroganoff it need me too much.'

Quill looked round the cell but said nothing.

'So I arrange the décor that it look like the suicide.'

'Like several suicides.'

'Alas,' said Stroganoff simply, 'it is the impresario in me.'

'Of course,' said Quill, 'it never occurred to you that you were doing your best to destroy any clues the murderer might have left.'

'Pas vrai,' snapped Stroganoff. 'I destroy nothing. I only add.'

This was a slight improvement. Quill produced his note-book and took a deep breath.

'Can you remember exactly what you added and exactly what you found?'

'Certainement,' said data-Stroganoff with dignity.

'Very well. Then, first—was it you who put the bottle of iodine beside the corpse?'

'It was I,' said Stroganoff. 'We get it when Arenskaya she run the sword in the Prince[1] when she rehearse Giselle. The Ballet Stroganoff it waste nothing. It was not the poison of the most convincing,' he apologized, 'but I can find no other bottle that bear the symbol.'

'The rope?'

'I fix that,' said Stroganoff. 'At first I plan to put in it the body but I shudder too much.'

'The overturned armchair?'

'I stumble after I fix the rope. But I think it good idea so I leave it comme ça.'

'The revolver?'

'It is mine,' said Stroganoff sublimely. 'But again I lack the courage to fire into the body. So I select a place on the wall where even the policement he could not miss it.'

'The gold-mine prospectus?'

'That I did not have time to read,' said Stroganoff regretfully.

'The glass of milk?'

'It is the mystery complete. Me I never drink the milk.'

'The cigar?'

'It is the kind that Button'ooke smoke. I put it there,' said Stroganoff, 'for loock. Also the ash, which I notice in my reading gives all the detectives mooch pleasure.'

'Why did you accuse Buttonhooke?' asked Quill, abandoning the list for a moment.

Stroganoff looked very pleased with himself. 'That was the coup d'état. I realize that with all my precautions I am still in the danger of arrest. Gustave he do not appear convinced. And

[1] Smithsky.

I ask myself if I am arrest what then will happen to the Casino Stroganoff? With me in prison the Casino Button'ooke it will have the walk-over. The only chance it is to put Button'ooke in the prison also. So I make the accusations against Button'ooke and the police they mistake me and think we are the accomplice. That, mon cher, is imbécile but it suits me well for the moment, so I do not contradict.'

'Your accusations, of course,' said Quill, 'were entirely without foundation.'

'Pas du tout,' said Stroganoff hurt. 'It is bien possible that Lord Button'ooke he is the assassin. It was he who advise me to muzzle Citrolo. Also Button'ooke he have the ballet too, and maybe he worry what Citrolo will write about it. Il a bien raison, aussi, mon cher. Citrolo did not wish to write well even of the Ballet Stroganoff. Picture you what he would write of the Ballet Button'ooke!'

Quill returned to his note-book. 'The open safe? The ransacked bureau?'

Stroganoff shrugged. 'Of that I know nothing. It is thus I find them. Doubtless the assassin he search for something.'

'Have you missed anything?'

Stroganoff clasped an anguished forehead. 'Mon Dieu, I have forgot to look!' He sat up. 'You go at once,' he said urgently, 'and fetch me here the two chapters of my memoirs, the mortgage papers of my Casino, my address book and the contracts Ostorojno, Lubova, but not Smithsky. Also . . .'

'Presently,' Quill promised. Only a few more questions and he would be ready to start work. Stroganoff was a fair-minded man. He groaned slightly and leant back on his couch.

Having reduced Stroganoff to passivity Quill set about his task. He explained that in every murder there were three basic facts on which the detective had to concentrate. Means, Motive, Opportunity. The passive one sprang to life to point out that there would be plenty of scope for enquiries along the motive lines. One with so little taste must have plenty of enemies. For example, Buttonhooke. . . . With some difficulty Quill got him to lie down and resumed his argument.

It was clear, he managed to convince Stroganoff, that this could not have been a premeditated murder. No murderer could have relied on Stroganoff drugging Citrolo and leaving him tempting and isolated throughout the night. It was therefore the murder of someone who saw an opportunity and was quick to act on it. This narrowed the circle from which the murderer sprang to the people who might reasonably be supposed to know of Citrolo's presence in his office. So would Stroganoff tell him the names of all the people who . . .

He questioned Stroganoff and bit by bit extracted from him an unbelievably large list of people who had been hovering around and butting in upon his private sanctum last evening. These he jotted down in his note-book for private pondering.

'You get busy soon,' urged Stroganoff. 'It is of importance the utmost. . . .' He broke off and with a triumphant exclamation pounded eagerly across to the grille.

'Bon jour, mon ami,' he greeted the manacled astrakhan that was being trundled down the passage.

Lord Buttonhooke glared.

* * *

Leaving Stroganoff and Buttonhooke to their amiable discourse Quill took shelter among the collection of disconsolate marble tops that called itself a bar.

Though it was raining, trade at the *Dernier Douzaine* was anything but brisk. At the desk Madame Dupont was saying so to an elderly but sympathetic waiter.

'Courage, Madame,' he said, 'Il en reste toujours les anglais,' and ambled up to overcharge Quill for the modest bock he ordered.

'Il a raison, il faut en avoir du courage,' nodded seventeen Madame Duponts in the green reflections of the mirrors that lined the walls.

Quill settled down to a good ponder. The more he pondered the more he disliked the case, and the less he felt inclined to blame Gustave for his precipitate arrest of Stroganoff. All the evidence pointed to Stroganoff. The means, the opportunity—

even a motive that was typically Stroganoff. It was only his knowledge of the latter that induced his belief in his innocence. But it was going to be a devil of a job to prove it.

To get down to it he would have to ferret out many more facts than he had at present. First, there was the dead man. All he knew about Citrolo at the moment was that he was a dramatic critic with a habit of expressing himself candidly. His first step, therefore, must be to find out something of his private life. Interviews with people who knew him were indicated and a visit to his rooms might be helpful.

Quill got up, paid his bill, and left the café. Almost immediately he was in it again. With him was Arenskaya. She had collared him outside.

'Champagne,' she ordered.

'What did I tell you?' signed the waiter to the seventeen sea-green Madame Duponts.

'Me, I always drink the champagne when my nerves they are tricky.'

Quill nodded. 'You are upset this morning?'

'But it is natural that I am upset,' said Arenskaya. 'My new friend—Citrolo—is dead, and Stroganoff is the idiot.'

'But,' said Quill to cheer her up, 'Lord Buttonhooke is the idiot too. He's in gaol as well,' he explained.

'Tiens!' Arenskaya was interested. 'You are sure?' she asked.

'Positive,' said Quill. 'When I left he was enjoying a quiet little chat with Stroganoff.'

'Bien.' Arenskaya gulped down her champagne. 'It is then the moment for me to get back Dovolno to the Ballet Stroganoff.' She arose. 'You will understand,' she said, 'that with Stroganoff absent it is I who deputize.'

Quill nodded.

'In Lyons there is the crisis effrayant. The fat girl she wish to dance "Blue Bird." Me I am all for it since it is Smithsky who will have to lift her and it gives me pleasure to see that one work. But my personal enjoyment I put aside and I forbid.'

'Who,' interrupted Quill, the detective, 'is Dovolno?'

Arenskaya looked at him saucer-eyed. 'But you do not

know? He is the dancer the most promising since Kasha Renevsky. His terre-à-terre has the most style since Massine, his turns leave Lichine standing, and Idzikovsky never jumped higher.' She broke off impatiently. 'I forget always that you are the ignoramus complete and know nothing of ballet. So I tell you something that interest you more. Dovolno—he want to sleep with the little Ostorojno.'

Quill blushed. 'I am interested in Citrolo.'

'He want to sleep with her too,' said Arenskaya. 'It is curious how experience turns to youth.' She ogled Quill invitingly.

'Then Ostorojno is the person to tell me most about Citrolo?' Past practice enabled Quill to ignore the ogle.

'Du tout.' The flamboyant feather in Arenskaya's hat quivered with the strength of her denial. 'She has a mother that one. And I too help to put the spoke in the wheel of Citrolo. Who is he to interfere with my choice of mates for my ballerinas?'

'Do you supervise all the love affairs in this ballet?' asked Quill startled.

'I help a little,' said Arenskaya modestly. 'And sometimes I stop it. Always the benefit of my experience I put at their disposal.' She simpered. 'But interfere—no? Have I not said that to one of my nature it is impossible. Never do I repeat to the ballerinas what they tell me about each other—only once when I tell Dyrakova. . . .' She stopped. 'Tiens,' she said, 'there is one who will be sorrowful this morning. Even she cry a little per'aps.'

'Who,' asked Quill, 'is Dyrakova and why will she cry?'

'Mais c'est incroyable!' cried Arenskaya. 'Not to know the great Dyrakova—the greatest of all ballerinas—who live in Paris like a Queen and refuse to dance for anyone.'

'But why will she cry this morning?'

'The death of an 'usband it is always sad,' said Arenskaya solemnly. 'Even one that is many divorces away.'

'Was Citrolo one of her husbands?'

Arenskaya nodded. 'Always she marry her lovers. She is a stupid woman. It is well known. Also she is not always the dancer that the critics claim. In Vienna . . .'

Quill listened patiently as Arenskaya plunged into a recital of Dyrakova's worst performances interspersed with highly improbable accounts of her own successes, and then tactfully steered the conversation in the direction of Citrolo's murder. But here Arenskaya had no definite theories to offer. Citrolo, she claimed, was the typical smooth type of villain whom almost anybody might have a reason for murdering.

'Also,' she said, a personal grievance rising to the foreground, 'he was the meanness itself. He order champagne and leave me to pay for it.'

Quill paid the waiter hurriedly.

'Meanness,' said Arenskaya, 'it is the one thing that I cannot tolerate. Meanness and mothers. To those that have neither I can forgive much. That is why, M'sieur, I bear with the approaches of that poor Vanilla who have eye on me. He do not earn very much, but always he find the money to spend and give me presents which I would accept from one many times richer. Regardez!' She thrust an arm proudly in front of Quill to dangle three large emeralds in an embossed band of gold. Quill looked at it.

'An expensive present?'

Arenskaya nodded. 'Bien sûr. Vanilla he give me all I ask. But all the same I do not trust him. We are friends, but I watch him closely.' She gathered her wraps. 'But, really, M'sieur Quill, I cannot linger here and listen to your talking. I have the business serieux to do. I go to deal with young Dovolno while he is still too sleepy to argue much.'

*   *   *

The Garçonnière rented by Citrolo for his enjoyment of the winter sunshine at Bazouche was situated high on the slopes, named in a burst of inspiration, '*Beau Soliel*.' It was raining. A perspiring Talbot-Darracq deposited Quill at the entrance. In the passage a scrubbing concierge splashed water indifferently about his feet. She shook a gloomy head at Quill's enquiry and pointed vaguely towards the sky.

'Cinquième étage,' she said. 'L'ascenseur ne marche pas.'

She detached from her wrapped round person a large key and, muttering something about a faulty bathroom tap, a m'sieur who detested getting out of bed to answer the front door, and her rheumatism, thrust it upon Quill and returned to her scrubbing.

Quill examined the notice that for the past two days had been hanging outside the lift gates. It read '*Arrêt Momentaire*.' Cursing his luck he started to climb the stairs. In a vile temper he reached the top.

Unaccustomed to the inauspicious entrances that French landlords, as a class, delight in supplying, Quill was surprised to find the apartment itself distinctly comfortable. The room was predominantly grey with pearly walls and ceiling. Deep armchairs beckoned Quill to rest from his arduous climb. On the wall hung an exquisite print of the *Pas-de-quatre*. The desk boasted a signed photo of Diaghilev and the mantelpiece an Arabesque signed 'Dyrakova.' A bijou piano almost tempted Quill to try out his five-finger exercises. It was the room of a cultured man who could afford to gratify his tastes. The battered typewriter was the only professional note in the restful amateur symphony.

Quill would have liked to potter happily among the books which progressed in an orderly manner from politics to pornography. He had indeed started at the latter end when his eye fell on a bulky volume entitled *L'Etude Complet De Chantage 1810-1907*. Quill picked it out. It appeared to be a neat analysis of the methods of all the brighter blackmailers of the past century, and though outwardly the author seemed to write with reproof the undertone was one of sterling admiration. It was inscribed 'To my son Pavlo—from his affectionate father. Saint-Sulphice. 1908.'

With reluctance Quill tore himself away from the fascinating pages and walked over to the desk. Meticulously he began his inspection. Soon he was engrossed in his task. It was a funny thing, he mused, the way you could bring a dead man to life by the objects that surrounded him. With every moment a clearer image of Citrolo was forming in his mind. His cigar and wine bills indicated the Bon Viveur, his invitations showed him to be one who was sought after—possibly even a man of charm. His pasted-up press book and the files of dancers' photographs indicated pride in his profession. The lack of love letters pointed to his discretion and his moustache-curlers to his vanity with a hint of pomposity. Quill glowed with pleasure at his own shrewd psychology. Come to think of it that was all that detection meant. Applied psychology and (here the Scotland Yard in him reared its official head), of course, endless routine work. Thank the Lord he was finished with that. It was Gustave's baby now.

Humming he returned to his research. Really it was quite a pleasure to work for such a corpse. Everything was in its place, tidily arranged and beautifully accessible. With every move the feeling grew in Quill that though the witnesses in this case left much to be desired the dead man could not possibly have been more thoughtful. It was almost as though, foreseeing his own death, he had determined to make the detective's job as easy as possible.

Where would such a man keep his valuable documents? Quill reflected. The answer was easy. Obviously he was due to find a safe delicately concealed behind some not too callisthenic cache.

He tried the strikingly modern clock, set in the mantelpiece. He was right first time. The clock face swung open and there was the secret treasure. It consisted of a small faded note-book. Quill took it. At first sight it seemed to be a record of a number of people who owed Citrolo money and were paying it back by instalments. Quill took it to the window where the light was better. One look at the street and the note-book was in his pocket and he was crossing back to slip the clock face into its original position. A perspiring bicycle (with an expiring motor attachment) had come thankfully to rest outside the house. From it leapt Gustave.

He pounced on the concierge. The concierge called off an Alsatian that had pounced on him. It was old, lean, and very friendly.

'Conquième étage,' she answered Gustave's order. 'L'ascenseur marche,' she added with considerable pride. 'Profitez de l'occasion.'

Some few minutes later Quill was considerably annoyed to hear the lift groaning its way up. He would have a few words with that concierge when he left.

'You!' cried Gustave, bouncing into the room and nearly bouncing back again as he recognized Quill. 'What for do you tell the concierge that you have come to mend the bathroom?'

'What?' said Quill.

'It was not the act of a friend,' Gustave shook his head reproachfully. 'If you wished to see this room there was no need to do it in secret. You had but to come to me. Would I not fling open every door to assist you?'

Most of them leading nowhere, thought Quill, and offered his apologies.

Gustave waved them away. 'It is not important. The appartement it is not interesting. It is only a matter of routine that brings me here.' He looked round the room with disapproval. No trellised wallpaper, no statuettes, no naughty pictures, and nothing of Louis Quinze. 'He had not much taste—the dead man—hein?' He turned to business. 'You have searched the room?'

'Yes,' said Quill.

'Bon,' said Gustave relieved. 'Then I go home now to prune my pear. Almost I fear I would not have time to attend to it to-day. I offer you a lift?'

Standing on the spoke projecting from the back wheel of the bicycle the unresisting Quill found himself being coasted back to the Casino. But he hardly noticed the journey. He was busy thinking out excuses for not lunching with Gustave.

CHAPTER VII

SAFE in his hotel Quill retired to the lounge and opened the note-book he had captured from Citrolo's safe. Closer inspection showed that the book was not confined to figures of financial transactions alone but contained some elucidating sidelights on the Citrolo philosophy. The first page was headed '*Apologia*,' and read as follows:

'If this book should ever fall into hands other than mine it would be displeasing to me that the possessor should think of me merely as a blackmailer. He must understand that I am as proud of my "blackmail" as I am of my essays on the ballet and everyone who has met me knows how much I value the latter.

'This, then, is not an attempt at vindication. It is an attempt to open the eyes of the unreflecting; to show them how strongly my despised profession, cleverly disguised under some happier name, has embedded its roots in modern civilization.

'Blackmail is an unfortunate word, ugly and unmelodious. It conjures up visions of pale-faced clerks driven to falsifying ledgers and ultimately to suicide; or trembling spinsters with lost virginities and church-going fiancés. And, of course, somewhere in the background an evil chuckle.

'But such scenes are only the minor manifestations of a great industry. Blackmail—real blackmail—works on a much larger canvas.

'Blackmail in its highest form is found in Politics. There it is called "Diplomacy."

'Governments balance their budgets with it. Here it is called "Income Tax"—a quarter of your earnings or . . .

'The working-man finds it impossible to get a job unless he belongs to a trade union—Subscription? . . .

'What is the difference between a trade union and an employer, and a blackmailer and his victim?

'How did France get its vacances payées?

'How did Lord Dash get his peerage?

'When does a gold-digger get the most out of her sugar daddy?

'Have I not proved my case? Is it not blackmail that makes the world go round?

'The world does not condemn what I have described. It shrugs its shoulders and accepts it. C'est la vie! Why then should it condemn the blackmailer, simple and undisguised, who in straightforward manner demands money with menaces?

'Try as I may I cannot see any difference.

'It was early in my youth that I discovered nature had endowed me with one undisputable asset—an ability to stumble on secrets others did not wish to share. Wherever I went it was never very long before the facts of any guilty endeavour in the neighbourhood, past, present and future, were in my hands. My luck was uncanny. My memory and my ability to interpret apparently insignificant details in the correct light did much to help. Had I been stupid or conventional I would have become a detective. Instead I became a blackmailer.

'I studied my profession as closely as a confidence trickster studies his victim. I was determined to avoid the mistakes of some of my brothers. Why end up with a cut throat, or in dock with a Mr. A. giving evidence against me? Presently I evolved for myself the following three golden rules:

'1. Never do business with the weak, the desperate, or the ruthless.

'2. Never be too greedy.

'3. Always make it clear to your sucker that he is paying for being found out and not for his guilt. This makes him more careful in future and occasionally even grateful.

'It was soon evident to me that my most profitable sphere was to be the underworld. Crooks are delightful people to work with—they seldom bear malice. There is no need to explain to them my third golden rule. They understand it only too well. Some of them are almost my best friends, and whenever I can do so without danger I am only too willing to put what business in their way I can. Of course, in such cases I charge a small percentage, but that is only reasonable. I make a habit of talking of "commission" rather than payment: they call me "Pourcentage" Citrolo. I am proud of the name.

'A proof of my efficiency is that most of my customers pay promptly—practically without complaint. Occasionally one lags—then I threaten gently. If the threats fail I close the account with a cordial letter, in which it is made quite clear that the ex-customer has nothing to fear from me. I never have any intention of carrying out my menaces—there is no profit in exposure, only unpleasantness. As in diplomacy I rely entirely on my menaces. If the bluff is called I retire with grace. But it is called seldom.

'If I have any faults as a blackmailer it is perhaps that I am a little timid in going after the really big commissions. I have in my possession information against some half-dozen "big shots," who, if they paid, would pay well. But would they pay? It is dangerous to try. With the big people externals are deceptive and it is difficult to be certain that you have got their pyschology. I made an attempt on such a one early in my career—it nearly cost me my life. It is possible that I am over-cautious now.

'But then I am anxious to die in my bed.'

*   *   *

Quill smiled as he finished reading. Poor Citrolo. With all his precautions he had still failed to allow for a distracted impresario with a box of sleeping tablets.

His thoughts now switched to a gloomier direction. Stroganoff had been shrewder than he knew when he hinted that there would be plenty of scope for enquiries along the 'Motive' lines. Probably every one of the many people who had been in the room that night had one. The same one. Quill was inclined to doubt Citrolo's boast of his excellent relations with his clients.

He turned the pages to the accounts section. This was exactly like a money-lender's ledger. There were the names of the customers in the left-hand column, each accompanied with the amounts of their payments and the dates. Some of the figures were underlined, which showed that the next instalment was overdue. There was also a column for comments. Here and there, Quill noted, a customer was marked as doing well and able to pay more, while in other cases a decrease was contemplated. It was all very businesslike. Only in the case of Kurt Kukumber, whose payments seemed practically non-existent, was there any evidence of the dead man's slightly malicious sense of humour. Here the comment read: 'For Amusement Only.'

Some of the names came as a distinct shock to Quill. Others occasioned less surprise. From his point of view the most interesting were those of people at present in La Bazouche and hovering around the fatal room last night. Two names in particular stood out. Vanilla, the croupier, and Baron Sam de Rabinovitch.

Vanilla, Quill saw, was a fairly recent customer. His payments dated back little under two years. This, Quill assumed, was probably around the date when he had first taken service in the Casino, then run by Baron de Rabinovitch. It was reasonable to assume that his racket, upon which Citrolo with his flair had stumbled, was in some way connected with the gaming rooms. Quill marked down Vanilla for early questioning and passed on to the Baron.

Baron Sam de Rabinovitch must have been practically Citrolo's oldest customer. The payments began in 1925, and formed a clear reflex of the rises and falls in the Baron's prosperity. Starting with a comparatively low figure they rose steadily till 1927, fell in 1928 and ceased altogether from

1929-31. (In gaol, thought Quill.) In 1932 they started again at
an even lower level than in 1925, but they rose very quickly.
In 1935, the year that the Baron had opened the Casino, the
payments soared abruptly and from then on showed a slight
yearly increase. That the Baron was still flourishing was shown
in the comment, which revealed that yet another substantial
increase was contemplated. Quill made a rapid calculation and
worked out that if the Baron agreed to the latest demand he
would be paying Citrolo over 10,000 francs a month.

There was yet a third section in the book. It was headed
pathetically:

'Alas—No Courage.'

It contained a list, presumably the 'Big Shots' mentioned in
the *Apologia*, that Citrolo lacked the pluck to tackle. Reading
through the names Quill began to understand why Citrolo
lacked the nerve. Some of the names were almost household
words. There was a European Dictator, who apparently did
not compose his own speeches. An International Financier
only recently found out. Lord Buttonhooke. And a learned
judge who thought the American régime had much to com-
mend it.

The remaining names were all well-known to a wistful police.
It was almost a Debrett to the evasive peerage of the underworld. There was 'Gold Tongue' Gene, who had once almost
persuaded Mongolia to start a navy with the contents of a
decrepit shipyard. There was 'Banco' Dacarpo, who having
put it across the simple-minded Greek Syndicate at Deauville
had vanished into the blue. And there was Dimitri Dmitrius,
who had lived on credit for twenty years, suing himself under
various names for fortunes he never possessed. And others
equally fascinating.

To think that here was a blighter walking about with
information about half the crooks in Europe—information
that the police would give their large-sized ears to possess—
and he had been careless enough to let the man die under his
nose before he (Quill) could bully, cajole, or bribe it out of him.

With a regretful sigh Quill laid aside Citrolo's note-book and produced his own. It was time to tabulate the information he had acquired.

His best friends had never called Quill a brilliant detective. But he was conscientious and capable. His reports of a case were invariably masterpieces of lucid presentation, hailed as such by Scotland Yard and passed on to abler detectives for solution. But there was only Gustave to help him here. Quill felt a twinge of guilt at withholding the note-book from Gustave, but he suppressed it firmly. With that note-book in Gustave's possession there would not be a citizen in Bazouche left at large.

Methodically Quill went to work. Whenever it was possible he liked to set out the crime in the form of a time-table, and he did it here.

11.15 p.m. Citrolo, Stroganoff and Galybchik in office.

11.30 p.m. Vanilla enters to ask for chips.

11.40 p.m. Madame Ostorojno arrives to demand daughter's contract. Stroganoff opens safe and puts contract in it.

11.50 p.m. Nevajno arrives and departs.

Midnight approx. Lord Buttonhooke and Baron de Rabinovitch visit the office.

12.10 a.m. Citrolo drinks drugged whisky.

12.20 a.m. Stroganoff begins dictating notice.

12.30 a.m. Prince Artishok and Sadie Souse arrive looking for Buttonhooke. Told by Stroganoff that the sleeping critic is drunk.

12.35 a.m. My friend, the Balleto-Medico, tries to enter office. Pushed out by Stroganoff.

1.00 a.m. Stroganoff finishes notice and departs. Claims to have locked door.

1.00 a.m.—9.00 a.m. Citrolo is strangled.

9.15 a.m. Stroganoff arrives to find Citrolo dead.

9.15 a.m. Stroganoff arranges scene.

9.30 a.m. Stroganoff telephones Gustave.

10.00 a.m. Stroganoff telephones me.

Plenty of material here, thought Quill, though of course as
yet no information at all of those critical hours during which
Citrolo met his death. Still there was an abundance of suspects
—the note-book probably contained a complete list of the
dead man's enemies, several of whom were about the premises.
Both Vanilla and the Baron de Rabinovitch had actually seen
Citrolo in Stroganoff's office and assuming that they felt any
interest in the matter, could have been in a position to note
than he had not left it.

Pondering thus Quill became aware of a short, wasp-waisted
figure, striding up and down in anxious concentration, pausing
irresolutely in front of his desk, clasping its forehead, audibly
changing its mind and striding up and down again. At last
Quill decided he could stand it no longer. He looked up
severely. The figure started elaborately and hastened to his side.

'What's the matter?' Quill asked.

Kurt Kukumber shook his head dramatically, turned away
and recommenced his striding. But not for long. Presently he
was back again at Quill's side.

'M'sieur Quill,' he said, 'can I trust you?'

'Why not?' said Quill.

Kukumber stooped and sent a searching beam into Quill's
eyes. What he saw seemed to satisfy him. He nodded emphatically twice and drew up a chair.

'M'sieur,' he said, 'on me a heavy responsibility has fallen.'

Where had Quill heard that opening before.

'My uncle,' began Kukumber.

'In Australia,' supplied Quill.

'In Toronto,' said Kukumber in all seriousness. 'He has
died. Suddenly.'

'Leaving a will?' asked Quill.

'An amazing will,' said Kukumber, dazed but persevering.
'An astonishing will. A will that is typical of his eccentric but
generous nature.' He sighed. 'A wonderful man, my uncle.'

'Lovable,' suggested Quill.

'His will,' said Kukumber, 'has left me the chief beneficiary
but . . .'

'There are many bequests to charity to which you have to attend first.'

'It is a clause,' said Kukumber solemnly.

'You have to distribute—how much is it?'

'Pardon?'

'And you want a trustworthy person to help you do it.'

'M'sieur,' said Kukumber.

'If I can produce—say twenty thousand francs to show that I am a man of substance. . . .'

'Er,' said Kukumber.

'And leave them with you for half an hour to show I trust you...'

'Enough,' pleaded Kukumber. 'M'sieur, I apologize. But how was I to tell that you too were one of our profession?'

Quill passed one of his visiting cards.

Kukumber blushed deeply and apologized even more profusely. He also remembered a pressing engagement. But Quill would not let him keep it.

'Sit down,' he said firmly.

Kukumber sat down.

'About Pavlo Citrolo,' said Quill.

Kukumber sprang to his feet.

'It is a lie,' he said. 'I did not kill him.'

Quill pushed him back into his chair again. 'How did you know he was dead?'

'All Bazouche knows.' Kukumber sighed. 'Alas—poor Pavlo.'

'You knew him well?'

'I was his best friend,' declared Kukumber stoutly.

'Yet he blackmailed you!' Quill threw his bombshell.

It failed to explode. 'I paid for his silence,' said Kukumber. 'It was only fair,' he added ungrudgingly.

It was this remark that started the high esteem which Quill was eventually to feel for the Blackmailer's *Apologia*.

'He was a fair man,' said Kurt kindly. 'He did not charge me as much as the others and would not reproach me too much if I fell behind with my payments. You see,' he said with the assurance of the artist born, 'I show great promise—it needs only time for me to be the big shot. So Citrolo was content to wait.'

Quill toyed with the idea of showing him the comment in Citrolo's note-book but decided that the moment was not yet.

'How's business?' he asked chattily.

'Bad,' said Kurt. 'The luck is against me. My infallible system has broken down again.'

'And your rackets?'

'One disappointment after another,' said Kurt, man to man. 'First I think I find an English sucker—and he is you. Then I start to sell a gold-mine and what happens? It is my prospect who gets sent to gaol.'

Light dawned on Quill. 'The gold prospectus in Stroganoff's office—you put it there?'

'Yes,' said the unwary Kukumber.

'When,' snapped Quill.

Kukumber hesitated. 'I gave it to him downstairs.'

Quill lit a cigarette wearily. Here he was back on the dear old familiar ground. The lying witness who in all probability had nothing important to conceal.

But Kurt clung stoutly to his denial. He had posted the prospectus. He had given it to the commissionaire. He had dictated it across the telephone. He had never seen it in his life. But he had not put it there! Finally Quill changed the subject and asked Kukumber to describe his movements during the last night.

'You suspect me?' asked Kukumber alarmed.

'Purely a matter of routine,' said Quill from force of habit. Kukumber reflected. 'I have the perfect alibi,' he said triumphantly. 'I watch the new ballet. It was beautiful,' he said wistfully.

Clearly this could not be true. 'You never went near it,' Quill diagnosed.

'Useless to attempt to deceive you,' said Kukumber. 'If you know that, then you know also that Citrolo and I had a little disagreement last night.'

Quill nodded. 'I know.'

'It was not a disagreement exactly,' said Kukumber. 'Just such a cloud as comes sometimes between friends. Citrolo was a little put out as he left the baccarat room. Doubtless Vanilla had been difficult again. I am not fond of Vanilla,' said Kurt Kukumber a trifle irrelevantly.

'Was Vanilla fond of Citrolo?'

Kukumber was quick to catch the inference. 'It is curious that he is the one man who never spoke well of poor Pavlo. It is he who did it,' said Kukumber inspired, and grasped Quill affectionately by the arm. 'Prove it, M'sieur, and you will earn the gratitude of many.'

Quill was surprised. 'Is Vanilla so unpopular?'

But it was not that. Under the easy-going direction of Stroganoff, the Casino, it appeared, had become the little crook's Paradise. Petty swindles flourished in every corner and even the croupiers could occasionally be cajoled into paying out over the wrong numbers. With Stroganoff in gaol the danger of Buttonhooke buying the Casino and reinstating the eagle-eyed Baron de Rabinovitch loomed only too imminent. It was not, Quill was given to understand, Vanilla's immediate arrest that mattered so much as Stroganoff's immediate extradition.

Quill extricated himself from the babble of words and returned to the business in hand.

'What happened during the interview between you and Citrolo?'

'It was nothing,' Kurt assured him. 'He wanted a little money on account, but I persuaded him to be patient.'

'How did you spend the rest of the evening?'

'I played my system. No luck. So I went home to sleep.'

'Did you know that Citrolo was in Stroganoff's office?'

'No.'

'Did you go near it?'

'No.'

'Then how did the Gold Mine Prospectus get there?'

'What prospectus?' asked Kurt blandly.

* * *

'It's a scandal,' Madame Ostorojno was saying. 'My daughter dancing for a murderer!'

'I don't believe Stroganoff is a murderer,' said her daughter.

'Murderer or not,' snapped the mother, 'you're not going to work for a gaol-bird. We're going straight to Buttonhooke.'

'He's in gaol, too,' put in Quill helpfully.

'It's a scandal,' said Madame Ostorojno again. 'I'm going straight to that policeman to tell him what I think of him.'

'Presently,' Quill sighed. Already he regretted the foolhardiness that had prompted him to place Madame Ostorojno's name at the top of his interview list for no better reason than that she was staying at his hotel. He ought to have known what to expect from a dancer's mother. 'Go where you like, but please answer a few questions first.'

'It's a scandal!' repeated Madame Ostorojno obstinately.

* * *

'Rien ne va plus,' said the new croupier. His name was Samson and a distracted Galybchik had handed him his diploma that morning. 'Rien ne va plus,' he repeated a shade apprehensively. To his astonishment everyone obeyed him. The new croupier relaxed. This was going to be easy.

It was five o'clock at the Casino Stroganoff. As Quill arrived Kurt Kukumber left. Quill put it down to guilty conscience, but he was wrong. Five o'clock was the hour when Kukumber always left—broke.

The green cloth tempted Quill. He had come in search of Vanilla, but he might as well allow himself the luxury of losing a few francs. He flung a counter on seventeen. A lean hand stretched over and removed it.

'It is foolish what you do,' said Nevajno to the switched round glare. 'I cannot bear to see you lose your money on a method so devoid of line.'

'Vingt-cinq,' said the croupier.

'Voila!' said Nevajno triumphantly. 'Now we put it on number seven.' He did so.

'Zero,' said the croupier.

'N'importe,' said Nevajno. 'You have another louis?'

Quill felt it was time to dissolve this superimposed partnership. He got up and pushed Nevajno into his seat. Nevajno accepted the situation philosophically and reached out a lean hand to move his neighbour's stake into better alignment.

'Excuse me,' said a breathless stranger to Quill, 'but would you introduce me to your friend—the great Nevajno?'

Quill looked curiously at this hunter of unusual lions.

'Have you got a cheque-book?'

'Why—yes?' The lion-hunter seemed surprised.

'Just show it to him,' said Quill, 'he will be delighted to meet you.'

In the *Salle de Baccarat* Vanilla was presiding over a moderate assemblage. His tie was tilting happily all over the place. The afternoon sessions showed Vanilla his greatest profit. Afternoon players were all small punters, far too absorbed in their own speculations to notice anything else. Quill's experienced eye picked out Vanilla's two accomplices almost immediately. The first might have been Kurt Kukumber all over again—a little wasp-waisted man across whose face eagerness and anxiety continually clashed. There was a seediness about the second. His suit was debonair, if dog-eared. Nicotine stained his fingers. There was a droop about his eyelids. A man, Quill decided, who had seen better days—probably aboard a Cunarder. He would have been willing to bet that Vanilla underpaid them both for their assistance.

'Banco,' cried the eager one.

'Idiot,' hissed the other.

But it was too late. Glaring, Vanilla pushed across the counters to a palooka in a pince-nez.

Thanks to Citrolo, Quill found little difficulty in following the rigours of the game. Abashed by his mistake, anxiety was now uppermost on the little man's face. He muffed three 'bancos' in succession. The thin veneer of immobility that masked over Vanilla's rage was a delight to Quill. Clearly he would have loved to strangle his accomplice. Quill looked at the hands that moved with precision and efficiency and noted the strength in the lean deft fingers. 'The perfect strangler,' he thought professionally.

Presently the syndicate scored a triumph. The eager one got a signal right. Determined to take no more chances Vanilla glanced at the clock and declared the session over. The players disbanded. Quill went over to Vanilla and introduced himself.

Vanilla was inclined to be curt. It was clear that he was eager to get away for a few words with his syndicate. But the official visiting card awed him.

'I know nothing,' he insured himself, before Quill had a chance to fire a single question.

Quill looked closely at the ferrety face and decided that a bludgeon would be best.

'You know a lot about Citrolo,' he said coldly. 'How much you know about his murder, we will discover presently.'

The ferrety face twitched.

'What is there to know about the murder?' he asked. 'The guilty one is already under arrest.'

'Citrolo had too many enemies to be certain of that,' said Quill. He paused. 'You were one of them,' he accused.

Vanilla was hurt. 'I was his best friend.'

'Shut up,' said Quill, 'you have been paying him blackmail for years.'

'You know that!' Vanilla was staggered.

'I know nearly everything about you—including your baccaret racket with your rather childish cheats.'

'They are childish,' agreed Vanilla, natural indignation rising above fear. 'Never will I be able to teach them.'

'Still,' said Quill smoothly, 'their mistakes do not matter much so long as you can rectify them by helping yourself from Stroganoff's box of chips.'

It was a bow at venture but it succeeded.

'You have found that out!'

Quill nodded. 'I also know that the emerald bracelet you gave Arenskaya is stolen property.'

'Even my private life,' muttered Vanilla, helpless.

Quill smiled to himself. These Latins were easy. He could never have pinned a Russian down like this,

'You can see that you are in a tough spot,' he resumed relentlessly. 'If I wanted I could make things very unpleasant for you.'

Vanilla nodded. He saw.

'But the law-breakers of France are not my concern. I am working for Stroganoff. Answer my questions and I won't make any trouble.'

Vanilla took up a pack of cards and absently tore them across.

'What is it you wish to know?' he surrendered.

'First,' said Quill, 'you went into Stroganoff's office last night.'

Vanilla nodded. 'That was to get some chips.'

'Tell me what you saw.'

'There was M'sieur le Directeur in argument with the critic Citrolo. With him was his *poule*.'

'His what?'

'His secretary,' amended Vanilla. 'I do not like her,' he added irrelevantly. 'She us not my type.'

Quill remembered Arenskaya. He nodded.

'I take my chips and I go. That is all.'

'Did you come back again?'

'No.'

'How did you spend the rest of the evening?'

'I am in the baccarat room till five. Then I go home.'

'The baccarat game broke up at five a.m.?'

'Yes.'

'There were many players?'

'Just the one table.'

Quill reflected. 'Can you give me the names of the late players at your table?'

But on this point Vanilla appeared to have lost his memory. Quill had not attached any importance to the late players so far, but Vanilla's reluctance to divulge their names made them suddenly significant. After all, the murderer would need some pretext to remain at the Casino and the baccarat table provided an admirable excuse. He would only have to leave it for a few minutes. Quill pressed the matter and gradually Vanilla began to remember. Eventually he produced the following list:

Lord Buttonhooke.

Prince Alexis Artishok.

Sadie Souse.

M'sieur André Dupont, Mayor of La Bazouche.

The Baron de Rabovitch.

Herr Van de West, and, of course, Vanilla's two accomplices, who, said Vanilla, had been quite outclassed by the formidable company. Had it not been for the Mayor and Lord Button-hooke the evening would have been utter ruin.

Quill wondered why Vanilla should have been so reluctant to give this list. The names were interesting enough—one name in particular—but he could see no reason why Vanilla should want to hold them back. However he did not press the point.

'The Baron de Rabinovitch,' he asked, 'he used to be your employer?'

'He did,' said Vanilla, 'the cochon.'

'He wouldn't let you get at the chips?' Quill guessed.

'He kept them in the safe.'

Quill nodded sympathetically. 'It is harder to guess a combination than to pick a lock.'

Vanilla stared at him.

'Perhaps I am underestimating you,' said Quill; 'no doubt you have had a duplicate key to the office door made long ago.'

For some odd reason Vanilla looked relieved. 'I have no key. M'sieur le Directeur forgets to lock the door so often there is no need.'

'Did he leave it open last night?'

Vanilla shook his head. 'Last night it was locked.'

'How do you know?' Quill snapped.

Vanilla floundered helplessly. 'Did I say last night? I am confused. I refer to the night before.'

'So you did go to the office last night?'

'It was the night before,' insisted Vanilla. 'Last night I go to the office only once when I ask for the chips. After the game I go straight home. I have a witness,' he added proudly.

'Who?' asked Quill.

'A witness of quality—of integrity unimpeachable—the Prince Alexis Artishok,' said Vanilla. 'He gave me a lift.'

'What on earth did he want to get out of you?'

Vanilla fidgeted slightly. 'He is a great gentleman. It was raining. Doubtless he did not wish me to get wet.'

For the time being Quill let it go at that.

* * *

Remembering Stroganoff's request for 'possessions of the most valuable' left in the office, and thinking that he could, without offending Gustave, combine this small act of courtesy with a quiet prowl round of his own, Quill made his way upstairs. In the alcove by the broken statue he came upon two figures. Nevajno and his public. For once Nevajno was not talking. He was listening speculatively while the lion-hunter propounded the theme he had been waiting to unloose for many years. The perfect ballet.

'We will call it,' he finished on a note of ecstasy, 'NEPTUNE AGONISTES.'

Nevajno pondered for a long time.

'You schange me large scheque?' he demanded ambitiously.

Reluctantly detaching himself from this artistic collaboration Quill went up to Stroganoff's office. From inside came the pounding of a typewriter. Quill entered. Galybchik looked up eagerly from her machine but her face fell as she recognized Quill.

'Oh, it's you,' she said. 'Haven't you got him out yet?'

'We will soon,' Quill assured her. He glanced round and noted that the office had been restored to an apple-pie order it had certainly never possessed while its owner was about.

'Who tidied the room?' he asked.

Galybchik pleaded guilty. 'Was it wrong?' she asked apprehensively.

'Very,' said Quill.

'But the police had taken away everything they wanted,' pleaded Galybchik. 'And they've had the nerve to go through our ledgers.'

'How do you know?'

'They didn't put them back,' explained Galybchik. 'I found them on the shelf we use for our kettle and we always keep them locked in the drawer.'

Quill remembered those ledgers. They had been on the shelf that morning so it was not the police who had put them there. He docketed the information for further pondering and produced his list of the things Stroganoff wanted.

Together they crossed to the safe.

'Here's the biography,' said Galybchik, producing a formidable sheaf of foolscap. 'It's marvellous,' she breathed. 'The whole Ballet Stroganoff seems to come to life as you read. And nobody has ever been so right about Nicolas. Listen,' she began to turn the pages feverishly.

'Er,' said Quill.

'After that memorable performance the Tsar he say to me, "Vladimir Stroganoff you are astonishing." No—that's not it.' Galybchik turned a few more pages. 'Vladimir you are superb. . . . No. Vladimir you are a genius. . . . No. Vladimir . . .'

'Find it later,' Quill pleaded.

With a sigh Galybchik laid aside the memoirs and delved into the safe again. She produced the mortgage papers and the contracts marked 'Lubova' and 'Smithsky,' rummaged some more and emerged with a puzzled expression.

'The Ostorojno contract is missing.'

'Really,' said Quill, on whom the magnitude of the disaster had not yet penetrated.

'But this is terrible,' wailed Galybchik, 'our best dancer gone. How shall I tell Stroganoff?'

'I'll tell him,' Quill promised.

'It's that woman,' flared Galybchik. 'She tried to sneak it last night.'

'What woman?'

'The Ostorojno creature. The mother. She saw Stroganoff put it in the safe and came back for it.'

'Does she know the combination?'

'*Sylphides?*' asked Galybchik. 'Why, yes, I should think so.

Even if she didn't know she could guess it. Mr. Stroganoff is much too confiding. He tells everybody that it is always the name of a ballet and there aren't so many of them with nine letters.'

Quill became practical. 'But even assuming she could work the combination how did she manage to get into the room? She, or her daughter?'

'Oh—it wouldn't be Olga,' said Galybchik quickly. 'I like Olga.'

That seemed to settle that.

'Then how did the mother get in?'

Galybchik had no constructive suggestions to offer. She walked to the window, gazed down the flat wall and shook a puzzled head. Her own key had never left her—she never lent it to anybody—not even Nicolas.

Quill interrupted. 'So you have a key?'

'Of course,' said Galybchik, 'Stroganoff trusts me implicitly.'

'Which makes you a very suspicious person from my point of view,' Quill smiled.

Galybchik began to tremble visibly.

'Tell me,' Quill coaxed, 'you did go back to this room last night—didn't you?'

'No,' said Galybchik tautly. 'That is—no.'

Quill knew she was lying. It did not worry him unduly. Whatever felony Galybchik had compounded it was certainly not murder and in any case it would not be long before she would be telling him all about it.

Bestowing a paternal pat on her indignant curls he left her to her conscience.

*   *   *

The restaurant was crowded. This is explained, not by the excellence of the cuisine, which was appalling, but by the lavish system of credit that prevailed. Remembering the hungry days of his ballet, Stroganoff could never bring himself to refuse a ravenous customer food. Even Nevajno was allowed to sign a bill for his dinner. But it had to be signed. Every franc lost had to be accounted for in the books.

Quill had come to the restaurant on the track of the glass of milk found beside the dead man. But at his entry Emilio bustled forward with the smile of welcome reserved for cash customers, and before he realized what was happening Quill was seated at a table under the orchestra, allowing himself to order caviare, bortsch and pirojki, sole Stroganoff, Kiev cutlets, and Bombe Arenskaya, washed down with vodka and (a belated attack of firmness, this) vin du pays. It seemed an expensive way of cajoling a witness into a good temper.

'There are a few questions,' Quill began.

'M'sieur need have no fear,' said Emilio, 'the fish it comes fresh every day from St. Tropez,' and vanished.

He reappeared some ten minutes later carrying a dish of sardines. Caviare, it appeared, was off.

Quill smiled pleasantly. 'No matter,' he said, 'tell me—were you on duty last night?'

'Every night,' said Emilio, with a distinct sense of grievance. 'Always I am the last to go.'

'Then perhaps you can tell me. . . .'

'Un petit moment,' Emilio darted off and neatly fielded a bowl of soup trembling on a waiter's tray.

'Gaston est enervé ce soir,' he told Quill confidentially. 'He has discovered that his wife is faithful after all.'

'About last night,' interposed Quill.

The orchestra struck up *Madame Butterfly*. It struck, too, a reminiscent chord in Emilio's breast.

'I sing that once,' he said, wistfully, 'in Milan. Not the Scala.'

'Quite,' said Quill. 'But . . .'

'Ssssh,' said Emilio, reproachfully, and wandered off.

Quill pushed away the sardines and waited for the bortsch. When it arrived it was tomato soup. The orchestra played *Tosca*. Emilio was too sad to talk. It was the favourite aria of the girl who had almost married him.

The sole Stroganoff arrived next. It was smoked haddock.

'Pardon,' said Emilio, 'a little mistake. Le chef est enervé ce soir.'

'His wife?' asked Quill sympathetically.

'Sa maîtresse.' Emilio shook his head. 'Elle est extravagante.'

'About last night,' said Quill. 'Do you remember a glass of milk? . . .'

'Tout de suite,' said Emilio, and ran.

He reappeared a moment later apologetically carrying a beaker. Kiev cutlets were 'off,' but here was the milk M'sieur demanded.

Quill nearly threw it at him.

'It is curious,' mused Emilio, 'how much you English like the milk. Last night par example . . .'

The orchestra attacked *Tannhauser*. It was the trumpet's big moment.

'And so,' finished Emilio, the rest of the story buried beneath the tramping feet of the pilgrims, 'I understand too late that it is really the milk she wants. So I give it.' And he darted away to supervise the coffee-tray underling—doubtless *enervé* also.

The Bombe Arenskaya lived up to its name. It exploded the moment Quill touched it.

'C'est bon?' demanded Emilio, determined that someone should enthuse over the chef's masterpiece.

Quill wiped himself energetically. 'Who was it you said asked for the milk last night?'

'Mais la petite Anglaise,' said Emilio. 'Elle est gamine celle-la. Mais froide,' he added regretfully.

'Who?'

'Mais Mademoiselle Galybchik. It was after one o'clock when she came to me with her big eyes to ask for milk. Naturally, I do not suppose that at that hour anyone can really desire milk. But what do you suppose, M'sieur?'

'She wanted milk.'

Emilio nodded sadly. 'She wanted milk. Only milk. Moi—I am enervé to-day,' he added, and dashed off.

The orchestra burst into 'On with the Motley.'

*   *   *

The Ballet—it must go on!

Arenskaya was assuring everybody within screaming distance that a mere imprisoned impresario meant nothing to her. To-night *Oiseau de Feu* would be danced as scheduled, and no worse than usual. Nerve storms, sundry crises, and private quarrels must be put off until the old man came back to cope with them.

The curtain was going up in half an hour. Where was Ostorojno? Where was her mother? Where was the *Régisseur?* Where was everybody? Smithsky hurried over to reassure her that he, at least, was there, but she did not seem to notice him.

'You,' she grasped a soloiste roughly by the shoulder. 'Look at your hair—it is a disgust!'

A tired urchin lurched wearily over. He carried a note of frantic instructions from Stroganoff. It was the fifteenth note he had brought her since tea-time.

'Pas de répose,' snapped Arenskaya, stuffing the note with the fourteen others in her handbag to be read later.

The tired urchin lurched blankly away. No doubt this meant another journey.

CHAPTER VIII

THE Ballet of La Bazouche by night is played against a spangled backcloth. With any luck the *Régisseur* will have cleared away all traces of rain, and there will be some fascinating *entrées* for the corps-de-ballet. Take, for instance, the stream of waiters going off duty, whizzing past another stream of waiters crawling on duty. Take the hopeful trickle of gamblers making their way to one or other of the Casinos. Take a vivacious sprinkling of ballerinas, making for opposition shows on one of the rare nights when they happen not to be needed in any ballet on the programme, or when injuries to arms, ankles, or feelings, have temporarily intervened between their ambitions and their careers. Their hopeful faces will be framed in the unemotional orbit of the box-office window. 'Two, please.' The embarrassed expression dodging behind them of the boy-friend.

Take the residents—but there are none. In season La Bazouche is given over strictly to its visitors—clients who come to play at the Casino. The good Bazouchian who is neither hôtelier nor croupier has the decency to go right away—probably to try his luck at Monte Carlo.

Take the restaurants, they are just beginning to empty, as their clients make their way to café or casino. Take the cabarets. They are still the sleep-bound hide-holes for makers of synthetic whoopee.

Take Quill. He has made his way down a twisting hill, along a promenade, and has paused for a moment before entering an erection of ferro-concrete with an Astorian frontage and an Odeon lighting scheme. The lordly commissionaire, every shining button in place, has obviously decided that the Casino

97

Button'ooke is the perfect *décor* for his treacle-coloured moustachios. He is right about this.

Up those milky marble stairs, through those chromium-plated swing-doors. Past the lines of needlessly superior flunkeys such as Press Barons require to help them forget their ancestral homes. Past the beaky scrutineer, enthroned in a chaste signal-box. Into the gilded halls of the gambling hell strode Quill.

Here he paused, a little bilious. The interior of the Casino Buttonhooke had clearly been salved from plans jettisoned by Maison Lyons on the grounds of gaudiness. Never can more spurious alabaster have been found suspended from one ceiling. Never was there so much pseudo-marble. Silken carpets positively pushed the patron's foot from its soft resting-place. Settees were opulent. Service was prompt and impersonal. The lifts were in working order.

Quill took one.

A flunkey, in the discreet tones of an usher at a fashionable wedding, had told him that the Baron would doubtless be found in his Lordship's private office.

In Lord Buttonhooke's sanctum the need for tinted glasses became increasingly evident. A large boiled shirt bulging from an oil painting challenged the eye of the caller and created, from the outset, the proper feelings of reverence. Beneath it, also bulging, but rather more actual, posed another, smaller boiled shirt. Baron Sam de Rabinovitch, deaf to Quill's punctilious knock, was practising that look of well-fed benevolence that had persuaded so many investors to plunge heavily in the Buttonhooke concerns.

It seemed a shame to disturb this touching tableau, but duty was duty. Quill coughed. The Baron, startled out of his pose, looked first sheepish and then angry.

'Well?' he snapped.

'The Baron de Rabinovitch?' asked Quill.

'Yes. What do you want?'

Quill produced his card and explained that he was conducting an enquiry into Citrolo's death. The Baron did not appear impressed.

'Well?'

'If you would answer a few questions?'

'But why should I answer any questions?' asked the Baron coldly. 'You appear to have no official status whatever.'

Quill tried an appeal to better nature. 'An innocent man has been arrested.'

'Two innocent men,' interrupted the Baron, 'and when Lord Buttonhooke gets out, Gustave is going to wish he had never been born.'

'The French are inclined to be impetuous,' said Quill, tactfully.

'I am a Frenchman,' said Baron Sam de Rabinovitch.

Quill decided not to waste any more time on tact. He crossed the carpet, sank into an armchair and lit a cigarette.

'Making yourself at home?' jeered the Baron.

'Definitely,' said Quill, 'you and I have a lot of things to discuss.'

'I've already told you I won't answer questions.'

'You might answer this one,' said Quill. 'What were you doing from 1929 to 1931?'

The Baron said nothing but a gleam of apprehension in his eye told Quill that the shaft had got home. Mentally he blessed Citrolo's note-book.

'I wonder,' he mused, 'whether Lord Buttonhooke knows that his trusted assistant is an ex-convict.'

'I was innocent,' said the Baron from force of habit.

'Of course. Still,' said Quill, 'why bring up these unpleasant memories? I only want to ask a few simple questions.'

There was a pause.

'Very well,' said the Baron, resigned.

Quill produced his note-book. 'It was about one o'clock when you left Stroganoff's office on the night of the murder?'

'About that. I went to play baccarat,' said the Baron. 'I played till the game broke up. Then I went home.'

'You did not return to Stroganoff's office during the evening?'

'Certainly not,' said the Baron quickly.

'Have you a key to the office door?'

'No. I gave both keys to Stroganoff when he took over the Casino.'

'You did not keep a third key for yourself?'

'No.'

'Is there anyone else you know who might have a key to the door?'

'No.'

Quill glanced round the office, pondering his next angle of attack. He found it unexpectedly as his eye fell on two large ledgers on a shelf immediately behind the desk. It was the exact position in which the ledgers in Stroganoff's office had been found that morning, moved there, according to Galybchik, by intruders. But if Rabinovitch always kept his ledgers in this position he had doubtless kept them like that in his days at the old Casino. And if it was Rabinovitch who had examined Stroganoff's ledgers last night might he not unthinkingly have put them back in what was, to him, their usual repository. At any rate it was worth trying.

'Why are you so interested in Stroganoff's ledgers?'

The question took the Baron by surprise. It took him several moments to compose his features into an expression of injured innocence. Satisfied that he was on the right track, Quill changed the subject.

'You knew the dead man well?'

The Baron shrugged. 'I knew him only as a critic. We were never intimate.'

'Had he, to your knowledge, any enemies?'

'Every critic has his enemies. Your client had as good a reason as any to fear him.'

'As good a reason as yourself?'

'What reason could I have?' asked the Baron blandly. 'We did not have one single interest in common.'

Quill nodded and put away his notes. The Baron had already said quite enough to prove himself a liar and there was no object in inducing him to repeat himself. The moment was not yet ripe for confronting him with Citrolo's memoirs.

'I shall want to see you again,' he promised, and rose to leave.

There was a knock at the door. A pair of aristocratic eyebrows arched at them impartially from the doorway.

The Baron remembered the conventions.

'Er—Prince Alexis Artishok,' he said.

Quill bowed briefly. 'Delighted,' he said, and left.

The Prince and the Baron circled each other warily.

* * *

The cocktail bar at the Casino Buttonhooke was a symphony of red leather and stainless steel.

Quill pushed his way to a vacant stool and ordered a double Scotch. The barman nodded and dived under the counter.

'Make him show you the bottle,' said a voice beside Quill. 'They've got some of their own stuff they unload on you if you're not looking.'

Quill obeyed orders and then turned from the discomfited barman to thank the pale green Schiaparelli from which the voice came.

'Not at all,' said Sadie Souse. 'I hate to see an Englishman soaked by foreigners. I adore Englishmen,' she added, dazzlingly.

Not exactly his taste, Quill reflected, but undeniably more attractive than Arenskaya. He smiled back.

'You're English—aren't you?' demanded Sadie.

'Certainly.'

Sadie studied the handsome profile with interest. 'How d'you get here, anyway? You look more the huntin', shootin', fishin' type to me.'

Quill explained that he was here on holiday at Stroganoff's invitation.

'And he gets into gaol just as you arrive,' Sadie commented. 'Inhospitable I call it.'

'Worse,' said Quill. 'I've got to spend all my time getting him out again.'

Sadie was thrilled. 'Are you a busy?'

'I used to work at Scotland Yard.'

'Gee!' Quill found his arm seized enthusiastically. 'Can you get Percy out too?'

'Percy?'

'Lord Buttonhooke,' explained Sadie.

'Are you interested in Buttonhooke?'

'Am I interested? Gosh!' Sadie looked at Quill incredulously. 'Don't you know?'

'Know what?'

'I'm his girl-friend.'

'Congratulations.'

'No foolin',' said Sadie. 'I'm serious. What use is Percy to me in gaol? What sort of a temper do you think he'll be in?'

'Foul—I imagine.'

'Exactly,' said Sadie, 'and I particularly want him sweet and generous just now. So you gotta get him out.'

'We'll try,' Quill promised.

'That's dandy. You know,' announced Sadie, gazing at Quill over her glass. 'I like you.'

Quill bowed.

'This English reserve of yours gets me every time. Thank heavens Percy hasn't got any of it.'

'No?'

'No. Gee! I'd never dare to try and persuade you to buy me the Otchi Tchernia diamonds.'

'What sort of diamonds?'

'It's a necklace,' said Sadie. 'A hell of a necklace. Belongs to a Russian dancer—Duraska or something.'

'Dyrakova?' said Quill, startled.

'That's it. Anyway, I've decided that I want Percy to buy it for me.'

'And will he?'

'You bet he will. Of course, he doesn't know about it yet. You see,' she explained, 'Percy is getting this Dyrakova down here to dance and the Prince says he can persuade her to sell it. Well, I mean I can't miss an opportunity like that—can I?'

'Would that be Prince Alexis Artishok?'

'Isn't he grand?' demanded Sadie. 'I thrill all over every time he touches me. Why is it,' she demanded petulantly, 'that anybody I really like never has any money? Have you any money?'

'Very little,' said Quill quickly.

'I thought so.' Disappointed Sadie ordered another cocktail. 'Guess I'll have to stick to Percy. He's not such a bad old stick,' she added philosophically, 'and he's so busy that a girl gets lots of time to herself.'

'Alas,' said Quill, 'what with getting Stroganoff and your Percy out of gaol like I look being a very busy man.'

Sadie laughed.

'Instead of flirting with you I've got to ask you questions.'

'Questions?'

'Nasty official questions. For instance I understand you went into Stroganoff's office with the Prince last night.'

'Sure.'

'And was Citrolo sleeping it off?'

'He wasn't sleeping it off,' declared Sadie unexpectedly. 'I've seen too many people sozzled to make any mistake about it. As I told the Prince, that guy had been drugged.'

Quill controlled his alarm at this disturbing insight into Stroganoff's big secret.

'Did the Prince agree with your impression?'

'He hadn't noticed.'

'Where did you go after that?'

'We looked for Percy and found him playing baccarat, so I played too. I won a packet,' she said proudly.

'You won!' Quill was surprised. What on earth had Vanilla been thinking about.

'The Prince brought me luck,' said Sadie. 'He won a packet too. Poor Percy lost though,' she added.

'Did you play late?'

'Darn late.'

'I wonder if you noticed whether any of the players left the room for any space of time.'

Sadie nodded. 'Most of them went out for a bit some time

or another. All except Percy. Percy played all the time without stopping and still wanted to play when the game finished. Maybe it was because he was losing.'

'It's asking a lot, I know,' said Quill, 'but can you by any chance remember the approximate times at which various players left the room and how long they were absent?'

'Have a heart,' pleaded Sadie.

'Please try.'

Sadie gazed at him intently. 'I get you. You think one of them may have slipped upstairs to bump off the critic guy.'

'I don't think anything,' said Quill, 'I'm just trying to assemble my facts.'

'Sure.' Sadie was not to be side-tracked. 'But you never told me you were looking for the murderer.'

'I told you I was trying to get Stroganoff out of gaol.'

'Sure,' said Sadie again. 'He's your client. I suppose you've got to try and pin it on somebody else.'

Quill was mildly annoyed. 'You sound as if you thought Stroganoff guilty.'

'He doped his drink—didn't he?'

Quill brought the conversation hurriedly back to the baccarat room and spent the next half hour in jogging Sadie's memory. On the whole, considering that she had not been concentrating on the players' movements, it proved remarkably good. She could vouch for the following:

Prince Alexis Artishok had gone out to get some air around two-thirty. He was away about twenty minutes. She was certain about this because her luck had mysteriously changed the moment he left, and changed back again when he returned.

The Mayor of La Bazouche had left the room about five times for intervals of about three minutes.

Around three-thirty the Baron de Rabinovitch had excused himself. Sadie did not notice how long he had been gone, but it did occur to her that the Baron seemed slightly distraught on his return and played without much concentration or success.

She herself had gone to the ladies' cloakroom about two o'clock. She mentioned this because she found it occupied by a grim old lady gloating over a sheet of paper. On seeing Sadie the old girl had hurriedly stuffed the paper into her bosom, glared, and waddled out. From the description it was not difficult to recognize Madame Ostorojno.

Quill enquired after Vanilla. Sadie remembered that at one period the croupier had left the game, leaving an assistant in charge. The time? It was just after the Prince had won a large bank against a funny-looking, wasp-waisted little man. It must have been about two-twenty.

'At any rate,' said Sadie, 'it was just before the Prince went for his walk. I remember the Prince left the moment the new croupier took over.'

'The Prince also gave Vanilla a lift home—didn't he?'

Sadie laughed, 'He did that. In Percy's car. Percy was quite annoyed about it.'

'But didn't he ask for permission?'

'Of course,' said Sadie. 'In that regal manner he's got which implies that a refusal never even occurs to him. Anyway, Percy was tired and wanted to get to bed, but he hadn't got the guts to say no.'

Just then the regal manner appeared at the top of the marble stairs and began a royal descent. A smile here, a bow there, even an occasional kindly word somewhere else. The court obediently made way for his progress.

'You're darn late,' said the plebian Sadie.

'A million excuses,' the Prince apologized. 'The Baron and I were discussing a matter of some importance.' He bowed coldly to Quill.

'The Otchi Tchernia diamonds?' asked Sadie.

The Prince frowned warningly. 'A matter of business.'

'But of course,' said Sadie, 'I'm silly. There's no need for the Baron to know anything about it. He doesn't like me so much, anyway.'

'Shall we proceed to the prison,' the Prince suggested.

'Sure.' Sadie jumped up. 'Must say good night to Percy. And I think,' she mused, 'I'll just drop him a teeny-weeny hint about the diamonds.'

The Prince frowned again.

'Mind if I walk with you?' asked Quill. 'I ought to say good night to Stroganoff.'

'How is your enquiry progressing?' asked the Prince courteously. 'Favourably I trust.'

'He's been asking me all sorts of questions,' put in Sadie. 'He's actually trying to find another murderer. He won't believe Stroggy did it.'

The Prince nodded. 'Personally, I, too, am sceptical of his guilt. He has not the temperament of the strangler.'

Quill was in no mood to swap theories. 'Shall we go?'

'But assuredly,' said the Prince.

They started off.

'You know,' mused Sadie as they left the Casino, 'I don't think I shall mention the diamonds to Percy to-night. I don't feel it's the right moment.'

The Prince sighed deeply.

* * *

'Mais mon cher,' Stroganoff was saying, 'soyez raisonnable. Fifteen francs for a small cigar it is too much!'

'Fifteen francs.' Gustave was adamant. 'I have to live. If it is too dear there are the cigarettes Celtique I can supply for ten.'

'It is the swindle,' sighed Stroganoff. 'Ten francs for the Russian tea, fifty francs for the chicken that was tough, two hundred for the champagne. You make the fortune from my misery.'

'I have to live,' said Gustave relentless.

Stroganoff sighed and extracted a note from a rapidly diminishing wallet. Gustave pocketed it without a change of expression, nodded affably to Quill, unlocked the cell door for him, and went off to escort the rest of the party to Lord Buttonhooke's quarters.

'Gustave he is the thief,' Stroganoff greeted Quill. 'He should be here instead of me. But without this.'

He pummelled a downy pillow, tucked in a lavish quilt, and peevishly tested a hot-water bottle. Incredulously Quill took in the Persian rug, the reading-lamp, the large bouquet of orchids (a present from Arenskaya) and passed on to the table laden with asparagus, wine, cold chicken, and hot-house grapes.

'No caviare,' said Stroganoff pathetically. 'Nobody they think of me.'

From the opposite cell came a roar of rage. It was Buttonhooke telling Gustave what he thought of the prison skilly. Prince Artishok and Sadie listened in dismay.

'Allow me,' said Prince Artishok, producing from his wallet the sprat destined to catch the Otchi Tchernia mackerel.

'You'll do nothing of the kind,' said Buttonhooke sharply. 'I'm determined this scoundrel won't make a penny out of me.'

'Comme vous voulez,' said Gustave the philosopher, and left them. 'If M'sieur should desire the English breakfast,' he said, through the grille, 'it will be thirty-five francs only.'

An unintelligible roar followed.

'Otherwise,' said Gustave, 'there is cocoa.'

'He is mean that one,' explained Stroganoff to Quill. 'He will not consent to pay Gustave's prices. But a man must live— even a policeman.'

'Thanks,' said Quill.

'Pas de quoi,' said Stroganoff magnificently. 'Why,' he enquired, 'have you English the expression "To live like a lord"? Never yet have I seen an English lord who knew how to live.'

The one in the adjoining cell was now shouting to Gustave about the nasty time his leader-writers were going to give him the day after to-morrow.

'He has the language inspired,' said Stroganoff approvingly, 'but,' he added, with a shake of his head, 'the vision of a little man. With all his money his ballet it is a joke. He has not the vision nor the daring of Vladimir Stroganoff.' He purred complacently. 'Never could he have had the courage, like I have had, to induce the great Dyrakova to dance for him.'

The Dyrakova motive again, thought Quill. It kept on recurring.

'All,' said Stroganoff magnificently, 'is arranged. This day I get from her a telegram. Look.' He passed it to Quill.

It read: 'Vladimir stop pestering me. Love. Dyra.'

'See,' pointed out Stroganoff, 'how she weaken.'

Quill felt that he ought to tell the old boy that Buttonhooke too was negotiating for Dyrakova, but weakly decided not to complicate life any further at the moment.

'Eh bien,' asked Stroganoff, putting the telegram away. 'Our assassin you have found him?'

'We're trying,' said Quill.

'Hurry, mon cher,' pleaded Stroganoff, 'I am worried by my ballet. The performance to-night it was all right—yes?'

'I didn't see it,' said Quill.

'I have the worry about Arenskaya,' confided Stroganoff, 'I fear what she might do without me. All day I write to her but she do not answer. M'sieur Quill—I beg you—keep the eye on Arenskaya for me.'

'Eh,' said Quill, startled.

'Restrain her if she would be impetuous. Paint the picture pitiful of how I fret in here. Make her feel for me the sorrow. It is as well that she should be well disposed towards me.' He cogitated and appeared to reach a decision. 'Yes—I will do it.'

'Do what?' asked Quill.

'Make her the present,' said Stroganoff. 'The present expensive. It is in third drawer of my bureau. I bought it for . . . but no matter. You will give it to her, Mr. Quill, and you tell her that I bought it for her birthday—no—she is sensitive— just tell that I buy it expressly for her.'

Quill promised.

'There is one other little matter,' said Stroganoff. 'It is the chips. Again to-day a large number is missing. You attend to that and find me the thief tout de suite for if it continue I am the ruin.'

'How do you know about the shortage?'

'Galybchik she send message. She will be here presently and you can ask her the questions.' He glanced at his watch. 'She should be here it is a long time,' he said irritably.

A lavender tie strode gloriously into the gaol, raised an eyebrow at the furnishings of Stroganoff's cell, passed on to hand Lord Buttonhooke his English mail and drifted back again.

'Mr. Galybchik,' appealed Stroganoff.

The lavender tie stopped dead. 'My name,' it reminded Stroganoff stiffly, 'is Hugh Bedford.'

'Mr. Galybchik,' said Stroganoff, waving the unnecessary English name aside, 'I ask you, have you in your duties come across my Galybchik?'

'Are you speaking of Miss August Greene?' asked the lavender tie.

'Mais non,' said Stroganoff, 'I speak of Galybchik—the little one with the head of curls. She should be here it is an hour.'

There was a scuffle in the passage. A tattered Galybchik darted down the corridor and finding the cell door unlocked sought Stroganoff's protection. Behind her lumbered a sheepish Gustave.

'He tried to kiss me,' pointed Galybchik accusingly.

'Everyone try to kiss her,' said Stroganoff to Quill with pride. 'Always I have to protect. Lord Buttonhooke he have not this trouble.' He added mischievously, 'nobody I think try to kiss Mr. Galybchik.'

The lavender tie made an icy departure, Gustave confusedly following in its wake.

Stroganoff became businesslike.

'You are late,' he said. 'Have I not taught you that punctuality it is the virtue of the Tsars? Me—I am never late.'

'Oh,' said Galybchik.

'Explain yourself,' said Stroganoff, 'and be certain that you have the alibi convincing or else——'

'Or else what?' asked Quill meanly.

'Poof,' said Stroganoff, 'just—or else——'

'I was searching the office,' said Galybchik. 'I looked everywhere—I couldn't find it. . . .'

'You have lost something?' asked Stroganoff, all sympathy.

'In the desk, under the carpet, in the armchairs—even the towel cupboard. But it had vanished.'

'Poof,' said Stroganoff, 'it turn up. And if not I buy you another. What is it, anyway?'

'I daren't tell you,' Galybchik trembled.

'Mais si—my little one. Do not be frightened.'

Stroganoff found no difficulty in leaping to conclusions of his own about the missing object. 'The young they must be young, and Nicolas he is careless—it is well known. So tell me.'

'It's too awful!'

'Mais non,' soothed Stroganoff, 'even if the worst it already happen, there is always Switzerland. I take you there myself. So do not fret any more, mon brave, but give me my Ostorojno contract.'

'But you don't understand,' wailed Galybchik, 'it is the Ostorojno contract that is missing.'

Stroganoff leapt to his feet. 'Comment!'

'I knew you'd be angry,' said Galybchik, 'but it wasn't my fault.'

'But this is the ruin. You are certain it has vanished?'

Galybchik nodded.

'You have looked everywhere?'

'Yes.'

'The desk, the armchair, the carpets.'

'You put it in the safe,' Quill reminded him, 'and it was certainly not there when we opened it.'

Stroganoff paced his cell pouring a stream of Russian invective at a fascinated Quill who would gladly have paid much for a literal translation.

'It's that woman,' said Galybchik, 'I know it is!'

Stroganoff stopped pacing and let out a howl of fury.

'The thief—the bandit—the pirate! You are right. She saw me put it in the safe.' He ran to the grille. 'Gustave,' he hollered, 'à moi.'

Gustave came rushing in with a revolver, but stowed it away on seeing that Stroganoff was not being attacked by Quill.

'What is it now?' he asked, querulously.

'You arrest for me immediately that woman,' demanded Stroganoff. 'She is the thief.'

Gustave looked incredulously at Galynchik.

'Pas celle-la,' screamed Stroganoff, beside himself. 'The fat one—the mountain—the mother!'

Light dawned on Gustave. 'The one that pester me all day?'

'Si, si,' Stroganoff mopped his brow.

'It will be a pleasure to oblige you,' said Gustave, licking his lips in anticipation. 'I arrest her the next time she calls.'

'You go to search for her,' pleaded Stroganoff.

'There is no need,' said Gustave, 'she will be here soon. Of what is it,' he asked, 'that you accuse her?'

'She has burgled my safe.'

Gustave looked slightly downcast. 'You have the evidence?'

'But what for you want the evidence?' demanded Stroganoff. 'Did you wait for the evidence to arrest me?'

Gustave was on his dignity. 'Without the evidence there can be no arrest.'

'Poof!' said Stroganoff. 'We invent some.' He turned. 'My friend here has much experience in manufacturing the evidence for his English Scotland Yard. Give Gustave your assistance so he goes quick to collect our mountain.'

There was a sound of distant pounding. Unfalteringly the mountain bore down on Mahomet.

Madame Ostorojno's gait contained determination and fallen arches in equal quantities.

'Once again,' she said, 'I demand that you release Lord Buttonhooke.'

'You have demanded it ten times,' said Gustave, 'and I tell you no. No one shall be released till M'sieu le Préfet he come to-morrow.'

'I shall come here every hour till you release him.'

Puzzled, Gustave turned to Stroganoff for information.

'What is there between the English lord and this woman? Why is she so eager for him? It is inconceivable that she should be his petite amie.'

'C'est un voleur,' said Stroganoff hotly. 'You arrest her.'

'Volontiers,' said Gustave, 'but for what?'

'She has stolen the Ostorojno contract.'

The mountain crossed to the grille.

'So you have lost it,' she jeered. 'Isn't that a shame! But now I can take my daughter to Buttonhooke.'

'Thief,' howled Stroganoff, shaking his fist. 'Give me my contract or else we put you in the manacles.'

'You allow that man to insult me?' cried outraged womanhood.

'Certainly I offer the insult,' said man, the brute. 'I offer it with much pleasure,' he embroidered amiably, 'and if you do not give me my contract I complain to the Consul and poof! you are exported.'

A great light dawned on Gustave.

'Votre carte d'identité, Madame?' he pounced.

Madame Ostorojno fumbled in her purse and presented it defiantly.

'It is two days out of date,' said Gustave with relish. 'The penalty it is the fine or the prison.'

'Not the fine,' said Stroganoff urgently, awful visions of having to pay it himself floating before him.

'Have no fear,' said Gustave, 'for this one, it is the prison. Shoo!'

The gaol was becoming quite full.

From his cell the local pickpocket launched a weary protest. Was he never going to get any sleep that night?

*   *   *

Every night, some three-quarters of an hour after the dancers in the rival ballet companies had acknowledged their polite curtains with weary radiance, the seventeen grey-green mirrors in the café-bar, *Dernier Douzaine*, abandoned their reflections of the fat Madame Dupont and her hopeful satellite[1] in favour of an assemblage of impertinent little hats perched upon tired, but eager little heads. The companies came here to eat after their shows. And not only to eat, but to work lovingly on every shred of scandal that could be produced, until a large-sized tapestry had been woven from the doings of the day. Even in

[1] 'Courage, Madame—il nous en reste toujours les Ballets Russes!'

uneventful times the sessions lasted long into the night. Someone had always fallen foul of Arenskaya, and—in this midnight
version—neatly imparted a crushing blow. Someone else had
just walked out of, and into, one or other of the companies.
Someone had had words with a principal. Someone had had
words with her mother. Someone had been 'relieved' of a rôle.
Someone had never had the luck to be given one.

Whatever the scandal, the verdict never varied—it was a
shame!

By the time Quill arrived in the wake of the hurrying
Galybchik, the session was in full swing. No single mirror
reflected the same collection of hats for more than a few
minutes at a stretch. As each fresh arrival burst in with a new
scareline, she was passed from table to table, where friends
from both companies were detailing, embellishing, drinking in,
and suggesting. Feuds were sunk, petty enmities forgotten, in
the common quest for sensation.

'Have you heard the latest—they're hanging Stroganoff at
dawn!'

'But surely, guillotining,' corrected a purist.[1]

'Hanging,' firmly. 'It is true—I was told so.'

'Without a trial?'

'This is France, my dear!' The saucy little hat shook sagely
and darted away to another table.

In a corner, Ostorojno was smiling mysteriously at Dovolno.
Gossip washed around them as the sea washes the Eddystone—
and with just about as much effect.

'I've got a surprise,' she was telling him, 'I great surprise.
But you mustn't ask me about it till after to-morrow night.'

'Have you heard the latest?' A gay little hat burst
triumphantly into the bar. 'Buttonhooke has . . .' a dramatic
pause ' . . . hanged himself!'

'Impossible!'

'It's quite true—with his silk braces—someone told me.'
After which irrefutable evidence the hat passed on with its
important trivia.

[1] Ernest Smithsky.

But Dovolno and the little Ostorojno paid no heed. They meant to make the most of their time before her mother appeared to cut it short. They looked so happy that Quill hated interrupting them.

'Your mother,' he told the girl gently, 'has decided to spend the night with a friend.'

Olga opened astonished eyes.

'Two friends to be exact,' Quill amended. But before he could break the news, a whirlwind interrupted him.

'They've found another,' it screamed, 'a body, I mean—dead! They say it's the English policeman—Quirk! . . .'

At a table by a screen Arenskaya was sitting drinking Russian tea with her pianist.

'But the Grand Duchess, she do not believe that I am going on for *Giselle*, and it is for this reason that my 'air it is down, and my gown défait,' Arenskaya was saying. 'And me, I do not blame 'er,' she added fairly, 'for you do not dance *Giselle* in the peignoire séduisante. . . .' She paused for the laugh. The pianist yawned.

'Have you heard the latest?' This time it was a pale young man who was playing the Greek Messenger. 'They have discovered the assassin.' He turned confidentially to Quill. 'The Englishman from Scotland Yard,' he hissed.

At their table in the corner Ostorojno received the news of her mother's incarceration with fortitude (Dovolno received it with gratitude). Almost, you might have thought, she was relieved. Soon she returned to the fascinating subject of her secret.

'You'll be awfully surprised,' she told Dovolno, 'and perhaps a little—just a very little—happy.'

He squeezed her hand expectantly. 'I too have a surprise up my sleeve,' he boasted. 'It's for you, darling, and you're going to be mad about it—only you mustn't ask anything till after to-morrow night.' They drank to one another in orange juice.

'Have you heard the latest? Stroganoff has confessed!' The words flew round the room. 'He killed Citrolo with a knife from *Thamar*.'

'A rope from *Tricorne*.'

'A pistol from *Jardin Public.* . . .'

'Come and join us,' sang out the warmhearted Galybchik, taking compassion on Quill's solitude, 'Nicolas is nervy,' she added.

On his way to Nevajno's table Quill stopped short at a nook near the buffet. Two middle-aged men were arguing hotly the points of the dancer, Dyrakova.

'I say it is her artistry that is unrivalled,' the Balleto-Medico was insisting.

'And me, I say it is her arabesque,' persisted Anatole, Stroganoff's commissionaire.

At an adjoining table a further argument was in progress. Kurt Kukumber was hotly debating the ethics of the gaming-room suicide with Vanilla, who had taken the late session off.

'A man has no right to call himself a gambler,' he insisted, 'if he behaves in a manner so indiscreet. He scares away the suckers from the luckier players.' The syndicate, also on furlough from a late session, nodded in weighty agreement.

'Good evening,' said Quill.

They did not seem particularly pleased to see him. Kurt Kukumber, however, made an effort at cordiality and invited Quill's opinion on the subject under discussion.

'It is not—what you call—sporting,' he argued. 'A man may kill himself if he likes—but he should not cause discomfort to others.'

'Even a well-organized suicide holds up the game for quite a few minutes,' said the eldest of the syndicate reprovingly, 'and it takes quite some time after that for the stakes to become normal again.'

'Well organized?' said Quill.

'But, yes,' explained Kukumber, 'the organization for the suicide is excellent here. Like in Monte Carlo.'

Quill turned to Vanilla. 'What happens exactly?'

Vanilla scowled uneasily. 'But nothing,' he said. 'We put the screen round and we take the body away—quick.'

'There is a secret door in the panel,' said Kukumber. 'They take it through that.'

'A secret passage?' Quill was interested.

'Of course,' said Vanilla nonchalantly. 'It leads into the garden. All casinos have such passages.'

Quill nodded and left.

'Dolt,' hissed Vanilla to Kukumber, 'must you talk of our secret passages to a detective?'

Galybchik smiled brightly at Quill as he joined her table. The gloomy Nevajno acknowledged his arrival with his left eyebrow.

'Champagne, M'sieur?' suggested the waiter, materializing hopefully by Quill's side.

'Oui,' said Nevajno, brightening slightly.

'Champagne,' Quill agreed, 'and,' he added maliciously, 'a glass of milk for Mademoiselle.'

'Milk, M'sieur?'

'Milk,' said Quill firmly.

Galybchik was visibly nervous. She essayed a smile. 'What makes you think I want milk?'

'But don't you?' asked Quill. 'I had an idea you always drank milk at this hour of the morning.'

'You are clearly insane.' Nevajno had no patience with faulty logic. 'How could such a thing be possible? Would I, Nevajno, tolerate as a companion a drinker of milk? Milk it does not stimulate either the mind or the senses.'

'Sorry,' said Quill, 'but that's the impression I got after chatting with Emilio.'

'Oh,' said Galybchik, 'so you've found out?'

'I've found out.'

'There wasn't any harm in it,' pleaded Galybchik. 'I only thought how awful that poor man would feel when he woke up after all that drug—alone and hungry. So I asked Emilio to get me a glass.'

'Is it of Citrolo that you are speaking?' demanded Nevajno.

'Yes,' said Quill.

'Do I understand that you carried milk to Citrolo last night?'

Galybchik nodded again.

'But why the mystery?' asked Quill. 'Why couldn't you tell me this before?'

'Naturellement, she did not tell you,' broke in Nevajno furiously. 'She does not even tell me. And I understand well why. A girl does not take refreshment to strange men in the middle of the night unless . . .' He turned his back and sulked.

'Nicolas,' appealed Galybchik.

'He'll get over it,' urged Quill. 'What time was it you brought the milk?'

'About half-past one,' said Galybchik. 'But you don't know Nicolas. He'll sulk for days.'

'Let him,' said Quill. 'You got in with your key?'

'Yes.'

'How was Citrolo?'

'Snoring.'

'You wish me to believe that?' said Nevajno. 'Ha!'

'But he was.'

'And you put the milk beside him and left?' asked Quill.

'I pottered about a little tidying up.'

'A little,' said Nevajno. 'Ha! And me I sit and wait for you in the cabaret and suspect nothing.'

Quill ignored him. 'Did you see or meet anybody on your voyage?'

'Well—no,' said Galybchik. 'It did seem to me once when I was in the room that I heard footsteps, so I looked out, but there was no one in sight. I suppose I imagined it.'

'The guilty conscience,' jeered Nevajno.

'You're an ass,' said Quill.

'Oh,' Galybchik wailed, 'now you've made it worse by insulting him.'

Fortunately the champagne arrived to cover the insult. Nevajno drank it with his back turned, easily resisting all Galybchik's efforts to mollify him. Wearying of the scene Quill paid the waiter and left them to it.

On his way out he stopped to interrupt Arenskaya in the middle of a reminiscence the pianist had heard three times already, and delivered Stroganoff's message.

'A present!' Arenskaya was thoughtful. 'It is many years since the old one he give me a present. What is it that he desires?'

'Read his letters,' Quill suggested, 'you might find a clue. Good night.'

'Oh—you not go yet,' Arenskaya grasped his arm. 'Wait the few minutes and we go home together.'

Quill fled.

*   *   *

Back in his hotel bedroom Quill settled down to tabulate the data he had accumulated. To think that only last night he had gone to bed with the happy prospect of a fortnight's joyous loafing ahead, and here he was, up to his ears in as eccentric a murder case as had ever happened. An abundance of suspects was presumably fairly normal in the murder of a blackmailer, but this one was positively lavish with them. In addition there were all sorts of people with guilty secrets, probably entirely irrelevant, wandering among the clues. Like Galybchik and her milk, for instance.

Quill wondered whether Stroganoff had told him the whole truth. It was quite possible that the wily Russian had committed some further imbecility he had not yet confided. Quill decided a little reluctantly that he must, for the moment, accept the Stroganoff version as the complete truth and build his case from that.

Stroganoff had left Citrolo sleeping in his office. At some time during the night somebody had come in and strangled him.

There were only two known keys to the office door. Stroganoff had one. Galybchik the other. There might be further keys. There was every indication of other people in the office during the night.

Assuming a means of admission the following were around the Casino last night and had every opportunity of paying a visit.

The Baron de Rabinovitch
Dino Vanilla

Lord Buttonhooke
Kurt Kukumber
Prince Alexis Artishok
Sadie Souse
Madame Ostorojno
or even the Mayor of La Bazouche.

All of them, except the mayor and possibly Kurt, knew that Citrolo was in Stroganoff's office and, if interested, could have observed that he had failed to leave.

Quill produced his note-book and conscientiously wrote down the case against each suspect. The result read:

Baron Sam de Rabinovitch

The nobility is doubtful—the career obviously chequered. Has been in gaol and has probably committed several minor swindles for which he was paying blackmail to Citrolo. Knew of Citrolo's presence in office. Left baccarat game at three-thirty—returned agitated. As previous owner of Casino, likely to have key to office. Interesting to note that ledgers in office were moved from usual place and put on shelf behind desk—the position in which Buttonhooke ledgers are kept. As emissary of Buttonhooke, who is anxious to buy back Casino, Rabinovitch would be interested in the Stroganoff finances. Quite a workable theory is that Rabinovitch had gone to the office to examine books, found his blackmailer drugged, and took his opportunity. He then, from force of habit, replaced the ledgers in the position where he was used to finding them.

In cross-examination this afternoon the Baron lied like hell, claiming only slight acquaintance with the deceased. This does not necessarily make him the murderer—naturally he would not wish to admit to being blackmailed.

Dino Vanilla

Croupier. Crook. Runs baccarat game with rather clumsy accomplices. Pays blackmail to Citrolo—probably for this. The solution of the Stroganoff missing chips mystery. Practically admitted this in cross-examination. Left baccarat game at two-fifteen for short interval. Large sum in chips taken from office during night.

This makes it almost certain that Vanilla entered office during night. Has he a key? Finding Citrolo asleep Vanilla might easily have taken his chance. He has the hands of a strangler—can tear a pack of cards across quite easily.

Apprehensive when questioned upon night's activities, but curiously enough rather relieved when it was suggested that he possessed key to office door.

Prince Alexis Artishok

Something very peculiar about this Prince. Appears to be lucky at baccarat—is intermediary in big Otchi Tchernia diamond deal pending between Lord Buttonhooke and the dancer Dyra Dyrakova. It might be merely a matter of a straight commission, but it would bear watching.

Prince left room (breath of air) at two-thirty while Vanilla was absent. Subsequently gave Vanilla lift home in Button-hooke's car, risking the latter's displeasure. Why? Did the two men meet outside the rooms when something transpired that made a further interview advisable?

Note: Prince knew Citrolo was not sleeping but drugged.

Memo: Investigate Prince's antecedents.

Madame Ostorojno

Saw Stroganoff put contract in safe. Was anxious to get contract back so as to transfer daughter to Buttonhooke ballet. Discovered in cloakroom by Sadie Souse gloating over piece of paper. Ostorojno contract missing this morning. Madame Ostorojno almost certainly the thief. Mystery—the means of entry.

Lord Buttonhooke and Sadie Souse

Not seriously considered.

Kurt Kukumber

Small time confidence trickster and roulette fan. On Citrolo's list—as joke. Unlikely murderer—sounded almost fond of dead man. Chief point of interest—Gold-Mining Prospectus found in Stroganoff's office. Obviously put there by Kurt. Kurt denies this vigorously. But why should he bother unless he had put it there some time during the fatal night? Makes no secret of his profession. Rather proud of it. But how did Kurt get in?

And that was that, thought Quill. Everywhere there was ample evidence to suggest numerous entries, but how had they been effected? Not all these people could have had keys.

Suddenly Quill remembered the suicide carried through a secret passage into the garden. There might be another secret passage in the Casino. Perhaps that was the solution.

Quill remembered how Vanilla had frowned while Kukumber talked of the secret passage and felt certain he was on the right track. A passage to Stroganoff's office would explain everything. With it all his suspects could have spent the night popping in and out of the place. Quill decided to go up to the office first thing next morning to try and find it. He was not very expert in looking for secret passages, but he had a firm conviction that if one prodded and pushed long enough something slid open.

Of course a secret passage would not solve the mystery, he had too many suspects for that, but it might help.

CHAPTER IX

QUILL pushed back the shutters. It was raining.

'Du thé,' announced the waiter proudly, trundling in with a tray.

'Coffee,' said Quill.

'Du thé,' corrected the waiter, 'et bien chaude.'

'Coffee,' said Quill.

'Always M'sieur change his mind.' The waiter shook his head sadly and went.

Quill shaved apprehensively, expecting a telephone call at any minute. It came when he was in his bath. Gustave.

'I am worried, mon cher,' he confided. 'Is it possible that the man Stroganoff is innocent?'

'It is,' said Quill comfortingly.

'He does not behave like a guilty person, that one,' expatiated Gustave. 'He eat, he drink, and all the time he grumble. This morning when I take him the omelette that I have made myself, almost he throw it at me—the toast, it appears, it was not Melba!'

'Why don't you release him?' asked Quill.

'M'sieur le Préfet arrives this afternoon, and I must have for him an assassin to justify his journey,' explained the hard-pressed Gustave.

'What about Buttonhooke?'

'There the evidence is not so irrefutable. Maybe I was hasty there—what you English call "trop de zèle." '

'But,' began Quill . . .

'But, you ask me, why then do I trouble you at this so early hour, on a morning when the rain refreshes à merveille our dusty oliviers? It is in case M'sieur le Préfet releases my two prisoners. Where do I look for my new assassin?'

'Where?' agreed Quill.

'M'sieur, I implore your assistance. All yesterday you were busy with the research—have you no theory yet?'

'Have you none?' countered Quill.

But it appeared that Gustave was baffled. Yesterday he had been unable to sift the evidence. First there had been his gardening, and then, even before the light began to fade, there had been Stroganoff. Every time he sat down to make a tabulation, the man Stroganoff wanted something. And his assistant—who, Quill must understand, was *bon gosse* and incidentally his godson—was still *en Vacances*.

Quill regretted that he had no concrete suggestions as yet. But the case was developing in an interesting manner—he would keep Gustave advised.

'Ah, bon!' said Gustave. 'I leave it in your hands, cher collègue. I go now to talk business with the woman Ostorojno.'

Quill completed his toilet and sauntered out into the street. He went back again to get his mackintosh.

'Useless to call to-day,' remarked Anatole, helpfully, when Quill arrived at the Casino. 'M'sieur le Directeur is still in prison. But do not lose heart,' added that kindly soul, 'next week, when he is released, you will doubtless get the order for whatever it is you sell.'

Quill was a trifle tired of the commercial traveller gambit. He handed Anatole his card.

'They sacked you?' asked Anatole, interested in the 'late of.'

'I resigned,' replied Quill, with dignity.

'Bien entendu,' said Anatole, with a buddie's smile to make it quite clear that he was not meant to believe a word of this. 'The resignation, it is fashionable. Signor Vanilla would have resigned too, had not the Baron himself removed to the other casino, and I resigned from the Moulin Mort after M'sieur le Patron find me with his petite amie. What was it that they catch you at, when you resigned from Scotland Yard?'

'Buying drinks after hours,' said Quill good-humouredly and made his way upstairs.

With his mind dwelling on secret passages Quill entered the office.

He rapped on a promising-looking panel. A barometer nearly brained him. He tugged at some ornamental moulding—it came away in his hands. He tried a bookcase—*The Ballet in Western Europe* missed him by inches.

Flushed with success he sought repose in an armchair. Almost immediately he found a knitting needle. Galybchik had been seeking it for weeks. There was still a certain amount of jumper on it.

A picture of the croupier's annual dinner—enlarged and coloured—looked promising. Quill peered behind it, and drew a dusty blank.

He washed his hands and went to work systematically. Conscientiously he rapped, tapped, and prodded every panel in the room. He slid immobile mouldings, pressed obdurate buttons and picked up splinters from perfectly innocent floor-boards.

Exhausted he leant against the filing cabinet. The next moment he was on the floor. The cabinet had swung inwards and here was his secret passage. It looked cold and damp and took most of the elation out of him. But manfully he pulled out his torch, stooped and entered.

It was evident at once that the passage had not been designed for comfort. The concrete was rough and the cracks, as Quill discovered almost immediately, were many. The ceiling was low, the walls mildewy, and there was no electric light. No house-proud charwoman had swept it for years—in fact, no charwoman of any kind had been near it since it had been built.

But there was every indication that the passage was in frequent use—mainly by chain smokers. Cigarette ends were all over the place. Quill stooped and conscientiously scooped up an assortment of samples for future inspection. He also collected the butt end of a cigar. His torch raked the surface as he progressed searching for further clues. A distant gleam lit his heart. A diamond! He stooped. Only a sequin. He picked it up and sighed for a Sergeant Banner to rifle innumerable wardrobes in search of sequin dresses. Women wore these things on scarves he remembered, and he had a vague idea that bull-fighters wore them too—doubtless to dazzle the bull. It would not surprise him in the slightest to find a bull-fighter embedded somewhere in the maze of this fantastic murder.

Further research showed that the mildew had been disturbed shoulder high in streaks along the passage, and in a crack he found the regulation shred of cloth. In his Scotland Yard days the shred would have been sent meticulously round to every cloth manufacturer in the country for identification, but Quill was damned if he was going to bother.

The passage turned abruptly to the left. Quill had not observed this. The exciting crimson dab on the wall came from his own nose. But on the floor beneath it was a piece of lace. Quill examined it and decided at once that it belonged to no ballerina. No tender breast ever rose and fell under it. It was much too coarse. No laundry, try as it might, could do a thing to it. Either the maid had struggled uncommonly hard or the seducer had been an octopus. Quill thought of Vanilla's strong fingers, but Arenskaya would never struggle—neither would she wear such lace. On the other hand, not only would Madame Ostorojno wear it with pride, but boast of the bargain she had picked up at the sales! The floor sloped upwards at this point and no doubt she had trodden on the lace-trimmed edge of her underskirt.

Quill went on with a vague sense of something missing. These discoveries were all very well, but there was something else he ought to have found. Something one always found. Presently realization dawned on him. There was no button. No sign of a button. He grew quite angry about this as he went on with his search. Why was there no button? He had never handled a crime yet without its exasperating, unclaimed, unassignable, and usually entirely irrelevant button. He could not feel normal until he had found one.

Instinct had not misled him. Back at the point where he had bumped his nose lay the missing clue. Quill purred with satisfaction as he stowed it lovingly away in his pocket. That it was ordinary black ebony and might belong to any suit was only to be expected.[1]

The passage came to an end at an impassable wall. Quill pushed it. Nothing happened. He prodded, pressed, slid, coaxed, reinvestigated and started all over again. No use. Finally he gave up and retraced his steps. But the other end had swung back too and presented difficulties. Quill swore softly.

Quill swore.

Quill swore loudly.

Quill stopped swearing and decided to chain-smoke too. Striking a match against the wall his hand came into contact with a bump in the plaster. Without much hope he pressed. The wall swung inwards. . . . He dodged it just in time.

*   *   *

Quill stumbled into the office and with a sigh of relief sat down to recuperate. He was tired and dusty, but on the whole not displeased. The mystery of the murderer's entry into the office was a mystery no longer. All he had to do was to check up on the numerous people who appeared to have used the passage and decide which one of them was the murderer.

He spread the evidence collected in the passage on the table in front of him and contrasted it with his own list of suspects. It fitted well enough, in fact there was almost too much of it. The cigarette ends were mainly of coarse French tobacco such as Vanilla might smoke, but there were also the remnants of expensive-looking Egyptian which Quill for the moment could not place. And there was a cardboard holdpiece from a Russian cigarette of the kind Stroganoff ought to smoke but did not. Quill had the impression that only recently he had seen someone with this kind of cigarette and racked his memory to remember. But the latter refused to function. Making a mental note to keep his eye open for the smoker, Quill passed on to the cigar-stub. It was the end of a Henry Clay. The Baron de Rabinovitch smoked Henry Clays—Quill remembered the box in Buttonhooke's office.

[1] Later he was to discover that it belonged to his own waistcoat.

'Ha!' thought Quill.

The lace was easy. It almost certainly belonged to Madame Ostorojno, and in any case it should be simple to check up on it. The sequin and the shreds of cloth were different. He would need some luck to identify them.

Quill collected his evidence and stowed it away. He would have to interview all his suspects all over again—confront them with his discoveries and get their reactions. Tentatively Quill sketched out his programme. First he would say good morning to Stroganoff and tell him about the passage. It was just possible that the old boy knew about it already, but for some vague reason of his own had omitted to tell him. Then he would have a few words with Rabinovitch and Vanilla. And it might also be as well to see little Kurt Kukumber, whose reticence about the Gold Prospectus in the office was now fairly clear. Almost certainly Kurt had used the passage to deposit his bait, had seen the sleeping Citrolo—might even have murdered him—or, as was quite possible, he might have arrived after the murder. Quill was confident in his ability to make Kurt tell all he knew—he only hoped he knew something interesting.

It might also be worth while to have a few words with Prince Alexis Artishok and get him to explain his sudden passion for giving croupiers lifts home.

*   *   *

Quill left the office and went downstairs. At the bottom of them was Arenskaya, tapping her heel impatiently for the pianist who was late for class. The fact that Arenskaya was twenty minutes early made no difference to her wrath. She would tell that woman what she thought of her when she came. Lovingly she curled her tongue round the preliminary sentences.

'Hallo,' said Quill.

'Ah!' Arenskaya beamed. 'My present!'

Quill had forgotten all about it. 'It's in the office. I'll get it.'

'We go together,' said Arenskaya.

Quill stepped back to allow her to precede him.

'Not the stairs,' said Arenskaya surprisingly. 'The stairs they tire me. I know a better way. Come.'

She put her arm through Quill's and led him into a corridor. Here she stopped in front of three sulky Cupids ignoring a *prima donna* bosom. It was a faded oil painting in the Rubens manner—but only just. Arenskaya stepped unflinchingly up to it, punched an unsuspecting Cupid in the eye, and the framework swung inwards to reveal the now familiar mildew stains.

'Entrez,' said Arenskaya hospitably.

Quill was distinctly annoyed. To think of the blood vessels he had nearly strained looking for it.

'How long have you known about this passage?' he demanded.

'Mais tout le monde know it,' said Arenskaya, astonished. 'Vanilla he show it me many weeks ago. I think,' she mused, 'it was because he could find no other way to get me in the dark.'

'Does Stroganoff know of this passage?'

'Mais non,' said Arenskaya, 'we take care not to tell him.'

'Why?'

'It is clear you do not understand our Vladimir,' said Arenskaya indulgently. 'He has the mind of a child. If we show him the passage he would play there for hours, he would install the electric light and the carpets. He would boast of it to everyone, and it would be a secret no longer. Also, my poor Vanilla he would not get his chips.'

'Good God,' said Quill, 'are you in on that too?'

'Mais bien sûr,' said Arenskaya. 'Anyways,' she added righteously, 'I make him promise not to borrow too much.'

'But your loyalty to Stroganoff?' asked Quill amazed. He had always thought that there was real affection between these two eternal combatants.

'Of what is it that you accuse me?' shrilled Arenskaya, indignant. 'My devotion to the ballet it is without questions. I have sacrificed all to its interests. Have I not stayed with

Stroganoff fifteen years—on and off? Have I not turned down the offers fabulous from Berlin, Vienna and even 'Ollywood? It is the impertinence what you suggest.'

'Hush!' pleaded Quill.

'I will not 'ush,' said Arenskaya. 'You apologize for your insinuation monstrous.'

'But,' pleaded Quill, 'don't you see what you're doing? You're helping Vanilla to rob the Casino.'

'The Casino it is not my concern,' declared Arenskaya. 'It is bad joke, anyway. And the gambling it interfere with the performance. The sooner Stroganoff tire of it the better, and besides this, for the moment he is rich.'

'He will not stay rich if everybody takes his chips.'

'He will not stay rich in any case,' declared Arenskaya. 'Mon ami, you do not know Stroganoff. Why should not my poor Vanilla get his share while the going it is good? Especially,' she added, 'when he spend so much of it on me.'

The rather peculiar moral code was altogether beyond Quill. He decided not to meddle with it any further.

'Come on,' said Arenskaya, and pushed him in.

They reached the study without accident. Quill opened the third drawer of the desk. Two brown-paper parcels loomed up at him. He selected the bigger.

'For me?' cooed Arenskaya from force of habit. 'Open it quick for I am impatient.'

Quill obliged. Several pairs of ballet shoes fell out.

Arenskaya screamed.

'But he has turned imbécile, the old one.' She picked up a shoe. 'They are not even my size.'

It dawned on Quill that he had made a bloomer. He extracted the other parcel. It was square and thin.

Arenskaya smiled again. 'Doubtless a first edition for my library. Open it—quick.'

Quill opened it. Weak with laughter he deposited the gift on the table and sat down to enjoy Arenskaya's expression as she crossed to gaze at it. It was a full-sized photograph of Stroganoff in his Admiral's uniform.

'The insult,' screamed Arenskaya. 'The slight unforgivable. The libel. That is how the miserable old gaol-bird repay me for all my loyalty. It is for this that I refuse Rheinhardt and walk out on René Clair. Pah!' she said, more calmly, 'it is foolish to be angry. He is in his dotage. A baby.'

Quill had a good idea. He opened quite another drawer. A jeweller's case was enshrined cosily in it. Quill took it out and extracted a large diamond 'D' in a cumbersome gold setting.

'The darling,' said Arenskaya. 'I run to kiss him. It is such a sweet thought. The "D,"' she explained, 'it stands for Dyshenka which is Russian for little darling.'

Remembering the words in which Stroganoff had instructed him about the gift, Quill thought it more likely that it stood for Dyrakova, but said nothing.

'I fly,' said Arenskaya, settling more comfortably in her armchair. 'I hasten to his side to offer him the embrace.' She lit a cigarette—an Egyptian, Quill noted. But that could hardly be called a discovery now.

'Shall I telephone a cab?' he asked.

'We stroll,' said Arenskaya. 'But first we drink a little champagne to celebrate. Come.'

'But your class?' said Quill.

'Mon Dieu!' said Arenskaya. 'I forget.'

She rushed out.

*   *   *

The prison was a hive of industry. Quill arrived to find both impresarios in the throes of composition. From his bench Lord Buttonhooke dictated laboriously to an upright lavender tie, whose shorthand was in no way strained to keep up with the output. Galybchik's task, though more luxuriously housed, was less easy. Her shorthand, for all practical purposes, did not exist and her typewriter galloped to keep pace with the peculiarly formed flowers of rhetoric that cascaded from Stroganoff's golden-hued memory.

'Vladimir, this is incredible!' dictated Stroganoff. 'Your Highness, I reply, it is nozzing. Wait till you see the dress rehearsal.' He broke off to greet Quill. 'Bon jour, mon ami. Sit down. We are busy.'

Quill sank into the most comfortable armchair and looked round in admiration. All the luxuries of yesterday were here, but in addition room had been found for a divan, a Flemish tapestry, and the roll-top desk at which Galybchik was working. The table had gained a magnum of champagne,[1] a porcelain monument of caviare, and a colossal water-melon. There was also a bottle of French Scotch and a syphon.

'Wiskyansoda,' said Stroganoff, interrupting himself. 'See how I remember you.'

From the adjoining cell the voice of Buttonhooke rose. It was apparent that he, too, was engaged on his memoirs.

'It was in the spring of 1933 that I first met that effervescent, eccentric, Vladimir Stroganoff.'

'What it mean—effervescent?' Stroganoff asked Quill suspiciously.

'Bubbling,' suggested Quill.

'Bon,' nodded Stroganoff. 'It was in London,' he dictated loudly, 'that I first met the bubble Buttonhooke.'

'Wassat?' Buttonhooke pounded across to the grille.

'I describe you in my book,' said Stroganoff, bouncing to meet him. 'I am very kind.'

'You called me a bubble,' accused Buttonhooke. 'I heard you.'

'But it is well known that you are the bubble,' explained Stroganoff sweetly. 'All the financiers they explode in good time.'

An inexpressibly shocked lavender tie rushed to his chief's aid.'

'Is that an assertion?'

'Read my book,' said Striganoff. 'We publish at eighteen and six, and that to you is nozzing.'

'You've found a publisher?' asked Quill, surprised.

'I have not yet selected,' announced Stroganoff magnificently. He turned patronizingly to Buttonhooke. 'You have chosen yours?'

[1] I work better when I am not thirsty.—STROGANOFF.

'Blurbson,' said the lavender tie crushingly.

'Me I do not care for Blurbson,' observed Stroganoff, and one could almost see them reeling under the blow. 'I think I send to my old friend, Michael Joseph—it is good he should read something which is not about cats![1] It will be for him the surprise stunning when he find it in his spring list.'

'Pah!' said Buttonhooke, and returned to his bench.

'Poof!' said Stroganoff and cut himself a large slice of water-melon.

'Presently,' he said munching, 'we return to work. Pour le moment I repose myself.' He stretched himself on the divan and closed his eyes.

'Hey!' said Quill.

'Sssh,' objected Stroganoff. 'Do you not see that I compose myself? You lucky policeman have no idea how the literary composition it exhausts. I am prostrate,' he said correctly.

Quill refused to sympathize. 'You're much more comfortable here than I've been this morning.'

Stroganoff sat bolt upright and beamed.

'I have made it cosy—no? And when they bring me the portraits of my ballerinas, my samovar, and my stamp collection, I shall be well enough here. Though I would not recommend it to you, mon ami. The cooking it is awful, and the tariff it is the ruin.'

'Do you know Prince Alexis Artishok?' asked Quill.

'Assuredly I know him,' said Stroganoff absently. 'All the Russian nobility they come to my box. What was the name you said?'

'Alexis Artishok.'

Stroganoff pondered. 'There is no such family. Arapoff, yes. Yusupoff, yes. But Artishok—no. You have made the mistake.'

'Don't be an ass,' said Quill. 'He's here in Bazouche. With Buttonhooke. He came into your office while you were composing Citrolo's notice.'

'Ah,' Stroganoff remembered. 'The big man with the beard. I like him,' he added. 'He is very polite.'

---

[1] Special joke to keep publisher in good humour.

'He calls himself Prince Alexis Artishok and . . .'

'Mais pourquoi pas?' Stroganoff shrugged. 'Doubtless he finds it useful to pretend to the aristocracy. And at least he has invented the name—he is not like some others that claim real titles.'

That was all Quill wanted to know for the moment. He changed the subject.

'Were you aware that there is a secret passage leading from your office into the corridor?'

'Comment!' Stroganoff was instantly alert. 'The passage secret?'

'The secret passage.'

'Like in the haunted house?'

Quill nodded.

'Bon.' Stroganoff rubbed his hands. 'Now I understand why the swindle Baron Rabinovitch wish to buy back the Casino. Clearly there is in it the hidden treasure.' He turned on Quill. 'Maybe you find it already and come hot-hand with the good news?'

Quill suppressed a smile. 'Sorry,' he said. 'No treasure.'

'No treasure!' Stroganoff was dumbfounded. 'Poof—you have no idea how to look.'

Quill was a little hurt. He pointed out that he had found the passage in a couple of hours while Stroganoff, in all his weeks at the Casino, had not even found an alcove.

But Stroganoff was already immersed in his dreams.

'There is always treasure,' he informed Quill. 'But it is hidden well. Always one must dig.'

'Dig where?'

'There is a spot. It is marked on the plan.'

'What plan?'

'But the plan secret. It will not,' he said judicially, 'be easy to read. It will be in the cipher—but this, M'sieur Quill, is where you will be so useful. You solve for me this cipher which you will find on your return, and I give you large share of fortune.'

'Thanks,' said Quill.

'De rien,' said Stroganoff.

There was a sound of heavy breathing and Gustave appeared

carrying a gosling which he held out to Stroganoff for inspection.

'Too old,' said Stroganoff, prodding it. 'Take away.'

'But it is perfect,' protested Gustave. 'I went to the Marché to choose it myself.'

'You were the swindle,' said Stroganoff. 'But no matter. I desire now a strong garden spade. I wish to dig,' he explained.

Gustave blanched. 'Not that! My garden implements they are not for sale. Never will I lend the rake, the hoe, or the lawn mower.'

'Mais,' protested Stroganoff, 'it is necessary that we dig for the treasure that M'sieur Quill has found.'

Gustave was impressed. 'You have found treasure?'

'No,' said Quill. 'What I have found is a secret passage that leads into the Casino office. The passage,' he pointed, 'through which the murderer of Citrolo gained admission.'

'Ha,' said Gustave. 'I knew it. Always I felt that the assassin he did not penetrate by the door.' He mused. 'It seems to me that somewhere I have heard of this passage before.'

'It seems to me,' said Quill, 'that you might have thought of that before you arrested two other people.'

'It is not kind to remind one of mistakes,' said Gustave reprovingly. 'Do I remind you of the time you arrested the innocent man in England?'

How on earth did he know that, Quill wondered? Out of the corner of his eye he caught a glimpse of a red-faced Stroganoff signalling furiously. All was now quite clear.

'Anyways,' said Gustave, 'if I have made the mistake M'sieur le Préfet comes this afternoon to rectify it. As for the passage I hurry myself to inspect it as soon I have finished pruning the roses.'

'Roses,' said Stroganoff eagerly. 'You grow the roses?'

'My roses,' boasted Gustave, 'are the finest in the *Midi*.'

'It is a small place the *Midi*,' said Stroganoff unimpressed. 'Now at the flower show in St. Petersburg every year I win . . .'

Galybchik seated herself at the typewriter.

Quill left them to it.

CHAPTER X

BACK at the *Hôtel Moins-Magnifique* Quill enquired for Kurt Kukumber's room. The reception clerk, new to Quill, regarded him hopefully.

'M'sieur is a relative of M'sieur Kukumber?'

'No,' said Quill hastily.

The hotel clerk was disappointed. 'M'sieur Kukumber is expecting a visit from his rich uncle. We, too, are anxious that he should arrive.'

Quill nodded understandingly and made his way to the back of the entresol. He knocked at a door. It opened a cautious two inches and Kurt Kukumber's head peered round the corner. He seemed almost relieved to see Quill.

'I regret,' he pointed round the tiny bedroom, 'to receive you in surroundings so unimpressive, but you understand it is only for the moment. Soon it will be the Royal Suite.'

Quill sat down on the edge of the bed.

'You will pardon my attire,' babbled Kurt. 'For the moment it is flannel but soon I shall wear pyjamas of silk. The dressing-gown I have already.' He crossed to the wardrobe and proudly encased himself in three golden dragons on a purple background.

'Chinese,' he explained. 'Robert Taylor has one just like it. The Armenian on the Promenade des Anglais assured me of that.'

'Beautiful,' admired Quill tactfully.

'Dubonnet?' offered the delighted Kurt.

Quill accepted. 'Soon no doubt it will be Napoleon Brandy.'

'No doubt,' agreed Kurt wistfully. 'If only I had a little capital. But my system it is for the moment not lucky.'

'Hard lines.'

'No matter,' said Kurt sunnily. 'I have put my finger on the weak spot and my system is now infallible. This afternoon you shall see.'

Quill nodded gravely.

'But,' said Kurt, remembering that his funds were too low to give the system a thorough try-out. 'I have this afternoon also an infallible horse at Deauville. In the last race.' He looked hopefully at Quill.

Quill said nothing.

'It has been arranged for many months,' urged Kurt. 'The horse is doped and the judges are bribed.'

'You think of everything,' said Quill.

'Mais non,' said Kurt. 'It is only by accident that I hear of it. It will start at long odds. A modest fifty francs will return a thousand.'

Quill laughed.

'You do not believe me?'

'No,' said Quill.

'You think it is a trick?'

'A very old one.'

'You are too shrewd,' said Kurt. 'But this time I do not mean to take—only to borrow. See I make you an IOU.'

Quill explained that he was short of ready money himself. Perhaps Kurt's rich uncle . . .

'You do not give me away?' asked Kurt alarmed.

Quill shook his head. 'Why should I interfere as long as you answer my questions? . . .'

'More questions. But I tell you everything yesterday.'

'Everything,' agreed Quill, 'except how that Gold Mine Prospectus got into the office.'

'Alas,' said Kurt, 'I cannot remember.'

'You took it there during the night.'

'Mais non.'

'Mais oui,' said Quill brilliantly. 'Through the secret passage.'

The bombshell went down well.

'But you are a real detective,' said Kurt admiringly. 'How comes it they sack you from Scotland Yard?'

'I resigned,' said Quill. 'Anyway, let's stick to the point. You used that passage the night Citrolo was murdered.'

'That night I did not go near it. I did not use it anyway. I have no reason.'

Quill took an envelope from his pocket and extracted a few shreds of cloth. He crossed to the wardrobe and pulled out Kurt's blue serge suit. They matched perfectly.

'I surrender,' said Kukumber, the philosopher. 'It is quite true I used the passage that night.'

'I thought so.'

'You understand why I am so reluctant to tell you. I do not wish to be mixed up in the murder.'

Quill nodded. 'Quite. But now that you are mixed up in it, the best thing you can do is to tell me the whole story.'

Kurt Kukumber sat down. 'What can I say?'

'Begin with the time.'

'It was late,' said Kurt. 'Almost two o'clock. My infallible system had failed me again. It seemed to me the moment to begin my plan on Stroganoff. For weeks I had been pondering his psychology, he seemed to me one to whom the gold mine would have much appeal. It said in the stars that this day was good to start a new enterprise, so I say to myself: "Kurt . . ." '

'Yes, yes,' said Quill. 'You decided to leave the prospectus in his office.'

Kukumber looked hurt at being robbed of his climax.

'If you interrupt,' he said, 'how can I remember? But you are right. I reach the painting. I peer round. There is no one in sight.'

'One moment,' said Quill. 'How long have you known about the passage?'

'But many months,' said Kurt. 'It is no secret. Everybody knows there is a passage. One year during the crise, they even show it to tourists for five francs—and then for three.'

Quill's pride in his discovery ebbed away. Kurt resumed his story.

'I turn to press the Cupid's eye. I jump back quick and stand in the shadow. There comes out the old lady.'

'What old lady?'

'The old lady with the pretty daughter. She looks very pleased as she goes down the passage. I wonder what it is she gets from the office. But it is not my business. It is my rule,' said Kukumber, 'to attend only to that which concerns me. Neither do I like to be questioned.'

'Quite,' said Quill. 'Continue.'

Kurt Kukumber sighed.

'In the office it is dark. But I have my electric pencil that I always carry. See!' He produced it proudly.

'Soon you will have one in gold,' said the exasperated Quill.

'Why not?' agreed Kurt. 'I lay the bait on the desk where Stroganoff will find it and prepare to retreat. Suddenly someone snores. Figure to yourself how I jump! I switch round my pencil. It is my good friend Citrolo sleeping it off. I wonder why he has selected this place but decide that doubtless he had some good reason of his own. Mr. Citrolo always had a reason for everything. Possibly, I think, he has caught Stroganoff in some little mistake. So I tiptoe away, not to disturb his rest.'

'Is that all?' asked Quill.

'That is all.'

Quill thanked him and rose to leave.

'See you at the Casino,' waved Kurt affably. 'You will see this afternoon, I shall win.'

*   *   *

The receptionist waved as Quill descended the stairs.

'Pardon, M'sieur,' he entreated, 'but did by chance M'sieur Kukumber mention his uncle?'

'He mentioned him,' said Quill non-committally.

'He did not specify when he was due to arrive?'

'Well—no.'

'The management becomes impatient,' confided the clerk. 'Already we wait three weeks to open the chest.'

'Chest?' asked Quill.

'But it is an interesting story,' said the clerk. 'It appears that the uncle of M'sieur Kukumber is eccentric. He desires to test the will-power of his heir who is M'sieur Kukumber. He gets a small chest of iron and he fills it with money. And he says to his nephew, "Kurt, I desire to test you. I give you no money—no allowance—you must support yourself for five years. But I give you this iron chest which you shall carry with you wherever you go. It is full of money but however great your need you are not to touch it. If at the end of five years I arrive and the seals are still intact the contents are yours. The five years,' said the clerk, 'were up last week—and now we all wait for the uncle to arrive.'

'Wonderful,' said Quill. 'Where is this chest?'

'It is in the hotel safe. It is nothing to look at, just old iron, almost rusty. Never would one imagine that it contained maybe a million francs.'

'Never,' agreed Quill.

'C'est la vie,' announced the clerk. 'To have a fortune in your charge, and to haggle for centimes with unpleasant old ladies who desire a deduction from the pension for nights that they spend in prison. But I am firm with her.'

'Hallo,' said Quill. 'That sounds like Madame Ostorojno.'

The clerk nodded, and wiped his brow. The scars of battle still showed.

Quill was interested to hear that Madame Ostorojno had been released. Come to think of it she must have been released just before he arrived at the gaol, for he had not heard her arguing during his visit. He enquired her room number.

'You wish to see her?' said the clerk, incredulous. 'Bien, that is your affair. The number is 214.'

'Why is it?' asked Quill, 'that no French hotel has a room number under two hundred?'

'I will explain,' said the clerk willingly.

'Later,' said Quill and left him.

*　　*　　*

'So,' repeated Mme. Ostorojno grimly, 'this is the way you take advantage of my absence.'

'Yes, Mamma,' agreed Olga.

'While your mother languishes in gaol you gallivant around the town till four in the morning.'

'Not till four, Mamma.'

'It's no use denying it. I got the time you came in from the hall porter.'

'Blast,' said Olga.

'What's more, you were with that small-time dancer, Dovolno.'

'He's not a small-time dancer.'

'Don't argue, child. Small time or not he's no use to you.'

'But I adore him.'

'Not while I can stop it.'

'Look here, Mother,' said Olga in level tones. 'Why don't you accept the inevitable? I'm no longer a child. I've a right to lead my own life.'

It was an open challenge—the first Olga had ever dared to throw. Madame Ostorojno did not quite know how to cope with it.

It was at this electric moment that Quill knocked on the door.

'I'll see who it is,' said Olga quickly and darted towards it.

'Morning,' said Quill.

'Morning,' smiled the young Ostorojno and flew down the stairs.

Quill's first impression of the room was a mass of photographs. There was an arabesque. It was the little Ostorojno aged three. There was a fourth position. Olga was five when she achieved this feat. A block shoe had been put on when Olga was seven. At nine her first dancing partner made his appearance. He did not stay long. At thirteen she was dancing with Anton Palook himself. (Madame Ostorojno practically financed the company to achieve this feat.) At fifteen she was alone again, posing on the diving-board at Eden Roc. At seventeen she was shown signing a contract with Stroganoff.

In the darkest corner of the room was a strong arabesque

perfectly placed. It belonged to Baronova. Mother Ostorojno displayed it to prove that she was not like other mothers in the ballet. She was unbiassed—she thought Baronova showed promise. But she kept her in the darkest corner because Olga's arabesque was not so well turned out.

'Morning,' said Quill brightly.

'What do you want, young man?' demanded Madame Ostorojno forbiddingly. 'More questions?'

'Just a few.'

'I won't answer them.'

'You might,' said Quill. 'You must be reasonable. After all, you have committed a criminal offence by stealing the Stroganoff contract.'

'Nonsense,' said Madame Ostorojno sharply. 'Anyway, I defy you to prove it.'

'It won't be difficult,' said Quill sweetly. 'I've got witnesses who saw you coming out of the secret passage and purring over the contract in the cloakroom.'

'Oh, you have, have you? So what?'

Quill was a bit baffled about this himself.

'All right, I stole the contract,' Madame Ostorojno pursued her advantage. 'It was an unfair contract. We signed it in a weak moment.'

'But you did sign it.'

'Exactly. That's why I had to steal it back.'

'Supposing I demand that you hand it over?'

'Demand away.'

'We might prosecute.'

'Don't be an ass,' said Madame Ostorojno contemptuously. 'You know Stroganoff wouldn't dare make himself a laughing-stock.'

Quill tried a new line. 'Doesn't it occur to you that it's very unfair to Stroganoff to take away his best dancer? Particularly at this moment.'

'What do I care about Stroganoff,' said Madame Ostorojno. 'What do I care about anything except Olga's career? In twenty years' time Stroganoff will still be putting on ballets.

But Olga will be finished then, she'll be teaching sniffy little girls in a Kensington studio.'

'Is that so inevitable?' Quill asked.

'Sit down, young man,' said Madame Ostorojno, more kindly. 'Smoke if you like, but listen to me.'

Quill did all three.

'I know,' began Madame Ostorojno, 'that it is the fashion to laugh at mothers in the ballet. I know that we are not liked. They accuse us of pushing, sneering, and eye-catching in useful quarters. They say we stir up mischief. All the unrest in the company they put down to us. They say we are the biggest nuisance the management has to contend with.' She paused. 'And they are quite right. We are.

'You see we have to be. A dancer's life is short. Twenty years, fifteen years, sometimes less, and she is finished. Even at the peak of her career her earnings are mighty small. There is no old-age pension in the ballet, only pupils, and they are hard to get. Look at Dyrakova, the greatest dancer of her day. She is in Paris now, teaching. An impoverished Queen ruling an apathetic little court. Her pianist is a Russian Countess, her manager a retired General from the Cossacks. And Dyrakova is lucky for she has a constant stream of English girls who come and who pay.

'Look at the free list of any ballet company. The faded brightness, the tired charms. All the tricks of the one-time favourites to look prosperous on nothing. Once they, too, had their opportunities but perhaps they had no mother to see that they did not waste them.'

'I see,' said Quill.

'You don't see,' said Madame Ostorojno with grim humour. 'But no matter. The young never see. My daughter never sees. So it falls on us to do the worrying and fussing, to praise them when the spirit is flagging, to smile in the right places, and to snap up the best offers.

'You cannot get your daughters to take any interest in these things. They are young and there is a young man. Or if there is no young man there is a rival. They are beginning to get the rôles they covet and old age is something that does not happen. Take my own Olga.'

'I thought we would soon,' said Quill.

'Oh, all right,' said Madame Ostorojno, taken out of her stride. 'I don't know why I bother to tell you all this, anyway.'

'I'm glad you did,' said Quill and meant it.

'Anyway,' said Madame Ostorojno, 'perhaps you understand now why I won't give you back your contract.'

'Fight it out with Stroganoff,' said Quill. 'It wasn't what I came about, anyway.' He produced the piece of lace. 'Does this belong to you?'

Madame Ostorojno inspected it. 'It must have happened when I heard the stitches go.'

'Just two questions,' said Quill. 'How did you know about the secret passage?'

'How did you know I knew about it?'

'It's where I found the lace.'

'If you must know,' said Madame Ostorojno, 'it was an accident. I wanted a word with Arenskaya.'

'About your daughter?'

'Who else,' said Madame Ostorojno. 'Arenskaya was in the corridor with that croupier, Vanilla. They saw me coming and ran away. A lot of people run away when they see me coming,' she added, almost with pride, 'but I'm used to that. I followed them round the corner and saw them disappearing into the picture. And that's how I found it.'

'The other point,' said Quill, 'concerns Citrolo. Did you see him while you were in the office?'

Madame Ostorojno shuddered. 'I was terrified he would wake up the whole time I was at the safe. But he just went on snoring. The drunkard,' she said indignantly. 'I'd never have thought it of him. And to think that I actually encouraged Olga to go out with him. . . .'

* * *

Quill's next call was on Vanilla. The apartment house on the sea front in which the croupier lived might well have been (and probably was) constructed by the same architect who had designed the residence of the late Mr. Citrolo on *Beau Soleil*. There was the same grimy exterior, the same lift (out of order) and an almost identical scrubbing concierge. There was, however, no Alsatian—only a rather seedy Pekinese.

Of course Vanilla had to live on the fifth floor.

The croupier was on the point of leaving when Quill arrived. He had what was obviously a new suit and the knot of his red silk tie had a precision that suggested many minutes spent before the mirror. He did not seem at all pleased to see Quill.

'What is it?' he asked. 'I am in a hurry. I have the lunch engagement.'

Quill thought lovingly about lunch himself.

'It's not very much,' he said. 'Only that I have found out all about your secret passage and the chips you stole on the night of Citrolo's murder.'

'Oh.' Careless of the crease in his new trousers, Vanilla sank into a chair.

'It was that idiot Kukumber with his talk who put you on the track.'

'Possibly,' agreed Quill. 'But whatever it was it seems to me that your one chance now is to tell me the whole truth about that night.'

'It is a lie,' said Vanilla. 'I did not kill him.'

'I didn't say you did,' said Quill. 'But a jury might not be so easy to convince. You had every reason for killing Citrolo and now it appears you had every opportunity.'

Vanilla shrugged. 'What is it you want of me? I am at your mercy.'

'Only the truth.'

'What use is that? The circumstances are against me. I cannot prove my innocence, only repeat it. There is nothing I can do to convince you unless,' he looked at Quill thoughtfully. 'Who knows of your visit to me?'

Quill glanced at those strong fingers. 'The concierge,' he said, 'Arenskaya. Gustave.'

'Enough,' said Vanilla. He pondered. 'I understand you were dismissed from Scotland Yard.'

'I resigned,' said Quill.

Vanilla nodded. 'Perhaps you would be willing to do business. I am not a rich man but . . .'

'Stop trying to bribe me,' said Quill. 'I haven't accused you of anything yet, anyway. Suppose you tell me your story.'

'But there is nothing to tell,' said Vanilla. 'That night, as always when the syndicate does not do too well, I go to the office for chips.'

'What time was that?'

'I do not remember,' said Vanilla. 'A little past two maybe. As always I use the passage. In the office Citrolo is asleep. I look and I see that he is drugged.'

'It must have been a great temptation,' said Quill.

'I do not deny it,' agreed Vanilla. 'I had little friendship for Citrolo.'

'Not unnatural as he blackmailed you.'

'As you say. And it would have been easy to kill him. But as the dead man himself told me, I have too much imagination for murder. Always I see the consequences. I do not deny,' said Vanilla candidly, 'that if I had been certain of safety I might not have taken my opportunity. But it was too risky, I decided. So I took my chips and left.'

Quill nodded. 'If you didn't strangle him someone else did. The best way of clearing yourself is to help me find the murderer.'

Vanilla started to pace the room. 'How can I do that? I am not a detective.'

'You can answer my questions. Did you hear or see anything while you were in the office or the passage?'

'No.'

'Did you meet anybody on your way back to the baccarat room?'

Vanilla reflected. 'I cannot see how it can in any way concern the crime, but Prince Alexis Artishok was on his way out to the garden.'

'Did you speak to each other?'

'The Prince,' said Vanilla with heavy sarcasm, 'was kind enough to point out that it was a lovely evening.'

'Is that all?'

'That is all.'

'Was this the first evening you had met the Prince?'

'Yes.'

'And yet,' said Quill, 'on the strength of this lively conversation the Prince went out of his way to give you a lift home?'

'Why not? It was raining by then.'

'So you told me before,' said Quill. 'Come on. Out with it. What was it that you and the Prince had to discuss?'

'A purely personal matter.'

'What? My patience has its limits.'

Vanilla thought frantically. 'You will not repeat this?'

'It depends what it is.'

Vanilla thought again. 'It concerns the baccarat. The Prince has a very shrewd eye and it did not take him long to spot my accomplices. He is the soul of kindness. On the journey he devoted himself to discussing their inefficiency and made many valuable suggestions for their improvement.'

'The Prince won that evening, didn't he?'

'He is a great player.'

'How comes a Prince to know so much about the finer aspects of the game?'

Vanilla shrugged. 'M'sieur, I do not ask such questions. Possibly you will ask him for yourself.'

'So,' said Quill, 'the Prince gave you a lift purely to teach you to cheat better. Do you expect me to believe that?'

'It is true,' said Vanilla. 'And I am grateful. Last night the profits were already bigger.'

'Is the Prince getting a rake-off?'

Vanilla started to look affronted but changed his mind. He said that he managed to persuade the Prince to take his share.

'But you will not tell him I told you this?' he said anxiously. 'The Prince would be angry.'

'I'll say nothing for the moment.'

'And the rest?'

'The rest,' said Quill, 'remains to be seen. I shall do nothing for the moment. Now run along to your lunch.'

'I am late,' said Vanilla and flew.

Quill descended the stairs thoughtfully. When he reached the street Vanilla was already out of sight.

Quill had intended to lunch at the café with the grey-green mirrors, but on nearing it he found Arenskaya telling a still puffing Vanilla what she thought of him for keeping her waiting. Taking no chances, Quill bowed, bought a packet of cigarettes, and went to the *Hôtel Moins-Magnifique*. The lunch was even worse than yesterday, but at least he had it alone. Kurt Kukumber, lunching in another corner of the room, did not come near him. He appeared to be explaining something to a saucer-eyed Dutchman.

Quill reflected ruefully that the case was not getting much clearer. It looked singularly as though he would end up with his multitude of suspects all prancing round the sleeping Citrolo, and he would have to decide for himself which one had done the strangling. Quill sighed. Psychology had never been his strong point.

Meanwhile there was the Baron de Rabinovitch to be interviewed. Quill finished his coffee, waved away the cigar trolley hopefully wheeled up, and went to the Casino Buttonhooke.

The Baron was in his usual position under the Buttonhooke portrait. He had almost concluded his day's practice in well-fed benevolence when Quill arrived.

'You again,' he said. 'What is it this time?'

'Plenty,' said Quill, switching on his most formidable expression. He had penetrated the craven heart beneath the astrakhan exterior and deliberately decided to run this interview on a bullying note.

'I have found out,' he began smoothly, 'that you are a liar, a crook, an ex-gaol-bird, and possibly a murderer.'

'Sir.' The Baron, outraged, rose to his feet.

'Shut up,' said Quill. 'Yesterday I let you tell me a string of lies. To-day you're going to answer a bit more accurately.'

The astrakhan began to moult curl by curl but it made one last gesture at affronted dignity.

'This is an outrage.'

'Shut up,' said Quill. 'Sit down. Listen. First so as not to waste time I'm going to tell you what I know about you and then you will tell me what I want to know.'

The Baron sat down.

'You claimed,' said Quill, 'that you only knew Citrolo slightly.'

'That is so,' said the Baron without much hope.

'So slightly that for a number of years you have been paying him blackmail to keep his mouth shut.'

'It is not true,' said the Baron.

'We'll get on much quicker if you'll stop denying the obvious,' said Quill. 'I'm in possession of Citrolo's account book. From it I gather that he has followed your ups and downs with a loving accuracy and charged you according to your success.'

The Baron made no further attempt at denial. He nodded. 'It could not be avoided.'

'You had therefore every reason to hate Citrolo.'

The Baron sprang to his feet. 'I did hate him. What then? Does that make me his murderer?'

'Probably,' snapped Quill.

'There were others who hated him too. Many of them are in Bazouche now. Why do you not accuse them?'

'One at a time,' said Quill. 'Sit down.'

The Baron sat down.

'Next,' said Quill, 'you told me you no longer had a key to Stroganoff's office. I have reason to believe that this was true.'

'A de Rabinovitch does not lie,' said the Baron, cheering up a little.

'But only because you know the way up through the secret passage.'

The Baron mopped his brow.

'At three on the night of the murder,' resumed Quill relentlessly, 'you left the baccarat room and made your way through the passage into the office. You stayed in it some ten minutes. You examined the ledgers, perhaps you also occupied yourself in some other way. Whatever it was you did, you were sufficiently agitated to put the ledgers back, not where you found them, but where you used to keep them. When you returned to the baccarat your agitation was clearly visible to the onlookers.'

'There's not a word of truth in all this,' declared the Baron.

'No?' said Quill. 'Then how came this cigar stub in the passage?' He held it up. 'Henry Clay. You smoke Henry Clay, do you not?'

'Never,' said the Baron, trying to screen the box on the desk by leaning forward.

'Stand up,' said Quill.

The Baron leapt to it.

Quill collected the box. 'Sit down.'

The Baron collapsed.

'Now,' said Quill, as the Baron once again mopped his brow, 'do you admit the truth of what I have been saying or must we go over the ground once more?'

'It is quite true,' said the Baron. 'Only I did not kill him. He was already dead when I entered.'

Quill nodded. 'Tell me about it in detail.'

Rabinovitch tried to pull himself to something resembling his former dignity.

'You are aware,' he began, 'that Lord Buttonhooke wishes to buy back the Casino Stroganoff?'

'I know,' said Quill. 'Why?'

'It is a nuisance,' declared the Baron. 'It detracts from the dignity of our Casino. Also too many people go to it.'

'You ought to have thought of that when you swindled Stroganoff into buying it.'

'I could not tell he would bring his ballet,' said the Baron. 'It is that which has upset our plans.'

'Go on,' said Quill.

'But Stroganoff will not sell. Buttonhooke wanted to increase his offer but I'm against it. I do not think Stroganoff can hold out much longer. So as I am on the premises it seems to me a good idea to have a look at his books, then I will be able to judge the position accurately.'

'You are a specimen, aren't you?' said Quill contemptuously. 'First you swindle Stroganoff and now you want to swindle him again. I suppose,' he hazarded, 'the idea was to see if you could persuade him to take a bit less than you'd tell Lord Buttonhooke and keep the difference for yourself?'

The Baron leapt to his feet. 'It is a lie. Buttonhooke is my friend.'

'Quite,' said Quill. He had a sudden inspiration. 'I suppose the big diamond necklace you and Prince Alexis are going to swing on him is merely a legitimate piece of business.'

The Baron looked puzzled. 'What's this about diamonds?'

'The Otchi Tchernia diamonds that belong to Dyrakova and that the Prince is going to persuade Buttonhooke to buy for Sadie Souse. Don't pretend you knew nothing about it.'

'But of this I have heard nothing,' said the Baron. 'It is outrageous!'

'Then what was it the Prince and you were discussing when I left yesterday?'

The Baron hesitated. 'Nothing. Just a friendly discussion, that is all.'

'What about?'

'But nothing. We must,' said the Baron, looking peculiarly determined, 'have another friendly discussion soon.'

'You seem somehow to be involved with the Prince.'

'But no,' said Rabinovitch. 'Not at all.'

'Oh, all right,' Quill gave up. 'To return to the passage. You entered the office . . .'

'I entered it,' said Rabinovitch. 'I switched on the light over the desk and got busy with the books. The position of Stroganoff is even worse than I thought. He cannot last out much longer.'

'What about Citrolo?'

'I did not notice him at first. It was only when I got up that I noticed a form in the chair on the other side of the room. I crossed to it and , , ,'

'Go on,' said Quill.

'I realized that the man is dead. You can imagine how I felt.'

'Yes,' said Quill, without sympathy.

'I realized I must not be caught, for my legal position would not be good. So I replaced the ledgers . . .'

'In the wrong place.'

'As you say, in the wrong place, and hurried out. And that is all. Naturally I am agitated on my return.'

Quill pondered. 'So on your own admission you were alone with Citrolo in that room. There is only your word that you found him dead.'

'It is bad,' agreed the Baron dismally. 'But it is true.' He looked at Quill anxiously. 'You believe me?'

'I'm keeping an open mind.'

'What are you going to do?'

'Investigate further.' Quill got up. 'If your story is true you have nothing to fear. If it is not . . .' He made for the door.

The Baron produced a second handkerchief.

*   *   *

In a corner of the Casino lounge, Royalty was enjoying its after-lunch cigarette. In front of him a minute portion of Napoleon glowed warmly from its large glass. An admiring waiter stood at a respectful distance hanging on the slightest lift of a finger.

Not in the best of tempers after his interview with Rabino-vitch, Quill thought he might as well have a few words with the Prince and strode over. The Prince raised a Royal elbow in greeting. The waiter jumped to it.

'Brandy,' said the Prince. The waiter darted away.

'The cellar here,' said the Prince condescendingly, 'is almost tolerable. Pray be seated.'

Quill already was.

The Prince passed his cigarette-case. Russian, Quill noted, and started to fill his pipe. To his fury the Prince lit a match for him.

Quill decided to cut short the civilized preliminaries. They took up too much time.

'You know that I am investigating the murder of Citrolo.'

The Prince nodded. 'I trust success will crown your efforts.' His left eyebrow implied that he doubted it.

'I'm checking up on the movements of everybody that night. Several of them call for explanation.'

'Meaning mine?' enquired the Prince.

'Meaning yours.'

The Prince sipped his brandy. 'If one can be of any assistance?'

'You can begin by telling me when last you saw the dead man.'

'But surely,' said the Prince, 'several people must have told you that already.'

'I'd like you to confirm it.'

'Très bien. It was about one o'clock. Mademoiselle Sadie and I went in search of Lord Buttonhooke. Our search took us to the office of our friend Stroganoff.'

'Your friend?'

'A form of expression. He was at work, doubtless on his biography, and Citrolo was apparently resting from his labours.'

'Apparently?'

'He was drugged. Mademoiselle Sadie told me that. A shrewd woman. She pleases me.'

'Did it please you to hear that Citrolo was drugged?'

The Prince raised a reproving eyebrow. 'How could it concern me in any manner?'

'All right,' said Quill. 'How did you spend the rest of the evening?'

'I played baccarat.'

'You were lucky?'

'What, M'sieur, has that to do with your enquiry?' All the traditional hauteur of the Artishoks was to the fore.

'You left the baccarat room at some time after two?'

'That is correct.'

'Where did you go?'

'I walked in the gardens,'

'You met Dino Vanilla in your walk?'

'Who is that?' The memory of the Artishoks was doubtless short. Quill said as much.

'You mean the dark croupier,' the Prince remembered. 'I believe now that we did pass each other in the passage.'

'You gave him a lift home.'

'Possibly, possibly.'

'In Buttonhooke's car?'

'Green is a vulgar colour,' said the Prince. 'But it runs well.'

'Why should you give a croupier a lift?'

A shade of annoyance crossed the regal face.

'M'sieur,' he said, 'I submit to your questions just so long as they can possibly concern your enquiry. Already I have allowed you considerable latitude. But when your questioning becomes impertinent it annoys us.'

'Is that so?'

'That is so.'

Quill tried another track. 'How,' he enquired, 'are "we" getting on with the Otchi Tchernia racket?'

The Prince raised both eyebrows. It was his strongest form of reproof. Quill practically wilted.

'I do not see how that can possibly concern you.'

'These swindles are in my line,' said Quill. 'I used to collect them.' He passed his card.

The Prince did not forget to adjust his monocle before reading it.

'I trust,' he said courteously, 'that the bribe for which you were dismissed was sufficiently large to compensate you.'

CHAPTER XI

A FAMILIAR figure hailed Quill as he emerged from the Casino. It was his old friend, the Balleto-Medico. After his utter rout by Prince Artishok, Quill was quite pleased to see someone unconnected with the crime.

Unlike the Prince the Balleto-Medico wasted no time on preliminary courtesies.

'Have you heard?' he demanded. 'What do you think of it? Isn't it shattering?'

Several features in Quill's mental landscape, including a pair of imprisoned impresarios, qualified under this description. But before he could single out the particular peak which was being mourned, the Balleto-Medico broke out again.

'The finest promise since Baronova. And her mother takes her to Buttonhooke. Buttonhooke! There ought to be a law against it.'

'There is,' said Quill, deducing correctly that his friend was babbling about Mademoiselle Ostorojno. 'But why should you be so upset about it? In what way is the Ballet Buttonhooke worse than the Ballet Stroganoff?'

'Pah!' said the Balleto-Medico, 'it is not a ballet at all.'

'You've always given me the impression that you considered the Ballet Stroganoff the worst ever.'

'So it is,' said the Balleto-Medico. 'But at least it has tradition behind it. Arenskaya passed through the Maryinsky—she is her pupils' link with the ballerinas of the past. They may not be able to dance their rôles but at least they approach them in the proper attitude. But the Ballet Buttonhooke—pah!—it is almost a revue.'

'Of course,'said Quill, 'I don't understand these things but . . .'

'Hush,' said the Balleto-Medico shocked. He looked round. It was all right. No one had heard.

'Still, doesn't Buttonhooke pay better than Stroganoff?'

'That's exactly what I'm complaining about,' said the Balleto-Medico. 'He bribes the few dancers Stroganoff does manage to get hold of, and sets them to work in pantomime transformations. Ivanoff at his worst couldn't touch the sort of stuff he puts on. I'm writing an article about it in my paper. I hope he sues me for libel.'

'But,' said Quill, 'at least there's no Nevajno in the Buttonhooke Ballet.'

'Don't misunderstand me,' said the Balleto-Medico. 'I roar and rave at Nevajno because the fellow is one mass of stupid conceit, but I have never denied he has something. It infuriates me to see him wasting his talent on Modernist nonsense. Did you ever see his *Bed Time Story?*'

'Nevajno's?' asked Quill, startled.

'Delicious,' said the Balleto-Medico. 'It was one of his very early works. It had all the simplicity of Fokine with the contortion of Massine on top.'

'It doesn't sound very like Nevajno.'

'It isn't now,' said the Balleto-Medico. 'He has been spoilt. It's partly Stroganoff's fault and partly the Press. Stroganoff praises too much and the Press too little. As a result Nevajno sees himself as Misunderstood Genius and his work gets more and more defiant—and more and more impossible.'

At the hotel over their tea, Quill explained that though he had come to Bazouche on a holiday, he found himself plunged into an infuriating murder case. He outlined the details and presented the Balleto-Medico with a synopsis of his investigations to date. As a Watson the Balleto-Medico was a distinct failure. He interrupted far too often and he did not say 'wonderful' once. But he grasped the essentials of the case very quickly if not exactly from the police angle. He seemed particularly interested in Citrolo's *Apologia* which Quill showed him.

'Typical,' he chuckled. 'Typical! You know I'm quite sorry the man's dead. I shall miss his critiques.'

'You knew him well?' Quill enquired.

'We both served the same mistress.'

'Not Dyrakova?'

'Not, as you say, Dyrakova—not Dyrakova alone, that is—nor yet Spessitsiva, nor Lopokova, nor Karsavina. Not even the gracious Riabouchinska, the dark Toumanova, the charming Baronova—the ethereal Markova—not any one dancer, but every dancer. Our Mistress,' continued the Balleto-Medico, waving aside Quill's interruption, 'is the Ballet.'

'Quite,' said Quill.

'And this is a love that puzzles you no doubt.'

'Well—I wouldn't say that,' said Quill, floundering. 'Though I must admit that I am a bit surprised at finding this single-minded love in the dead man.'

'Why?'

'Citrolo was a bad lot,' said Quill, 'a blackmailer who drove his victims just as far as his common sense showed him it was remunerative to go. He had no clemency. He lived the meanest way a man could choose—on the forgotten mistakes of others. Yet from all accounts this man refused to accept a bribe—or—er—a ballerina, when it came to revising his opinion of a ballet.'

'And that seems strange to you, my friend?'

'It does.'

The Balleto-Medico waved a forgiving hand at Quill. 'To me it is perfectly logical. Bribe or bed—what do these count against the accumulating passion of a lifetime—a passion that has had time to spread its deep roots in your heart? Citrolo had this enduring passion.'

'Yet he was very critical.'

'Not "yet," ' corrected the Balleto-Medico, ' "Of course." '

Quill felt that he was beginning to understand.

'Critics are of two kinds,' explained the Balleto-Medico. 'There is the man who owing to the particular key in which his temperament is set responds readily to the stimulus of his chosen art, and there is the man who may be equally discerning but less engaged with his own sensation. The first type of critic wishes only to express what he feels when he sees a work. If he can convey and spread even the smallest part of his own response to his beloved stimulus, he has achieved his aim.'

So far Quill could follow the Balleto-Medico perfectly. There had been nights when he himself on his way back from one of those films that somehow contrive to get you . . .

But the Balleto-Medico was off again.

'But there is the other type of critic. He leaves his heart on his desk, and takes only his eye, his memory, and his Oxford Dictionary. He takes his memory because the art of the ballet is repetitive. You must understand that the literature of the dance is small and that the ballerinas inherit their rôles as a miser inherits his fortune. The ballet critic will remember many a vanished grace while he is watching a new performer. He weighs her in the scales of a fine tradition. He knows that this tradition is in his keeping. A promise too early acclaimed—a gift too long ignored—a work too easily assimilated—these are the critic's pitfalls. His knowledge of technique guides him to the less apparent aspects of a promise. He in turn directs the attention of the ballet-goer. A dancer appears from the rut. For this he needs his eye. His experience of the ballet that cloys, the ballet that keeps its freshness, the ballet that dates, or that continues to amuse—for this he needs his memory. For what, in a new work, will endure, what is perishable, for the just distribution of praise or blame among the dancers, choreographer, composer—for this he needs his eye, his memory, and his flair. Then, when he has written his notice, he can go back to his desk and exercise, in the privacy of his own memory, the forgiving functions of the heart. The performance he has just witnessed will become another signpost on the path towards impeccability.'

'And Citrolo?' asked Quill.

'Citrolo was a man in whom self-control was a trade as well as a virtue. He would not so far forget his own fallibility as to take his heart either to ballet or bed—and certainly never to business. His unswerving sense of the balletic and his unwavering defence of his flair in face of any bribe—any kindness, is in keeping with his mode of conducting his life.'

'I see,' said Quill. 'What do you make the chances of an enraged ballerina—or her partner—finding him drugged, and strangling him?'

'Ballerinas,' said the Balleto-Medico. 'No. Their partners—never. But a really enraged mother, with the strong conviction that her daughter is being systematically libelled, given the necessary strength—and how strong our ballet mothers look. . . .'

'I see,' said Quill.

'But in the case of Citrolo I think we can count the ballet mother out. There is only one really formidable mother and she has too much faith in her daughter's gifts to bother to kill a critic in defence of them.'

'Madame Ostorojno?'

The Balleto-Medico nodded.

'I'm inclined to agree with you there,' said Quill. 'But if mothers and daughters are exonerated what do you feel about croupiers? Croupiers with strong wrists and ferrety eyes.'

The Balleto-Medico lit another cigarette. 'My hobby,' he began, 'has led me into, and out of, more casinos than I can count.'

'And—er—your practice?'

'You must understand I have no regular practice any longer. I only took my degree to please the old man. After he died,' the Balleto-Medico waved an extenuating hand in the direction of filial memory, 'well, it was no longer necessary that I should starve the rich and cosset the poor. But my study of dietetics has stood me in good stead in my chosen sphere. Not a dancer but shivers in her shoes at the awful word "Thickening." And these little ones, they bring their ankles, their backs, and even their husbands, and put them in my charge.'

'Must be very interesting,' said Quill.

'Where there is a ballet, there will I be found. And where there is a casino, sooner or later some hard-pressed impresario trying to save his company from those dreaded one-night stands—those stands that bring the big money with them—but also the thickened legs, the weakened muscles and the untidy technique—those one-night stands that sap the pride and the vitality of a company as surely as a blackmailer saps the pride and bank balance of his victims, those . . . Where was I?'

'At the Casino,' said Quill firmly.

'Ah, yes,' said the Balleto-Medico, 'Casinos. Take for instance that one at Monte Carlo. . . .'

'I refuse,' said Quill.

The Balleto-Medico looked startled and then smiled. 'Of course, I had forgotten. This is a murder enquiry. You were asking about croupiers.'

'Exactly. And you told me all about thickening muscles.'

'Sorry,' said the Balleto-Medico. 'About croupiers then. I've known croupiers all over the world. It may seem curious to you but most of them are absolutely honest. They are surrounded by bribery and an atmosphere of easy money, but they are well paid. Their job is comparatively cushy, and they know that if once they get dismissed from a casino, even on suspicion, they can never get a job in another—except possibly in a private gambling house. So they train themselves to develop a sort of protective armour, like bank clerks who deal in other people's thousands, and do not allow themselves to translate the counters into money. They like the heavy winners. They look on their pourboires as an investment built on other people's risks.'

'And the dishonest croupier?'

'He's a rare bird but he's dangerous. Once a croupier starts on the downward path there is nothing he is not capable of. You see his opportunities are so many, and the man who drugs his conscience every day will be its master in an emergency. If the murder was unpremeditated your dishonest croupier might well have done it.' He paused. 'Yes—Dino Vanilla is certainly a possibility.'

'He had every opportunity, at any rate,' said Quill. 'He was alone with the drugged man whom he hated. He's easily excitable, and he has the strongest wrists I've seen on any man.

I swear he would have used them on me this morning if I hadn't pointed out the number of people who would know for a certainty that he had done it. And yet,' he mused, 'I'm not convinced he's guilty.'

'Got a better suspect?' asked the Balleto-Medico brightly.

'The Baron de Rabinovitch.'

'Splendid,' the Balleto-Medico approved. 'I never did like him. Just tell me what you've got against him.'

Quill repeated the evidence against the Baron. Once again there was the opportunity and an even stronger motive than in the case of Vanilla, for the Baron paid far larger sums in blackmail than the croupier, a further increase was mooted, and as his prosperity under Buttonhooke's patronage increased so would the payments. A blackmailer was far more menacing to a man on the verge of big success than to the petty thief. Quill ended up with the details of his interview with the Baron that afternoon.

'I've scared him stiff,' said Quill. 'He admitted everything to me except the murder—he claimed that Citrolo was already dead when he entered the office.'

The Balleto-Medico nodded. 'There's only one point in the Baron's favour. He's hardly the type to strangle a man. A cautious knife in the back is more his mark.'

'Citrolo was drugged,' Quill pointed out. 'That makes strangling quite safe.'

'You may be on the right track,' agreed the Balleto-Medico.

'I'm almost sure I am,' said Quill. 'But I think I'll have to act quickly to get him. He's scared stiff and may do a bunk at any moment.'

'I've known the Baron off and on for years,' mused the Balleto-Medico. 'I should think he's been run out of more small casinos than any other man on the Continent. But I've never known him to attempt anything really dangerous—yet. And somehow I can't visualize those podgy hands really meaning business on a man's throat.'

'In that case,' said Quill, 'what of bogus Russian nobility?'

'Prince Artishok?' said the Balleto-Medico. 'Is he bogus? Of course, that would explain it.'

'Explain what?'

'His extraordinary ignorance of the ballet. Mind you he knows enough to keep up a superficial patter, but I hadn't been talking to him a few minutes before I realized that the man was fundamentally unsound. It puzzled me a bit at the time to find this pretence in a Russian nobleman, but of course if he's phoney that explains it.'

Quill let it go at that.

But the Balleto-Medico was not willing to leave so promising a thread. Before Quill got rid of him he had weighed the Spaniard's love of the dance against that of the Russian, found it wanting, and assessed England as a good second and catching up fast. Towards the end, Quill was hardly listening. He was wondering if it would be possible to coax Gustave into yet another arrest before there was a vacuum beneath Lord Buttonhooke's portrait.

*   *   *

'Mais mon ami,' Stroganoff was saying, 'c'est bien intéressant ce que vous me racontez. You are certain of your facts, no?'

'Positive,' said Kurt Kukumber, with assurance. The few hundred francs in his wallet that the goggle-eyed Dutchman had handed over to invest on his infallible horse, had given him fresh confidence. 'This mine that has been derelict so long—these shares that have been worthless—soon they will hit the sky.'

'Naturellement,' said Stroganoff, 'if they have found gold—then it must be so.'

'The richest vein of gold in California,' stressed Kurt.

Stroganoff was suddenly cautious. 'This engineer who makes you the secret report—you are certain that he is not the swindle?'

But it appeared that Kurt had never been more certain of anyone's probity. The engineer who had double-crossed the company by giving Kurt advance information of his discovery, was quite the most honest man Kurt had ever known.

'He is my sister's husband,' said Kurt, clinching the matter.

'Entendu.' The man of affairs was satisfied. But the psychologist still had his doubts.

'If these shares make the fortune,' he demanded, 'why do you come to me?'

'There is plenty for both,' said Kurt quickly. 'If I were not so broke,' he added with a great show of candour, 'I would keep this good thing to myself. But I need money. My infallible system at the roulette is for the moment not lucky. So I make you this offer, my friend, because I like you.'

'Also you like my ballet?' said Stroganoff hopefully.

'I adore it,' said Kurt. 'The Sylphides. And—er—the Sylphides.'

'Superb,' agreed Stroganoff. 'Bon. We do business. I buy all your shares. 'Ow mooch?'

But here Kurt rose to his greatest heights of plausibility. He could not, he declared, sell all. He had to keep a few for himself.

'All,' insisted Stroganoff, back to big business. 'All or nozzing.'

Kurt pretended to weaken.

It was at this moment that Quill chose to walk in.

Kurt could have killed him.

*   *   *

'Mais, mon cher, M'sieur Quill,' said Stroganoff, 'Ce n'est pas raisonnable. It is the fortune that you prevent me buying.'

'Like the gold shares you bought in London?'

'That,' agreed Stroganoff, 'was the swindle. Mais cela n'est pas du tout le même chose. M'sieur Kukumber has the information confidential.'

'Hence the term "Confidence Man," ' said Quill.

'I have in him the confidence implicit,' said Stroganoff. 'He look me straight in the eye when he talk and honesty it is written on his face. I fear now only that you have offended him and that he sell to Button'ooke.'

'Good heavens!' said Quill, 'don't you know a swindler when you see one.'

But Stroganoff was not convinced. 'You suspect too much. Everything to you it is the fish. Doubtless it is the policeman in you. But I, Vladimir Stroganoff, have the mind broad —the vision. Also I am the business man. I do not buy the pig in the bush. I have read the prospectus and it is most glowing.'

Quill sighed.

'Besides,' said Stroganoff, 'I have the insurance. This is an investment where I cannot lose.'

'Even if the mine is dud?'

'I do not contemplate such a possibility. But even if you should be right in your view so pessimist then I shall come out the quits.'

'How's that?'

Stroganoff chuckled.

'The good Kukumber, he have the system infallible at roulette. So the moneys I pay for the shares it come back to me, anyway.' He winked at Quill. 'Is it not droll how people always believe they can get quick rich?'

Quill gave it up. But he decided to have a word with Kurt in private and dissuade him from further enterprise.

Gustave made an agitated appearance.

'Prepare yourselves,' he hissed urgently. 'M'sieur le Préfet arrives.'

'What must I do?' asked Stroganoff worried.

'Stand to attention,' said Quill. 'Speak when you're spoken to. And don't invite him to your box for the performance.'

Stroganoff crossed to the mirror, patted his bald dome, adjusted his tie, took a second look at it, tore it off, selected another from the wardrobe, and passed it to Quill for his approval.

'What you think?' he asked.

It was at this moment that the *Préfet* came in. Stroganoff

rushed hurriedly to the mirror, his back firmly turned, his fingers busy with his tie.

'This,' said Gustave embarrassed, 'is the man Stroganoff.'

'Stroganoff,' said the frail white moustache in some surprise, 'Vladimir Stroganoff?'

Stroganoff turned round defensively. One look and the apprehension vanished.

'Mon vieux!' An ecstatic rush followed. Bald dome and white moustache embraced one another. Eventually the moustache disentangled itself to point an accusing finger at Gustave.

'Imbécile—what made you arrest him?'

'The evidence,' babbled Gustave. 'Could I guess? . . . Could I tell . . .?'

'Poof!' said Stroganoff forgivingly, 'it is no matter. The good Gustave he try to do his duty. That he is stupid, it is not his fault.' He dismissed the subject. 'But let us sit down—no—not here—the divan, it is more comfortable. Have some brandy— some caviare—a cigar.' He passed the opulent-looking box. 'Big joke.'

The white moustache and the bald dome sat down contentedly side by side.

Gustave and Quill gazed at each other.

'Ah, it is good to see you,' said the moustache, sipping contentedly. 'You ballet is with you?'

'Mais toujours,' said Stroganoff. 'You come to my box,' he added, shooting a triumphant look at Quill.

'What is it you are giving?' asked M'sieur le Préfet.

'*Sylphides*,' said Stroganoff, '*Boutique Fantasque* and *Les Matelots*.'

'You tempt me,' said the *Préfet*. 'Excuse while I telephone my wife.'

Gustave intervened. 'M'sieur le Préfet, the man Lord Buttonhooke waits to be seen.'

'Plus tard, plus tard,' said the *Préfet*. 'But first, the telephone.' He trotted off happily in Gustave's outraged wake, while Stroganoff explained to Quill that the *Préfet* was an old balletomane—one who had a real appreciation of the art—not like that Citrolo, who so carelessly got himself killed and disturbed the routine of busy impresarios.

'I suppose,' Quill hazarded, 'that this old friend will release you and Buttonhooke.'

'Me—yes,' said Stroganoff sunnily. 'Button'ooke I think I ask him to keep.'

Buttonhooke was at the grille taking a deep interest in the conversation.

'Help me out of here,' he wheedled, 'and I'll let you have Dovolno back.'

'And Shashlyk,' said Stroganoff, 'and Kashkavar?'

'Certainly.'

'Bon,' said Stroganoff, 'it is the bargain. I give you Smithsky in exchange.'

The *Préfet* returned regretfully. It appeared that his wife had guests.

'Bring them all,' invited the hospitable Stroganoff. 'My box it is big. No? Olright—then you come to-morrow?'

'Entendu,' agreed the *Préfet*. He seated himself. 'Now my friend you and I have a little business to discuss.'

'What is that?' Stroganoff was interested.

'Concerning Pavlo Citrolo.'

'Ah ça!' said Stroganoff, 'Alors?'

'Did you kill him?'

'Non,' said Stroganoff forcibly.

'Of course. The idea was absurd.' The *Préfet* turned on Gustave reproachfully. 'Quick arrests after a murder are very useful—they keep away the Sûreté—but one must always arrest with discrimination.' He remembered Buttonhooke. 'What of the other prisoner?'

'He is innocent,' said Stroganoff. 'He runs a ballet, too.'

'You are certain?' asked the *Préfet* keenly. He was a conscientious man.

'Absolument.'

'Bon! Then we must release him.' He turned on Gustave. 'Does not that leave us without an arrest?'

'It does,' said Gustave mournfully.

'Then hurry,' said the *Préfet*, 'and clear up the little mystery. Else the Sûreté will be down on us.'

Gustave shuddered.

'The Sûreté,' explained the *Préfet* to Stroganoff, 'is to us what the dancer's mother is to you. They come in, and they meddle, and they spoil all the arrangements we have made. That is why we must make every effort to solve this murder quickly.'

Stroganoff decided it was time to introduce Quill.

'M'sieur Quill,' he explained, 'has promised to find for us the assassin. He is the great detective. Once he was with Scotland Yard.'

'Was?' said the *Préfet* keenly.

'I resigned,' said Quill.

The *Préfet* looked his disapproval. 'And what was it, M'sieur, that made it necessary?'

*   *   *

'Doucement! Doucement!' The man with the turned-up shirt-sleeves reproved his companion.

'Alors, faites passer vous même.' The sweater flung his cigarette stub on the floor and stamped on it temperamentally.

Stroganoff and Buttonhooke had made a hasty departure, and now the furniture men were removing the last traces of their sojourn. They had been at it for an hour under Gustave's anxious supervision. Quill chafed impatiently. He badly wanted a few words with Gustave concerning the wisdom of arresting Baron de Rabinovitch, but until the removal was over Gustave would be in no mood to concentrate.

At last the van trundled away. Gustave saw them off, turned on his tracks, ruefully inspected a large flake fallen from the stony wall of Stroganoff's cell and went clucking back to Quill.

'Now, mon vieux,' he said, relapsing on to a chair. 'What is it you want of me?'

'I think,' said Quill, 'that I've got your man.'

If he expected to startle Gustave he was disappointed.

'Bon,' said the gendarme placidly. 'We arrest him to-morrow.'

'To-morrow may be too late. You see,' Quill explained, 'I've frightened him, rather.'

'Méchant,' said Gustave reprovingly. 'Who is this assassin?'

'The Baron de Rabinovitch.'

Again Gustave exhibited no surprise. 'Celui-ci? Ah, bon! You have the proof?' he enquired as an afterthought.

'There is a certain amount.'

'Recount it to me,' said Gustave. 'This time I must be careful to be correct or else the Sûreté they will surely get vexed.'

Quill suppressed a smile. Scotland Yard, he felt, would have started to get waxy long ago. Soberly he outlined the evidence against the Baron, dwelling on his unquestionable opportunity and his indisputable motive. He produced Citrolo's note-book with its record of payments by the Baron. Gustave promptly collared it.

'This,' he announced happily, 'I read later—but you are right, mon cher. There is enough to hold him on suspicion,' he declared. 'We take him to-morrow.'

'At once,' insisted Quill.

'Pas ce soir,' Gustave shook his head firmly. 'Aujord-hui c'est mardi. Mardi je m'amuse.'

'That's all right,' said Quill. 'Arrest him first and amuse yourself afterwards.'

'Non,' said Gustave. 'J'ai mes habitudes et mes heures. I am too old to change.'

'Look here,' said Quill, 'if you don't take him to-night he may be gone to-morrow. And then the Sûreté will be very cross indeed.'

Gustave began to waver. 'Perhaps I come afterwards.'

'What time will that be?'

'Ça dépend,' said Gustave. 'Eleven may be.'

'Better come at once.'

'Non.' Gustave reached for his overcoat. 'It is already time for my appointment. Do not distress yourself. The Baron will not fly so soon.'

Still arguing, Quill followed him into the street.

'Vous venez avec moi?' observed Gustave. 'Ah—bon!'

He strode off vigorously. Quill followed. If he stuck close enough and nagged sufficiently he might succeed in dragging this zealous policeman away half-way through whatever party it was he was making for.

They turned down a side-street and stopped before some shuttered windows. Gustave pushed open the door. A bell tinkled down the back. A violent crimson carpet burst on Quill. So a moment later did Madame.

'Vous êtes en retard,' she rebuked Gustave. 'Mademoiselle Fifi vous attend dans la salle Chinoise depuis dix minutes.'

'Pardon,' said Gustave, making for the stairs. He paused to wave a vague hand at Quill. 'Vous vous occupez de mon ami. Il est Anglais.' He darted off.

Madame was affability itself. Had M'sieur any preference?'

'Er?' said Quill.

'J'ai une petite Russe charmante.'

Quill gulped and tried to explain.

'Je suis trompé,' he began laboriously.

Madame was a philosopher. 'Ça arrive à tout le monde. Ici on oublie. Peut-être une mignonne Japonaise?'

Quill shook his head desperately.

'Alors,' said Madame, 'vous préférez choisir.' She clapped her hands.

A confusion of shuffle, giggle, and perfume, trooped in.

Quill gave up any further efforts at explanation. He ran for his life.

CHAPTER XII

THE restaurant at the Casino Buttonhooke presented an animated appearance. News of the magnate's release from gaol had spread quickly and every inch of sable, every swell of starch, had gathered from miles around for a glimpse of the extricated Daniel.

The floor of the restaurant was packed solid with diners-out unanimously leaving their lukewarm *consommé*.

But clients expecting to see the Press Lord haggard and exhausted after his gruelling ordeal in the local gaol were doomed to disappointment. Incarceration had not affected Lord Buttonhooke outwardly in any material manner. Plump and jovial, he sat at the head of a table bestrewn with sheafs of lilac and showers of roses, beaming seraphically at one and all.

On his right, Sadie Souse emerged from a confection of pink chiffon, pale orchids, and no shoulder straps. On his left, Prince Alexis Artishok's monocle was clearly disclaiming all responsibility for the table's flower scheme. At the far end of the table the lavender tie was waiting to be spoken to before it answered. And beside the Prince, Baron Sam de Rabinovitch absently crumbed his roll.

The Baron was not himself to-night. There was no carnation in his buttonhole. He was not even making a dab at the Buttonhooke benevolence. When he smiled it was in a sickly fashion. He took no interest in his food. Frequently he leant forward as though about to speak, but each time he changed his mind. Lord Buttonhooke was eating Homard à l'Americaine. His digestion was due to pay for it later, but he felt that his palate was entitled to it now.

'Encore,' he instructed the waiter recklessly.

169

The Prince raised an eyebrow.

'Is it wise?' cautioned Sadie Souse. 'Had you better?' Visions of having to coax diamonds from an indigestion-racked Daddy floated before her saucer eyes.

'You're very beautiful to-night,' said Buttonhooke between mouthfuls. 'Pretty as a picture.' He placed a podgy hand on her knee. Sadie slid a practised little paw on top of it.

'I'd look a darn sight more beautiful in the Otchi Tchernia diamonds. I suit diamonds,' said Sadie modestly.

'Have you missed me?' pursued Buttonhooke, without much hope.

'Sure,' said Sadie, 'I got kinda lonely with only the Prince to look after me, and no Otchi Tchernia's to try out.'

'Poor little girl,' sighed Buttonhooke, 'never mind—I'll make it up to you, now I'm back again.'

'Darling,' the pressure increased with a practised percepti-bility. 'Prince, Prince,' added Sadie urgently, 'Percy's just promised me my Otchi Tchernia's.'

Rabinovitch edged uneasily towards his idol's eye-level, but Lord Buttonhooke did not observe him. He was bawling for brandy.

But the magnate's brandy was due to be delayed, for as his waiter moved smoothly away in search of it, a bald dome bobbed at him.

'Et mes framboises?' it demanded impatiently. 'J'attends toujours.'

'Pas de framboises,' explained the waiter slowly, loudly, and for the third time. But Stroganoff still looked hopeful.

'Pas de framboises,' repeated the waiter, 'ni de fraises, ni même de cerises.'

Shocked, Stroganoff voiced his complaint to the rest of his party. The audience reacted in their accustomed ways: Galybchik said it was a shame, Nevajno absently finished Arenskaya's champagne. Arenskaya boxed his ears. Order was restored with difficulty.

'Doubtless,' began Quill, the memory of his dinner at the Casino Stroganoff still vivid, 'doubtless, the greengrocer is enervé.'

Stroganoff looked about him distastefully.

'To eat at this place,' he said, 'it was the big mistake.'

'Then why we do it?' asked Arenskaya.

'It is the finance,' explained Stroganoff. 'Emilio he tell me the free list it must be reduced. But had I for a moment suspected that there would be no framboises. . . .' With sudden resolution he pushed aside his chair and strode over to Buttonhooke.

'Your publicité,' he complained, 'it makes the lie unpardonable.'

Buttonhooke goggled.

So, but less believingly, did the Baron.

So did Sadie.

So did the lavender tie.

Even the Prince raised an eyebrow.

'You announce us that your cuisine it is unrivalled, and poof!—there are no framboises!'

The lavender tie was the first to recover.

'In March,' it began crushingly. . . .

'Mistaire Galybchik,' appealed Stroganoff, 'what matters to me the calendar? It is the framboises that I command, and not the diary.'

'And if you wanted oysters in July?' argued the logical lavender tie.

'Oysters,' said Stroganoff with a sigh, 'do not agree with me.'

'Too bad,' said the Baron, absently.

'The dinner,' continued Stroganoff, outraged, 'was a disgust. The hors d'œuvres, the sole délice, the Caneton Sauvage, and the omelette surprise—poof!—it was not fit to offer a journalist.'

'Look here,' began Buttonhooke hotly. . . .

Stroganoff waved a magnanimous hand. 'Do not distress yourself,' he said forgivingly, 'we Russians are used to suffer.' An evil glitter lit his eye. 'Tiens!' he exclaimed. 'We prove it— we all stay to see your *Lac des Cygnes* to-night. Big joke,' he explained to Sadie, who was the only one who seemed to find his quip at all amusing.

'The house is sold out,' said the lavender tie.

'No matter,' said Arenskaya, materializing at Stroganoff's

elbow. 'Do not apologize. Not always can the stall hospitable be found. Instead,' she finished sweetly, 'we come to your box.'

'Enchanté, Madame,' murmured Prince Artishok into the stunned silence.

*   *   *

Al Fineberg hit his drum a disconsolate whang. 'Let's give 'em something hot?' he pleaded.

Bennie Schweitzer took up his saxophone and lovingly scaled to the highest note in his compass. Not content with that he slid down again like an avalanche in a silly symphony.

'A rumba,' said Moishe. He played the concertina.

'High, Wide, and Handsome,' suggested Abe Abelson, picking up his trumpet.

Isadore at the piano settled the dispute by striking up a hotted version of 'Two Guitars.'

By hiring Abe Abelson and his American College Boys for the Casino Ballroom Lord Buttonhooke had unwittingly done a keen stroke of business for his baccarat. Only in the gambling rooms could you escape their strains. Merciless amplifiers festooned the walls in every other place.

The hotted up version of 'Two Guitars,' which blared out as Stroganoff's party emerged from the restaurant, stirred the gipsy in Arenskaya.

'We dance,' she announced. Brooking no opposition, she clutched the weakest (Galybchik) and made off towards a table on the illuminated floor. Perforce the others followed.

'Consommation Obligatoire,' said Stroganoff, eyeing the notice on the wall with considerable disapproval. 'Me—I will not drink the orangeade. We go.'

'The first ballet it is *Les Sylphides*,' said Arenskaya cunningly. 'You will no doubt enjoy *Les Sylphides* Button'ooke. As for me—j'y reste.'

Stroganoff shuddered and sat down.

Arenskaya gazed invitingly at Quill. Quill looked the other way. Arenskaya advanced towards him, the gipsy very much in evidence.

A ferrety shadow loomed up in time to save Quill. It was Dino Vanilla.

'Carissima,' he muttered and wafted her away.

'He has the nerve that one,' muttered Stroganoff. 'It is but two hours since I give him the sack and déjà he dances with my maîtresse de ballet.'

'We dance?' suggested Galybchik to Nevajno.

'Quelle drôle d'idée,' said the intellectual, amused.

'We dance,' said Quill. Galybchik leapt to it.

Nevajno glared at the couple, his lean fingers drumming nervously on the table.

'But you dance beautifully,' said Galybchik, surprised.

'Long practice in night clubs disguised as a gentleman,' explained Quill.

'You dance wonderfully,' said Vanilla to Arenskaya, 'but it is only as I expected.'

'Foolish boy,' said Arenskaya, well pleased. 'Tell me why are you not at work?'

Vanilla looked pathetic. 'I have been sacked.'

'Vladimir dare to do that?' Arenskaya's shrill indignation almost drowned the trumpeter's solo passage. 'We go back and I arrange everything.'

But it appeared that tact would be needed. The English policeman had meanly told Stroganoff all about the chips and the latter had now conceived the darkest doubts concerning Vanilla's honesty.

'So now you throw the ball here?' asked Arenskaya. 'Poor boy, but no matter,' she consoled him, 'we still have your night off.'

But it appeared that every night was off. That pig Rabinovitch, who by a curious coincidence was harbouring much the same sort of doubts as Stroganoff, would see to that.

'I attend to everything,' Arenskaya assured him. 'I threaten Vladimir that I go to Hollywood and he take you back double quick. Without me Vladimir is an empty "O." It is well known.'

The empty 'O' was at the moment homesick for a real tzigane orchestra.

'In Moscow,' he was remembering, 'there was a little

kabachok where we dance, we drink, we sing far into the night. My baritone it was much admired then.' He cleared his throat.

Unfeelingly the American College Boys plunged into the 'Big Apple.'

*   *   *

In her dressing-room the young Ostorojno was dabbing powder on an agitated nose.

'You know,' she said, 'we haven't been too clever this time.'

'Nonsense,' said the old Ostorojno, 'there was no future with Stroganoff. I thought I'd made you see that.'

'Not Stroganoff,' sighed the young Ostorojno. 'I was thinking about David. Maybe we ought to have had a rehearsal.'

'Nonsense,' said the old Ostorojno, looking slightly guilty. 'You know your Swan Lake backwards. And you wanted to surprise Dovolno to-night, didn't you? Anyway, I thought you danced very well with that young understudy.'

'The orchestra!' groaned young Ostorojno, showing that she was growing up fast.

Mother and daughter settled down to a nice companionable grumble about the musical director.

'Still,' old Ostorojno concluded, 'you have danced with worse orchestras before now. Remember La Bourboule.'

'And Carlsbad,' said the young Ostorojno.

'And the pier at Eastbourne.'

Young Ostorojno brightened. 'It could be worse. And it will be nice to dance with David again.'

'Won't he be surprised to see you come on,' said the old Ostorojno encouragingly.

'I hope he won't dry up,' said the young Ostorojno, all nerves again.

'Now look here,' said old Ostorojno, 'don't bring that up again. After the way you had to persuade me to persuade the régisseur to let you dance with an understudy solely so that you could surprise Dovolno to-night, I won't stand for it.'

The call-boy knocked on the door.

'Your shoes?' flurried Madame Ostorojno. 'Your hair? Stand up. Let me look at you.'

The Ballerina was on her way.

*   *   *

Lord Buttonhooke's box was feeling the strain. Arenskaya, with difficulty detached from her Vanilla, had seated herself firmly in the front row with Buttonhooke on one side and Stroganoff on the other. Nevajno, foiled in his attempt to prise Buttonhooke from his seat, had wedged himself into the corner nearest the stage and obstinately closed his eyes. 'It is Petipas,' he explained. In the second row an eager Galybchik perched beside a bored Sadie Souse. The Prince had deserted her for baccarat, and Quill, lounging against the wall, did not seem to be paying her the attention she had every right to expect. The door space which had at first been occupied by the Baron de Rabinovitch was now held by the lavender tie. Muttering that something needed his attention in the office the Baron had left the party. Quill did not like letting him out of his sight, but surely Gustave could not be long now.

The conductor waved his baton. The oboe quaveringly announced the Swan Queen Motif.

'Your orchestra—it play bad—no?' said Stroganoff with much satisfaction.

The curtain went up.

In the wings Ostorojno stood screened behind a batch of friendly skirts. From her position she could just see a few inches of grey leotard belonging to the huntsmen. The purple splendour of the Prince was hidden from her. She giggled in anticipation. What a start David Dovolno was going to get.

Her cue.

A last trial of the foot, a last touch of the hair, and into the white light she ran, achieving a perfectly placed pas de chat. Vaguely she seemed to hear a scream of rage, but one could not be bothered with that. David would be standing against the wings looking at her. A few more bars and they would be face to face.

And now the Prince was hurrying forward. She bowed to him. He bowed back. There was something peculiar about that bow. Olga Ostorojno looked up—straight into the beaming face of Ernest Smithsky. Click went an amateur camera—it was a big moment.

* * *

At the Casino Stroganoff, his own secret well kept, a cursing Dovolno was endeavouring to rotate the fat girl.

* * *

The playing of the prelude had put Stroganoff into a fine humour. The first fiddle had been noticeably flat and the two harps had both come in two beats late. He discussed the matter fully with Arenskaya just in case Buttonhooke had not noticed it.

The view-hallo of the huntsmen increased his pleasure. He slapped Buttonhooke affably on the back when Ernest Smithsky as the Prince hurried invisibly on.

'You have done well, my friend, to take that one. His technique it is superb—it is a pity only that his personality is imperceptible.'

The jeers seemed to have little effect on Buttonhooke. He chuckled and almost rubbed his hands.

'Wait till you see the Swan Queen.'

Stroganoff was interested. 'You have a new dancer?'

'New to me.'

'She has talent.'

'A very great talent.'

'Poof!' said Stroganoff. 'She cannot compare with my Ostorojno.'

'Hush,' said Buttonhooke, 'here she comes.'

Stroganoff leant forward and nodded approvingly as a perfectly-placed pas de chat landed in its clear-cut fourth position. He leant further forward as the face of the dancer looked at the audience. He almost fell out of the box.

'Thief! Villain! Assassin!' He clutched Buttonhooke's right shoulder and tried to swing him round. He failed, for Arenskaya was pulling at the other.

Prince Artishok, entering the box, raised an enquiring eyebrow. Sadie explained it gleefully.

Lord Buttonhooke, though a little torn, went on chuckling.

'You laugh,' said Stroganoff infuriated. 'You think you spell for me the ruin. But soon you sing the other side of your face. Wait till you see the Giselle that come to me from Paris.'

'What's that?' said Buttonhooke.

' 'Ush,' cautioned Arenskaya. 'The plans of the Ballet—they are for us alone. And also per'aps she do not come.'

'She come,' said Stroganoff, 'she cannot resist me much more.'

Arenskaya changed the subject.

'It is a pity,' she said tactfully to Buttonhooke, 'that your cygnets they are out of step yet again.'

Lord Buttonhooke clapped defiantly as the ballet came to an end.

Ostorojno took her curtains alone. Only Smithsky was with her.

* * *

'Come, come.' As the contents of the box emptied themselves into the foyer Lord Buttonhooke patted the gloomy Stroganoff on the back. 'Cheer up. It's all in the game. To-day I've put one across you. To-morrow maybe you'll put one across me.'

'Then to-morrow I laugh,' said Stroganoff.

'It's stupid to bear malice,' urged Buttonhooke. 'Look at me. You got me into gaol, but . . .'

'I get you out,' said Stroganoff. 'And to thank me you steal my Ostorojno.'

'Forget it,' said Buttonhooke. 'Let's all go to my office and have a drink.'

'Champagne?' asked Arenskaya.

'Champagne, by all means,' boomed Buttonhooke. 'This way.' And off he marched towards the marble staircase.

'Me—I do not care to drink with the thief,' complained Stroganoff to Quill.

'What matters?' said Arenskaya broadmindedly.

Nevajno nodded agreement. Champagne, he announced with the air of one making a great discovery, was always champagne.

'Come on,' said Quill. He was anxious to get to the office to see if Baron de Rabinovitch was there. Gustave ought to be arriving any minute now.

They moved towards Buttonhooke who was waiting on the marble stairs. A figure catapulted past them. Quill stretched a lightning arm and tweaked it back. Brought to a standstill it turned out to be Kurt Kukumber.

'Just off to meet your uncle?' asked Quill, 'or is the Spanish Prisoner after you?'

Kurt gulped.

'What do you here?' demanded Stroganoff, visibly annoyed. 'Did you not promise me to play only at my Casino?'

'I sought to change my luck,' pleaded Kurt, 'also our arrangement it was to date from the time you bought the shares.'

Stroganoff was a fair-minded man. 'Bon,' he said, 'I overlook it this time. Now go.'

Kurt was quite willing. After a pathetic effort to borrow his cab fare from Nevajno he strode into the night.

'Funny little man,' said Buttonhooke, 'wonder what scared him?'

The cavalcade resumed its marble ascent. A flunkey gravely approached carrying a telegram. Before he could reach Buttonhooke, Stroganoff, who automatically assumed that all telegrams must be for him, had reached over and ripped it open.

He let out a howl of triumph.

'She comes, she comes!' he crowed. 'Dyrakova dances *Giselle* for me on the twenty-eight.'

'Let me see that wire?' said Buttonhooke almost brusquely.

With a flourish Stroganoff handed it across. Prince Artishok moved over and stood behind Buttonhooke's shoulder to help him read it.

'Ah—mon pauvre ami,' said Stroganoff, 'I understand only too well how bitter for you must be this defeat. But it is all—as you say—in the game. So console yourself. You have fought well. It is no dishonour to lose to Vladimir Stroganoff.' He beamed round for applause.

'This wire,' said Prince Artishok coldly, 'is addressed to Lord Buttonhooke.'

Stroganoff stopped beaming and snatched the wire. He read it incredulously.

'It is the mistake,' he declared. 'The post office confuse themselves.'

'There is no mistake,' said Buttonhooke, 'I have been negotiating with Madame Dyrakova for over a month.'

'Me, I have negotiated with Dyra all my life,' retorted Stroganoff. 'It is preposterous that she could come to you. You have but to read the wire to understand this. Listen:

> DELIGHTED TO DANCE GISELLE FOR YOU. EXPENSES IN ADVANCE. DYRAKOVA

Let us apply to this the logic,' Stroganoff urged his gaping audience. 'First—she is delighted. Now I ask, is it possible that our Dyra should be delighted in a Ballet à la Button'ooke?' He appealed to Arenskaya. 'Is it likely?'

Arenskaya was thoughtful. 'She is a stupid woman. It is well known.'

'Next,' demanded the logician, 'she ask for her train fare. Would she reveal to a stranger her poverty?'

'Never,' said Prince Artishok quickly. 'She has the pride of the devil.'

Stroganoff beamed on this unexpected ally. 'But Dyra and I we have no secrets from each other. I am to her like a father. When she speak I listen.'

The flunkey reappeared with another telegram. This time the lavender tie took no chances and reached for it. But it was addressed to Stroganoff and had been sent on from his Casino. He passed it over.

'Voilà!' said Stroganoff, 'now we will see. She realize her mistake and she hurry to correct.' He extracted the message, glanced at it, crumpled it into a ball, and threw it on the floor. Galybchik picked it up. It read:

> 'VLADIMIR—SHUT UP. DYRA.'

'A slight hitch?' asked Buttonhooke, as the party resumed its climb.

'Pour le moment peut-être,' admitted Stroganoff, 'but do not yet hatch your chicken,' he added defiantly to Buttonhooke. 'To-morrow she change her mind and she come to me. You will see.'

'I don't care where she goes as long as she brings the Otchi Tchernia with her,' said Sadie to the Prince.

At the door of Buttonhooke's office the party halted.

'This way,' said Buttonhooke and flung open the door.

The next moment he had halted too. 'Good God!' he said. 'What's that?'

They all crowded in and gazed incredulously.

Sprawled over the desk, his head on the blotting-pad, his arms hanging loosely by his side, was the Baron de Rabinovitch. On the floor beside him lay a broken tumbler. On the table was a decanter of whisky and a syphon.

'Il est malade?' asked Stroganoff.

With a horrible conviction Quill pressed forward and leant over the body.

'He's dead,' said Quill. 'Cyanide, I think.'

'Dead!' said Buttonhooke incredulously.

'Dead?' gasped Galybchik.

The party eyed each other.

'I am unwell,' said Arenskaya suddenly.

Stroganoff supported her to a chair. 'Some brandy.'

His eyes roved the room and alighted on the decanter. He made towards it. Quill interrupted him.

'Do you want to poison her?'

He was thoroughly fed up. It seemed to him that all his life he was to be pursued by the hoodoo of suspects that got themselves murdered the moment he planned to arrest them.

There was a knock on the door. Quill opened it. A weary Gustave was standing on the threshold.

'Je suis venu,' he announced simply.

CHAPTER XIII

QUILL pushed back the shutters. Sunshine streamed into the room.

'Good God!' he said astonished. To think that this could happen in the South of France!

He glanced at his watch. It was eleven o'clock. The hard fried remains of the h'English breakfast leered at him from a bacon-ringed plate. Abandoning all further efforts at waking him up the waiter had left them there in despair.

Quill sighed as the events of last night crowded in. Faced with a second body, Gustave had lost his head entirely. First he had turned on Quill, accusing him of gross carelessness, lack of foresight, and scaring the corpse into committing suicide. Next he reproached himself for releasing the two impresarios, who had misused their liberty to perpetrate a further assassination, and ended with a grand dust-up with Arenskaya, who wanted to go home. It had taken all Quill's resources to steer Gustave safely through the necessary formalities that to the police are the concomitants of death. But he had managed it somehow, and then, with the gallery safely dispersed to their respective homes, Gustave had thrown a *crise de nerfs* and Quill had had to take him home and put him to bed with a cup of cocoa. In bed, Gustave had become calmer. After all, as he pointed out to Quill, even if the Sûreté did come, which now seemed inevitable, they could find no fault with his handling of the case. Considering the way he was overworked, running the gaol single-handed, he had done as well as could be expected. Next week things would be easier. His assistant, who was also his godson, would be back to take charge of the routine work and the weeding, and he would have time to put the finger irrevocable on the murderer himself.

It was five o'clock before Quill got to bed.

As he dressed Quill felt thankful that he was, to all intents and purposes, out of the case. His client was out of gaol, he had solved the chips mystery, and he had nothing to fear from the Sûreté. It was none of his business who murdered Citrolo or Rabinovitch. Even if the Sûreté should decide, as they easily might, that Rabinovitch had committed suicide to avoid arrest there was no reason for him to interfere.

But to his growing irritation his mind refused to abandon its speculations. He could not for a moment accept the suicide theory. Rabinovitch was not the type—he was too much of a coward. No—he was pretty certain that both murders bore the same signature, and it seemed a pity to waste all the work he had put in on the first. He had all his suspects nicely tabulated —including the dead man—it went against the grain to hand it all over to Gustave's assistant. Besides, he was interested in crime. Why should Rabinovitch be murdered? Who was he menacing? Had he seen the murderer in Citrolo's death room? Damn it—this was his holiday!

But as he left his room he had an uneasy conviction that he would not be able to resist going on pottering.

* * *

'Bon jour,' said Anatole, the Commissionaire, brightly. 'You have heard the news?'

'I found the body,' said Quill.

'Ah, ça!' said Anatole, 'I do not speak of the Baron. Neither do I weep because he is dead.'

The Baron seemed to have been popular with his staff.

'I speak of the ballet,' explained Anatole. 'The wonderful news—that Dyrakova she dance for us.' A loving look came into his eyes. 'It is ten years since I have seen that développé.'

'I thought,' said Quill, 'that she had agreed to dance for Buttonhooke.'

Anatole smiled knowingly. 'That is but a rumour, spread,

no doubt, by the enemies of our Casino. M'sieur le Directeur has just assured me of that.'

Quill said nothing.

'If you do not believe me,' said Anatole hotly, 'demand of him yourself. He is in his office.'

Stroganoff was in a frenzy of activity. The biography had been abandoned for the long-distance telephone.

'Ah—c'est toi, Dyra. Ici Vladimir. Ecoute, cheri. . . .'

From the doorway Quill heard the clonk that terminated the Paris end of the conversation.

Stroganoff looked up at Quill like a hurt child. 'As soon as she hear who I am she do that. It is not fair. How can I persuade her with my eloquence if she hang herself before I use it?'

'What's this?' said Quill, startled.

'Always she hang herself,' repeated Stroganoff, 'but this time I will be more cunning.' He returned to the telephone. 'Montparnasse 23-107.'

'Encore?' said the operator.

'Toujours,' said Stroganoff.

'Vous avez tort, mon vieux,' counselled the operator. 'Elle est de mauvaise humeur. Mieux envoyez un petit cadeau et essayez encore demain.'

'Mais qu'est-ce que ça vous fait?' howled Stroganoff, exasperated. 'Je paie chaque fois.'

'Poor darling,' said Galybchik. 'This is the fifth time he's 'phoned this morning.'

'Allo,' said Stroganoff, 'je desire parler à Madame Dyrakova. C'est urgent. Qui parle?' Stroganoff reflected.

'Bernard Shaw,' suggested Quill.

'Bernard Shaw,' repeated Stroganoff, automatically. 'Mais—non—non!' he bellowed. He placed a hand over the receiver. 'What is it you make me say?' He removed his hand. 'Ici—Massine.'

'Vladimir,' said an exasperated voice at the other end. 'I can stand it no longer. Wherever I go there is the telegram—always from you. And now the telephone. Will you understand? I won't dance for you. Never! Never! Never!'

'Entendu,' said Stroganoff, 'mais sans blague I have for you the proposition intéressant. To dance *Giselle*. . . .'

'Plonk.' Dyrakova had hanged herself again.

Stroganoff signalled furiously. 'Montparnasse,' he bellowed. '23-107.'

Quill thought it time to leave.

'You despair too easily, my friend,' reproved Stroganoff. 'Me I do not give in. Dyra she dance *Giselle* and she dance for me. We are confident. Already we design the poster.'

He applied himself to the telephone again.

'Montparnasse,' he said stubbornly. '23-107.'

*   *   *

In his office Lord Buttonhooke was giving the lavender tie his instructions. The death of the Baron, the only man who had ever seemed to like him for himself, had been a real blow to Buttonhooke, but he was not going to let it interfere with his publicity.

'See that it's large,' he ordered. 'Plenty of colour. And see to it that the name hits the eye. I want the whole town plastered with it by to-morrow.' He gloated. 'Dyrakova in *Giselle*. Have I ever seen *Giselle?*' he asked the lavender tie. . . .

*   *   *

Up in the practice-room Madame Ostorojno was not at all pleased. In making the headlines of the local paper, the Baron de Rabinovitch had pushed her daughter right out of the print. On top of that, the little silly was sulking because Dovolno was no longer in the company. She actually wanted to go back to Stroganoff. And as if that were not enough, there was the threat of Dyrakova. True she was only supposed to appear for one performance, but once a retired ballerina started re-emerging. . . . If Dyrakova stayed on with the company, gone was her child's chance of the leading rôles at anything but matinées. And there were no matinées at La Bazouche. Perhaps they would have been better off with Stroganoff, after all, even if he was practically bankrupt. She sighed heavily. What was a mother to do?

At the other Casino, Arenskaya was engaged in her daily tussle with the pianist. Murder, earthquake or flood, the morning classes take place as usual.[1]

'When I say ta-ra-ra——' she was screaming, 'why do you play tootle-ootle-oo?'

The pianist snorted and banged down the loud pedal.

The fat girl led off. But not for long.

'And what,' demanded Arenskaya, 'will Dyrakova say to me when she sees those deboullés of yours?'

'Dyrakova is coming.' The whisper ran round the class.

*   *   *

'Dyrakova is coming,' jubilated Sadie Souse. 'Prince—you're wonderful!'

The eyebrow very nearly winked.

*   *   *

With great care Vanilla had enamelled his hair with perfumed brilliantine. He was off to impress Lord Buttonhooke. With the Baron out of the way there seemed no reason why he should not land a job at the Casino Buttonhooke. After all he had a long career as croupier at the back of him, and if it was not all precisely honourable, who was going to bother to tell Buttonhooke now?

His gloves. His walking-stick. His carnations. Tiens! He had almost forgotten his spare pack of cards.

'Have patience,' Kurt Kukumber was pleading with the manager of the *Hotel Moins-Magnifique*. 'My uncle he comes for certain any day now.'

*   *   *

Gustave looked up wearily from the list of suspects he had arduously compiled. Soon, he reflected thankfully, his nephew would be here to tell him which one to arrest. The Englishman was no good.

[1] 'The ballet it must go on. . . .'—STROGANOFF.

CHAPTER XIV

On Thursday morning an interested crowd of marketers gathered round an enticing leg, a giddy little wreath and a tu-tu. Underneath it all was the unlikely legend, 'DYRAKOVA in GISELLE.' Above in crimson letters: 'Lord Buttonhooke has the honour to present:'

No sooner had they passed opinion on this work of art than their attention was distracted by Ludwig, the bill-poster, at work on the hoarding opposite. They veered over to watch.

'It is a circus,' hazarded a hopeful.

'Non,' said Ludwig, 'that is not for three months.' He slapped on a wisp of tulle.

Layer by layer, a Wili emerged—a ghostly dancer standing before what appeared to be a graveyard. It was.

The audience shivered deliciously.

'Grand Guignol,' said the hopeful.

Ludwig shook his head regretfully. 'That comes not here again. It was not the success financial.' He slapped on a name:

'DYRAKOVA IN GISELLE.'

'Ah, ça!' The crowd began to melt.

But the bombshell was coming.

'VLADIMIR STROGANOFF has the honour to present:'

'You have mixed up your sheets,' said Madame Bonne-femme, pointing to the poster opposite. 'She dances at the Casino Button'ooke.'

Ludwig went on firmly with his work. Madame Bonnefemme repeated her remark.

'Madame,' said Ludwig coldly, 'I have put up posters in La Bazouche for twenty years and NEVER . . .'

By the afternoon the town was placarded with neutralizing

186

announcements. Gustave's godson, alighting from his train, stared at the station-yard in some bewilderment. All the time-tables, all the Côte d'Azur, all the Dubonnets, had turned into Dyrakova dancing *Giselle* at different Casinos on the same night. Doubtless his godfather would have much to say on the subject. At this hour he would be in his garden. He hurried to join him.

Mademoiselle Mignon, the postmistress, had never had such a busy day. She could hardly find time to read all the telegrams that arrived and were sent out—let alone scrutinize the post-cards. As the day went on, and his wires increased in pleading, her sympathy for a certain Vladimir grew. Here at last was the persistent lover that every woman dreams of. A man who would not take 'no' for an answer. Not like her own Alphonse, who so many years ago had taken her first hesitating 'no' as final.

Here was another of them.

'DYRUSHKA. DYRUSHKA. What is it you do to me? Vladimir.'

But the creature had no heart it was clear. Here was her response.

'Mille fois—non. Send your next wire reply prepaid. Dyra.'

And the stupid one did. This was no way to win a woman. Mademoiselle Mignon nearly 'phoned up to tell him so.

The telephone girl, too, was having a hard time. There was Buttonhooke getting through to London, the Englishman talking to Paris and Scotland Yard, the Sûreté trying to talk to Gustave, and a Dutchman trying to talk to Kurt Kukumber. And, of course, there was always the Russian with his eternal Montparnasse 23-107.

*   *   *

On Friday Lord Buttonhooke's temper was slightly frayed. His liver was no better. His girl-friend would keep harping on one subject.

'But I've never had a real diamond necklace,' she was saying as he shaved.

In town things were no better. It was raining. That clown

Stroganoff had plastered his ridiculous posters everywhere. Some people might even believe him. Fiercely, Lord Button-hooke ordered an addition to his publicity. DEFINITELY AT THIS THEATRE—his posters reassured in purple splashes.

SANS DOUTE ICI—Stroganoff's posters retorted almost immediately, in vivid jade.

In his office Buttonhooke snapped at his assistant manager, snapped at his head croupier, and nearly bit the head off the lavender tie. He was even reckless enough to snap at Prince Artishok, who had dropped in, apparently to stress the immense favour he was doing Lord Buttonhooke by egging him on to purchase a fabulously expensive diamond necklace that he had never seen.

'Nice of you to take so much trouble,' jeered the exasperated Buttonhooke, 'particularly as you're getting nothing out of it yourself.'

The eyebrow worked overtime. 'Are you suggesting that I will profit by the transaction, personally?'

'That's it,' said Buttonhooke. 'Rake-off.'

The eyebrow fell to street level. 'Well, I might be offered a small commission. . . . Why not? Still, if you feel that way about it, I had better wash my hands of the whole affair.' He turned to leave.

Lord Buttonhooke thought of a diamondless Sadie.

'Oie,' he said, 'wait a minute. Have a cigar? You know, I gotta have that necklace now. And I don't mind your rake-off. You know I'm man of the world enough to understand these things. But what gets me is why I can't haggle with the old girl myself? I'd beat her down in no time.'

Up soared the eyebrow.

'I thought,' said Prince Artishok, 'that I had made it clear that Madame Dyrakova has the pride of a Romanoff. It will take all my persuasion to induce her to sell and even then she won't want the sale to be blazoned abroad. She'll know you're the purchaser, of course, but it's my opinion that she won't even mention the subject when she sees you—either before or after the transaction. To her it would be too sordid—too painful.'

'But she'll take my money!'

'She'll take it only if it is offered with delicacy,' said the Prince, 'and only through my mediation. She could never bear the squalor of bartering with—er—a tradesman.'

'What's that?' said Buttonhooke.

Prince Artishok smiled.

By the afternoon, the rain had set in properly. Quill spent a moist four hours dodging from bar to bar, avoiding Gustave's godson, who was panting to swop theories with him. Finally he sought refuge in Stroganoff's office. The impresario had been there all day. 'At any moment she ring me to change her mind,' he announced hopefully.

* * *

On Saturday the Press arrived. It was not the news that Dyrakova was dancing that brought them. It was the two murders at the small plage. They lunched with Gustave and in return printed his views.

Stroganoff was beginning to lose confidence. Gloomily he admitted to Quill that there was just a chance Dyrakova might not dance at all. She was a stupid woman.

Sadie was impressing on Buttonhooke the need for tact. 'Remember what the Prince says,' she kept on repeating. 'Don't go shooting your mouth off to the old lady. I'll die if I don't get those diamonds. The Prince . . .'

'Damn the Prince!' said Lord Buttonhooke.

* * *

On Sunday the Sûreté arrived and reorganized Gustave.

Stroganoff was still telephoning. So was the Dutchman.

By four-thirty the Balleto-Medico could stand things no longer. He, too, telephoned Dyrakova. The number was engaged.

At the post office a great light dawned on Mademoiselle Mignon. 'The poor Vladimir,' she sighed. 'She play him double. Here is a wire for the Buttonhooke.'

'Missed train—coming to-morrow. Dyrakova.'

Two hours later hope was restored. Another wire came.

'Decided train journey too exhausting. Staying in Paris. Regrets. Dyrakova.'

Perhaps she loved Vladimir after all.

But Sir Jasper Buttonhooke went on tempting.

'Yacht will meet you at Marseilles. Wire at once. Buttonhooke.'

No girl can withstand a yacht, thought Mademoiselle Mignon. Poor Vladimir. A sudden resolve was born. She must warn him of his new danger. Putting her shawl about her she went to the telephone.

*   *   *

At six o'clock. Quill entering the Casino found an exhausted Kurt Kukumber recuperating in the bar.

'The Sûreté,' explained Kurt. 'Three hours they question me.'

'Did you tell them about your uncle?'

'Mais non,' said Kurt. 'It was all right. They let me go. And as I leave my luck turns. Picture you, I run into the sucker phenomenal.'

Another Dutchman, thought Quill, and passed on.

'Imagine,' babbled Kurt excitedly. 'He desires to play pinochle with me.'

*   *   *

Stroganoff had almost given up hope when Mademoiselle Mignon took up the telephone. He sat slouched at his desk, his tea unsipped, unhappily doodling all over the opulent box of cigars. It brought tears to Galybchik's eyes to see him so despondent. He would not even work on his biography.

'It is the ruin,' he kept on repeating. 'And what is worse, we lose the face.'

'It is the Casino,' declared Arenskaya. 'Always the Casinos they bring us bad luck. Why you not sell?'

'Jamais!' said Stroganoff, outraged.

'It was at Deauville,' said Arenskaya, 'that the décor fall on Nevajno. It was at San Sebastian that we have the fire without the insurance. It was at Monte Carlo that Palook drop Dyrakova.'

'Is this the moment to remind me of these things?' exploded Stroganoff. 'When my Dyra she goes to dance for a succinsin and I am left here like a stuffed Petroushka.'

Somewhat startlingly Arenskaya burst into tears. 'Is this the moment to remind me of my poor Puthyk—my dear husband— who you never allowed to dance the rôle?'

'Pardon,' said Stroganoff. 'I forget.'

They kissed each other and lapsed into a companionable gloom.

The telephone rang. Stroganoff leapt up.

'Dyra!!!'

But it was a Mademoiselle Mignon.

'What she want?' asked Arenskaya.

'I find out,' said Stroganoff. 'Quoi?' He put his hand over the mouthpiece. 'She is mad,' he explained. 'She try to sell me a yacht.' He turned back. 'Mademoiselle—I am not in the market—not even for the battleship.'

Eloquence poured from the other end. Stroganoff shrugged his shoulders helplessly.

'It is the Buttonhooke yacht that she sell. It is ridicule. Quoi? Qu'est-ce que vous me dites? Mais c'est certain ça? Ah, bon! Merci. Merci—mille fois merci.' He hung up triumphantly.

'We haven't bought it—have we?' asked the apprehensive Galybchik.

'Mais si,' beamed Stroganoff. 'We have bought the whole world and all its diamonds. We have our dear ballerina.' Ecstatically he seized Galybchik and pranced her round the room.

It was at this moment that Quill came in.

'A private lesson?' he asked Arenskaya.

Stroganoff flung an arm round his neck. 'We are saved. Sit down. Wiskyansoda? Listen.'

'What 'as 'appen?' asked Arenskaya, hurt. She, too, wanted to know.

'The victory. Button'ooke we have him by the hair.'

'He has murdered somebody?' asked Arenskaya.

'Better,' said Stroganoff. 'Mooch better. He sent his yacht to meet Dyra at Marseilles.'

Quill gazed blankly at him.

'You do not understand,' burbled Stroganoff. 'Dyra she is the sailor lamentable. I remember well, on the boat from Vladivostok to Yokohama . . .'

'But the sea is beautifully calm here.'

'Calmness to Dyra it is nothing. It is the nerves that is all. She will be unwell—it is certain she will be unwell—it is necessary that she must be unwell. When she arrive she will be fatigué and then. . . . Ah, my friend, never will I be able to thank you for helping me to accomplish this thing!'

'Helping!' said Quill, startled.

'Sit down,' said Stroganoff. 'Listen. I have the idea.'

For half an hour Quill argued, protested, and elaborately washed his hands of the whole project. But it was no use. Stroganoff alone he might have withstood, but when Arenskaya and Galybchik, both of whom seemed to think that the preposterous plan Stroganoff had unfolded was quite sound, joined in the pleadings, he allowed an incautious 'perhaps' to escape him. Stroganoff promptly took this for an unqualified acceptance and bounced him off to a celebration dinner.

In the restaurant, Emilio came hurrying over with his cleanest menu. 'And for the little miss,' he turned to Galybchik and beamed, 'a glass of milk?' Galybchik giggled.

*   *   *

That evening both Casinos were crowded. In search of silence, Quill went to the reading-room. The dinner party had been hilarious and prolonged and Quill needed a quiet spot to meditate.

In the doorway he paused. In the far corner of the room across a card-table a bewildered sickle was facing an upright— and almost regal spear.

Kurt Kukumber was playing his sucker.

The sucker was Prince Artishok. Quill left him to it.

Two hours later Quill returned to the reading-room. The

game was over. The sucker had gone. Kurt Kukumber was still sitting at the card-table making sad additions on the margin of his cheque-book.

'Any luck?' asked Quill.

Kurt shook his head. 'Would you lend me five mille? It is debt of honour.'

Quill whistled. 'That's a hell of a loss.'

'On the contrary,' said Kurt Kukumber, 'it is almost an investment.'

Kurt nodded happily. 'Many have paid far more for a lesson from the great Banco Dacarpo.'

*   *   *

The great Banco Dacarpo. A very thoughtful Quill left the Casino Stroganoff. Surely that was one of the big shots in Citrolo's gallery of untouchables. Curse Gustave for pocketing that diary!

On an impulse Quill turned in his tracks and made for the Casino Buttonhooke. Prince Artishok (or Banco Dacarpo) was helping Sadie to play baccarat. Quill tapped him on the shoulder.

'Could you spare me a moment?'

'Is it essential?' asked the eyebrow coldly.

'Very.' Quill lowered his voice. 'Signor Dacarpo.'

The eyebrow never moved. 'Excuse me,' the Prince apologized to Sadie and made his way regally to a table in a far corner. Then he sat down and relaxed.

'How did you rumble?' said Banco Dacarpo, cheerfully.

'Kurt Kukumber,' said Quill. 'You big bully. Why don't you pick someone your own size?'

Dacarpo laughed. 'He was rather sweet.'

'He's quite proud of himself now that he's found out who you are,' said Quill.

'That's why I told him,' said Dacarpo, 'but I can't understand it—I never thought he'd blab on me.'

'He didn't blab,' said Quill. 'He was boasting. The last thing in his mind was to give you away.'

'But one doesn't boast to policemen.'

'That's where you made your big mistake,' said Quill. 'I'm not a policeman to Kurt. We're practically buddies. He looks on me as quite a promising amateur who's made a good start by getting himself kicked out of Scotland Yard. At any moment now he'll be offering to teach me the finer points of his trade.'

'Weren't you kicked out?' asked Dacarpo.

'That's my affair.'

'And Prince Artishok is mine,' said Dacarpo. 'At least, I hope so. It's taken me years to build him up and I'd hate to lose him.'

'Oh, I shan't interfere,' said Quill. 'It's not my affair.'

'You are wise,' agreed Dacarpo.

'But I can't help being interested in the Otchi Tchernia.'

'A sideline,' said Dacarpo. 'Nice little commission. But, of course, I've got to have Prince Artishok to work it on the old walrus.'

'No swindle?'

'My dear fellow—what a mind you've got! The Otchi Tchernia diamonds are world famous.'

Sadie Souse approached the party. Dacarpo vanished in a twinkling and Prince Artishok stood up to greet her.

'Prince,' urged Sadie, 'come back to the tables. I can't do a thing right since you left.'

CHAPTER XV

'When I say tum-ti-tum, I mean tum-ti-tum, and I do not mean tootle-ootle-ootle-oo. Is that quite clear?'

It seemed to be. The pianist snorted and banged down the loud pedal. Dismally the girls at the *barre* waved their legs—to think that this was Art!

'But this is terrible! Horrible! Stop!'

Everybody shivered. The scene might have been the practice room of the ballet Stroganoff—the culprit, the fat girl—and the shrill scolding voice that of Arenskaya. For that matter much the same scene was even now being enacted at La Bazouche.

But this particular crisis has been brought about in Montparnasse—the cause, a little miss from Sadler's Wells—the outraged teacher, Dyrakova.

Nothing was allowed to interfere with the ballerina's eleven o'clock class. Even the fact that to-day was Monday and she had to catch a train a bare four hours from now, only made Madame twenty minutes late in starting. To-morrow perforce a substitute teacher must be risked, but Dyrakova would be back again on Thursday to give them hell as usual.

Time had dealt lightly with the ballerina. Though nearing forty she had retained her neat, well-controlled figure, her vitality, and her looks. Only her voice had grown shriller—her temper worse—though it would have been difficult to convince Stroganoff that this was possible.[1]

'I am in despair,' declaimed Dyrakova, 'I give it up. I teach no more. My method it will be lost. It is a tragedy, you tell

---

[1] 'She lose the temper—I lose the temper—and poof.—It is terrible.'—STROGANOFF.

me—a calamity—but what avails that I give myself to the last
shred, and all for a row of wooden dolls—two rows of wooden
dolls?' she demanded. 'You,' she pounced on a pair of terrified
blue eyes, 'you have learnt my method three months already,
and look at your 'ip—look at your shoulder—look at your
over-balance. . . .'

The blue eyes filled.

'The man he comes to put my method on the news-reel,' she
continued, 'and what would you have me show? This,' Dyrakova's stick came down on the offending member with a
thwack—'and this'—thwack—'and this. . . .'

It was at this moment that she noticed the polo-sweater
planted in the doorway. It was accompanied by a movie
camera.

The news-reel was taking in the method.

The girls produced their tucked-away radiance. Dyrakova
put a hasty hand to her coiffure.

'Eh, bien!' she said, preliminaries over, 'and what would
you have us dance?'

'Just proceed with your class usual, Madame—take no
notice of us at all.'

'Ah, bon! Back to the barre, my darlings, to-day we make
'istory! Développé à la quatrième en devant—en seconde—
passer à la quatriême en derriere. . . .'

The darlings sighed.

'As for you,' she turned on the pianist, 'darling—when I say
tum-ti-tum, I mean tum-ti-tum—darling—and I do not mean
tootle-ootle-oo—do I make myself clear—darling?'

The pianist bowed, and played three chords tenderly. The
darlings applied themselves to the *barre*.

'But this is beautiful . . . lovely . . . exactly my method . . .
so . . . and now, we turn, my darlings. . . .'

The darlings turned.

The camera turned.

Dyrakova beamed. 'Ras Dva! . . .' But suddenly the beam
hardened. The voice rose. The delicate hands clenched themselves into fists,

'What is this you do?' screamed Dyrakova. 'You!' She pointed to a trembling pink leg. 'But you are 'orrible! You are impossible! Take your wrong-placed 'ips out of my beautiful class at once! And do not bring them in again. Or your knees. Or your thighs. Or your stupid, staring face. . . .'

'Cut!' said the polo-sweater.

The camera looked depressed.

A benevolent white head appeared in the doorway, waiting for the storm to subside. General Dmitri Dumka was used to Dyrakova's eloquence. He had been her business manager for twenty years. He was not a good business manager—this was the reason he had stayed so long with the ballerina.

'Better get ready,' he warned. 'The train it leaves in three hours and five minutes.'

'Mon dieu!' Dyrakova fled. 'Marya,' she called. 'Mes valises . . . my bouillotte . . . un taxi. . . .'

But one taxi was not enough. It took no less than three to take Dyrakova, her baggage, and the little court anxiously waiting to escort her to the station.

As the procession trundled into the yard of the *Gare de Lyon* a porter detached himself from the wall and ambled incuriously over to meet it. It was the last time he was to be incurious that morning.

Before he had time to think, a hat-box whizzed past his ears, three attaché-cases piled themselves in front of him, and two valises and a hot-water bottle were thrust into his defensive arms, while the cabman bellowed for his assistance with a large American trunk.

'Le rapide pour la Côte d'Azur,' instructed the temperamental toque thrusting out of the window. 'Il faut se dépecher —hein?'

'Deux heures d'attente,' said the porter.

Furious the toque turned on the benevolent white head.

'Why do you hurry me like this?'

'Could I foretell that you would leave when I asked?' demanded the white head, not without justice.

By this time the other cabs had disgorged their contents, and a courteous group of Russian *emigrés* disposed itself about the bookstall. With practised ease Dyrakova totted up the pieces.

'Seventeen,' she announced in horror. 'One is missing.'

Little round Marya bustled forward.

'Nothing important, chérie,' she said, 'only the old black trunk with our Press cuttings.'

'Mais vous êtes folle,' screamed Dyrakova. 'Never I travel without this. How else can I entertain the rich dark stranger that my tea-cup tell me I am due to meet?'

'You will be your sweet, gracious self,' said the General, without much hope. 'It will be enough for him to meet the peerless Dyrakova—he will not need her album.'

'Useless to argue,' said the ballerina, with an ominous calm. 'You go back at once and bring it to me.'

'How should I know which trunk it is?'

'There is but one,' said Dyrakova. 'It is in the attic.' 'Goodbye,' she pushed the General into the cab and turned back on the porter.

'Alors! Qu'est que vous attendez, vous?'

*   *   *

The General was a bad manager. He had omitted to reserve a compartment. A twittering of the ballerina's pupils informed the horrified Dyrakova that she was destined to travel with a plaid waistcoat, it's wife, and a large packet of sandwiches.

But this catastrophe was soon averted. . . . An old Etonian tie was discovered with a compartment to itself. A puzzled conductor found himself arranging the transfer for the smallest bribe ever accepted in the annals of the wagon-lits. What had come over him?

A porter came down the platform carrying a slate. D.Y.R.A.K.O.V.A., danced the white chalk letters. The ballerina hailed him. But it was only a telegram.

'Vladimir again,' hissed Dyrakova, tearing open the wire. She was right.

BON VOYAGE. KEEP CALM. VLADIMIR.

A yelp of helpless fury brought the Old Etonian to his feet.

'Sit down,' said little round Marya. 'Madame s'énerve—c'est tout!'

'Tais toi, Marya—do not mix yourself with my emotions. And you, M'sieur, I thank you for your sympathy.'

The Old Etonian subsided.

With only an hour to go and the General not yet back, Dyrakova could hardly concentrate on her parting presents. She leant out of the window exchanging compliments with her little court, but always her eyes roved to the end of the platform. He was going to be late. She knew it. And the charming man with the pretty tie would be deprived of reading her cuttings.

At last she spotted him. But what was this he was bringing? A perspiring porter trundled up a trolley of luggage.

'There were seven trunks,' panted the General reproachfully, 'four of them black. I've brought the lot. Choose.'

'Celui-ci,' said Marya.

'Mais non—celui-là,' said Dyrakova.

There was nothing for it but to open the lot.

The first contained old ballet-shoes.

So did the second.

So did all the others.

'Mon dieu!' gasped Dyrakova. 'I recollect. Last week I send it to the man who write my memoires. But you,' she turned to the General. 'You go at once and fetch it back. Immediate!'

Obediently the General turned.

The porter arrived with another telegram.

BON APPÉTIT. RELAX. VLADIMIR

*   *   *

'Another cup of Russian tea,' suggested Dyrakova hospitably.

The Old Etonian needed it badly. For the last three hours he had been unable to snatch a wink of sleep. But though it was half-past four in the morning, Dyrakova showed no signs of slowing down. She was still at the dear old Maryinsky and had the whole of her European career in front of her. If only he had known what he was starting up, thought the Old Etonian ruefully, never would he have asked her if she knew Nijinsky.

Nijinsky had lasted till tea-time. And he was followed by Johanssen, Legat, Bolm, and Diaghilev. It was the last time, reflected the Old Etonian, that he would attempt to console a weeping unknown, who, it turned out, was not emigrating from her loving and rather large family for ever, but making a flying visit to some Riviera town for a triumphant appearance in a ballet.

The Old Etonian was not very fond of ballet. Sheer courtesy had prompted him to put the fatal question to the dancer. And Dyrakova had been talking ever since. The only time the monologue varied was when the train stopped at a station, when Dyrakova would temporarily abandon her career in favour of cursing a man called Vladimir who had sent telegrams to all of them. The last one read:

REPOSEZ VOUS. STOP TALKING. TRY AND SLEEP,
VLADIMIR.

The Old Etonian wished wholeheartedly that she would take this sound advice.

But there was not a chance. She was still at it when the train puffed its way into Marseilles.

'Here I get out,' said Dyrakova, regretfully. 'You come to my class in Paris and I recount you further triumphs. Tiens! almost I had forgotten—Marushka, my photograph.' But little round Marya had already extracted a photograph from a valise and was sitting with a fountain-pen poised above it.

*   *   *

The train stopped at Marseilles about forty minutes. It was just long enough to marshal the ballerina's luggage.

This accomplished, 'No photographers?' she said, gazing up and down the platform in horror. 'We go back at once.'

'At once!' echoed little round Marya.

An apologetic lavender tie appeared on the scene. The photographers, he explained, were massed on the *quai*. They would take Madame embarking, embarked, and trying on a lifebelt.

'To go on your boat I must be crazy,' declared Dyrakova, 'I will be ill. I know it.'

'The sea is like a mill-pond,' said the lavender tie, reassuringly.

A porter appeared waving a slate. The wire read:

DO NOT FORGET YOUR MOTHERSILL. GO WITH GOD.
VLADIMIR.

Petulantly Dyrakova threw her bottle on the ground and stamped on it.

A monocle picked its way delicately through the valises and stopped within convenient kissing distance of Dyrakova's hand.

'Allow me to present,' murmured the lavender tie. . . .

'It is not necessary,' said Prince Artishok, 'Madame and I have met before.'

Dyrakova had met too many people not to have acquired a technique for glossing over inconvenient gaps in her memory.

'All is well with you, I hope,' she said without committing herself, and held out her hand.

The hand was duly kissed.

'And now,' said Dyrakova, 'the photographers! We must not keep them waiting. My hat—it is becoming?'

'Divinely,' murmured the Prince.

CHAPTER XVI

O<small>N</small> Tuesday morning the inevitable happened. Gustave's godson called on Quill. He made certain of his quarry by arriving simultaneously with the h'English breakfast.

Gustave's godson was ambitious, intense, and long-winded. He was not going to spend all his life in a mouldy little village pottering among the vegetable-marrows. He was taking correspondence courses in Economics, International Law and Mass Oratory—all he needed was a jeune fille sérieuse with a nice *dot*, and he was going to end up Chief of the Paris Police. Meanwhile, there was this little mystery to be solved for his godfather. He had to beat the Sûreté to it. Not that this should be difficult. The Sûreté were altogether too laborious. They were still busy with trifling details of the first murder, obscuring the broad sweep of the case with their eternal finger-prints, and inessential details of private lives. All the world knew Citrolo was a blackmailer. All the world knew that the Baron de Rabinovitch was a nasty bit of work. Find someone who disliked them both, and . . .

But just as the much-tried Quill thought he was going to elucidate the 'Means, motive, opportunity' theme Gustave arrived.

'Bon jour, mon ami,' he hailed Quill. 'Bon jour, Gaston. Il fait beau—hein?'

Clearly he was in the best of humours for it was raining.

'By to-morrow,' he announced, seating himself on the edge of Quill's bed and pouring himself out Quill's cup of coffee, 'all will again be peace. The murderer will be arrested. The Sûreté will be gone and at last I will have time to show the man Stroganoff how to grow roses. The first prize in St. Petersburg—pah!'

Clearly the grievance still rankled.

'The Sûreté making an arrest?' asked Quill.

'The Sûreté,' Gustave snorted. 'It is I, Gustave Clemenceau, who pounce.'

'And I,' said the godson.

'Entendu,' agreed Gustave. 'We pounce together. To-night we arrest the criminal.'

'Which one?' asked Quill.

But Gustave was giving away no secrets.

'Mon cher Watson,' he said chaffingly, 'you have all the facts. You have but to draw the inferences. They are irrefutable.

'In that case,' said Quill, 'why wait till to-night?'

'There are reasons,' said Gustave mysteriously.

Quill remembered it was Tuesday. 'You amuse yourself again?'

'Non,' said Gustave, looking apprehensively at his godson.

'Ça serais samedi cette semaine,' said the godson, unmoved.

'Tais-toi,' snapped Gustave. He turned to Quill. 'To complete the case there is still one witness to be seen. We await anxiously the arrival of the widow of Citrolo.'

He was not the only one. The entire town was waiting.

*   *   *

The widow of Citrolo lay in a cabin of *The Ziegfeld Girlie*. The luxury yacht balanced itself precariously on top of a mountain which was soon to subside into a valley.

The lavender tie had stopped telling Prince Artishok what a good sailor he was. He too was prostrate as the boat climbed laboriously up the mountain again.

Prince Artishok sat in the saloon drinking brandy.

The blast concentrated on a mast. It won easily.

'Only once in all my forty years' experience,' began the Captain heavily. . . .

The first officer was damned if he was going to listen all over again. Ever since the Captain had decided to write his memoirs, life was just one long reminiscence.

'C'est le Mistral,' shouted the man at the wheel.

'C'est le Sirrocco,' shouted the man who had come to relieve him. 'Nous serons bien en retard.'

* * *

Inside the peaceful harbour of La Bazouche the little launch bobbed comfortably at its anchor. Adjusting its riding-lights was Jean. Jean was an honest man. He had been with Button-hooke for six weeks now, and loathed every one of them. Taxi-ing Sadie Souse to and from the yacht was no occupation for a seaman.

Outside the little port the sea churned blackly. It was past seven o'clock. The yacht should be arriving any minute now.

'She ought to be here soon.' Four mackintoshes battled along the quayside.

'Supposing he won't be bribed,' asked Galybchik, eaten up by last-minute doubts.

'Leave it to me,' promised Stroganoff. 'I am the briber experienced.'

'I will deal with the finance,' contradicted Arenskaya, 'it will be cheaper.'

'Poof!' said Stroganoff, 'you are extravagant. It is well known. Did you not pay the swindle bijoutier. . . .?'

The wind drowned the rest of the reminiscence from Quill's ears.

'Voilà,' said Stroganoff, 'we are arrived.' He gazed doubtfully at the plank that served as gangway. 'You go first,' he suggested to Quill.

But honest Jean had climbed out to meet them.

'Pas à louer,' he said brusquely.

It was very soon evident that honest Jean merited his name. All that Stroganoff wanted was that Jean should risk his job by taking strangers on a joy-ride to the yacht, taking off only one of the three passengers wishing to go ashore, and riding without lights to some strange mooring-place. Practically money for marmalade. Yet it was not till Stroganoff raised his initial offer of two hundred to two thousand francs that honest Jean showed signs of listening. At twenty-two hundred he was willing to consider. At twenty-five the whole thing was off. And at twenty-six hundred they clinched. There was a slight hitch when it transpired that Stroganoff had forgotten to bring his wallet but Quill had incautiously brought his.

'Here she comes now,' said Jean. Nobody could see anything but they took his word for it.

Quill jumped into the boat and helped Galybchik in. Stroganoff put a cautious foot on the plank.

'What you do?' screamed Arenskaya. 'You ruin us. You wish Dryakova to see you?'

'You do not estimate my cunning sufficient,' said Stroganoff, hurt. 'I come prepared. Regardez!' He pulled from his pocket the bright red beard that had been specially dyed for the King in *Coq d'Or* and clamoured for a mirror.

Arenskaya settled the argument by snatching the beard from him and throwing it into the sea.

'Go back,' she commanded, 'and play with your Casino. And do not dare to show your face till Dyra she is on the stage.'

'But it is essential that I go,' argued Stroganoff. 'Without me all is bungle.'

'I go,' decided Arenskaya, picking up her skirts.

Quill hastily ordered Jean to push off.

Out in the choppy seas Quill marvelled at himself. What a holiday this had turned out to be. First he was pitch-forked into a murder case, next he was pitch-forked out of it, and now he was on his way to kidnap a seasick ballerina. If only Scotland Yard could see him now. But then he doubted if Scotland Yard would approve of his growing friendships with card-sharpers and diamond double-dealers.

'Do you think Dyrakova will rumble?' The anxious Galybchik interrupted his thoughts.

To Quill this seemed inevitable but he did not want to sound discouraging. 'Not a chance,' he said reassuringly. 'She's never seen either of us and we'll get her on to the stage so quickly she'll never realize she's in the wrong theatre. That is if Stroganoff has the sense to stay out of sight.'

'He's wonderful,' sighed Galybchik, 'no one else could have thought of such a plan.'

Quill felt inclined to agree.

* * *

The Ziegfeld Girlie, staggering slightly, let down a ladder. The passengers were waiting to alight. The one in three overcoats was Dyrakova.

Groggily she allowed Quill's steady arms to lower her into the boat. After her, little round Marya, less groggy, less precious, but stubbornly persistent, awaited assistance. Quill took her too, and her numerous valises.

The lavender tie stepped confidently forward. But the launch had gone. So had his balance.

'How's the water?' asked Prince Artishok blandly, leaning over the rail. There seemed to be a long swim ahead of him.

* * *

In the launch a swaying Dyrakova clung to Quill.

'Terrible, terrible,' she sobbed. 'We have been ill. You promise me it will be smooth. You are naughty, Mistaire Buttonhooke, and I not forgive you soon.'

'I am not Buttonhooke,' explained Quill.

Marya bristled immediately. 'Why he come not to meet us? This we do not understand.'

'He's very busy,' said Galybchik.

'I am a busy woman too, but I remember my manners,' declared Dyrakova. 'I regret much that I come. The journey was a nightmare, and the ordeal horrible is in front of me. To dance *Giselle* without the rehearsal and with a musical director I do not know—only Dyrakova would undertake this.'

'Wonderful,' said Galybchik.

'I spoil that Mistaire Button'ooke. De Basil he would have come to Marseille for me. Vladimir he would have come to Paris. Mon pauvre, Vladimir,' she sighed, 'to do what he ask, it was impossible. But my heart it bleed for him.'

To lend plausibility to this statement she rummaged in her

bag for a hanky. It was a large bag—black and forbidding, bristling with odd pockets and substantial locks. Almost a portable safe, thought Quill, examining it with interest.

'The Otchi Tchernia diamonds there?' he asked.

'Once yes,' said Dyrakova sadly, 'but that long time ago. It is five years since I sell them, you silly boy.'

'You've sold them?' With a final click Quill's jig-saw puzzle fell into place. Everything was now so clear that even Gustave could be made to see it.

'But they still live,' continued Dyrakova, 'they are now my studio in Paris, where every day I teach my method.' She turned anxiously to Marya. 'Think you, Anna, she will remember to begin with the *plié?*'

'Who knows?' said Marya darkly.

The launch ran into a choppy passage. With a groan Dyrakova forgot all her other worries and subsided into her seat.

* * *

In a deserted cove a powerful car awaited the arrival of the launch. The driver sat jauntily in his seat combing out a moist red beard. One look at it and Quill hastily bundled Dyrakova into the back seat.

The driver experimented with his gears. Dyrakova screamed as the car backed boisterously towards the water. In the nick of time Stroganoff remembered the brake.

* * *

Eight o'clock at the Casino Stroganoff. Anatole, the Commissionaire, on duty outside the stage-door is pushing back the whiskered foam of Russian generals. No one is to be allowed back-stage, not even the dancers.

At the Casino Buttonhooke the little Ostorojno is fixing her eyelashes for *Giselle*. Already she has been sick three times. Even though it is by no means certain she will have to go on for Dyrakova in the great dramatic rôle, she is terror-stricken. Even after weeks of preparation *Giselle* supplies a high note in temperamental crises. Though tough ballerinas, bustling on for their three hundred and sixtieth performance in this tinted lithograph, may acquire an outward veneer of nonchalance, the youngsters cannot be expected to achieve these heights. They are going through hell and they show it. Anecdotes of other dancers' failures in similar circumstances for once fail to cheer them up.

And here is the little Ostorojno not really knowing whether she should indulge in nerves or disappointment. No signs of Dyrakova yet. She wished she would come. She wished she wouldn't. If only David were dancing with her. . . .

Eight-fifteen at the Casino Stroganoff. The shining dome of M'sieur le Directeur arrives beaming through the throng. 'But assuredly Dyrakova dances. Have I not promised it?'

Arenakaya is back-stage knocking firmly on Dovolno's door. Dovolno is relieved to hear the news. Nothing would have induced him to go on with the fat girl.

And here is Ernest Smithsky, rapping timidly on the door of Olga's dressing-room at the Casino Buttonhooke. He has come to wish the trembling dancer luck—to reassure her that he will be there on the stage to give her courage. Really it was a shame she did not hear him.

*   *   *

At half-past eight the flowers began to pour in. Yielding though the local soil might be, the town's chief florist found it difficult to cope with all the duplicated orders for bouquets to be delivered to the same person at the two Casinos simultaneously.

*   *   *

Twenty to nine at the Casino Stroganoff. The Balleto-Medico is telling Stroganoff what he will do to him if there is no Dyrakova.

At eighteen minutes to nine there is a familiar pounding down the corridors of the Casino Buttonhooke. Madame Ostorojno arrives to do all a mother can to assure the triumph of a daughter.

'Are your shoes all right? Did they freshen that wreath? Now just relax for five minutes and mother will dress you.'

'Mamushka . . .'

'Of course you'll be all right. I've never known a dress rehearsal go better. Why, do you know what Prince Artishok said to me at the end of your mad scene? . . .'

Mothers have their uses.

At a quarter to nine Bazouche is unable to make up its mind which Casino to patronize. The town has been whipped into one vast purée of excitement. The same star, in the same rôle, in the same ballet at the same hour—in which Casino? The announcements are similar; only the design on the posters differed—and, of course, the Casino. Rumour has been more emphatic, more highly coloured, and more contradictory than ever. The rich, the *chic*, and the near-celebrities invade the Casino Buttonhooke—at least they can be reasonably sure of making the gossip columns of the Continental *Daily Mail*. The ballet-goers plonked heavily for Stroganoff.

But in both factions Dyrakova and her famous *developé* were the common coin of conversation.

At ten to nine the amateur photographer parked himself outside the stage-door of the Casino Buttonhooke—his 'Nose for noos' had twitched him there. The solid phalanx of flash-men already stationed only served to confirm his faith in his *flaire*.

Five minutes to go and no Dyrakova. Already the little Ostorojno was seeing herself on the stage facing a disappointed audience. Dovolno was seeing the fat girl.

At nine o'clock a short huddle of cloak and shawl made its way through the Casino Gardens. It swayed, it lurched, it staggered. Clearly the earth was not its element.

Behind it a shorter, rounder bundle swayed, lurched, and staggered. Clearly the earth was not its element either. Bringing up the rear, cast in the rôle of amateur sheep dog, came Quill.

One look at the figure and Anatole sprang to offer a quivering arm. 'Madame,' he breathed, 'permettez?'

And so Dyrakova—shaken, shrill, and reeling, entered the Casino Stroganoff. The first person to greet her was Arenskaya.

'Ah—c'est toi,' said Arenskaya, with relief.

'Ah—c'est toi,' said Dyrakova, with dislike.

They went through the motions of a warm embrace.

'I am dressed—I am made-up—I am ready—Dyrakova is never late,' she announced—and fainted. . . .

Stroganoff's anxious dome appeared round a piece of scenery. 'She is all right?'

'Perfect,' hissed Arenskaya. 'Get down.' The dome bobbed down.

At the Casino Buttonhooke a sheepish white waistcoat regretted to a sceptical audience the sudden illness of Dyrakova. Her rôle would be taken by that talented dancer . . .

Ostorojno was popular but the audience had come to see Dyrakova. The gallery started to tell the white waistcoat what it thought of Buttonhooke. With great presence of mind the conductor started the overture. The curtains parted to reveal the stage with its lollipop house and blasted oak school of *décor*.

At the Casino Stroganoff the conductor began to beat a vigorous baton. Clearly he was making up for lost time.

The brought-round Dyrakova was calling loudly for Lord Buttonhooke. She'd come all this way to dance for him and he wasn't even here to wish her luck.

'He come,' promised Arenskaya. 'Soon he come racing in (how right she was!) but now he is in his box, waiting.'

'And Vladimir?' asked the fast-recovering Dyrakova. 'You have left him at last, I see. C'était bien le temps. Me, I think that Vladimir is phut!'

An adjacent piece of scenery trembled with emotion.

Arenskaya pushed it upright. 'Vladimir,' she said sharply, 'is the fool.'

This point settled, she escorted the guest artist to her seat in the wings.

'So many of my little ones,' sighed Dyrakova, catching sight of a bunch of *corps-de-ballet*.

'They, too, have follow me to Button'ooke,' said Arenskaya, 'they could not bear to give up my classes.' This explained all, she felt.

But now Dyrakova was about to get going. She tested her shoe, she scolded Marya, she fumed, she fretted, and she ripped off a piece of her fichu. It was too bad that she had not had time to rehearse with Dovolno. But he was an old pupil of hers and she knew him to be reliable. Besides, what did it matter if they did go wrong? The public were the blind ones, and now there was no Pavlo Citrolo to tell on her.

The bunch of ballet-girls flocked into the bright lights. It was at this moment that Dyrakova decided it was high time to remember she was a widow.

'I have had many husbands,' she wept on the unprepared Arenskaya. 'But only one have I ever loved. Pavlo—Pavlo—I am desolate.'

'The stage,' said Arenskaya several bars too soon. 'It waits.'

* * *

At the Casino Buttonhooke Ernest Smithsky bounded boyishly on and knocked at the door of the little lollipop house.

At the Casino Stroganoff Dovolno rat-rat-tatted on the door. The Balleto-Medico swallowed.

At the Casino Buttonhooke a roar of welcome greeted the little Ostorojno. The fair-minded gallery had decided that it was not her fault.

'Dyrakova,' breathed a late arrival to the stalls. 'She's very well preserved for her age.'

At the Casino Stroganoff a great ballerina took her stage. She was thirty-eight. She was life-ridden. She was seasick. But she took her stage.

* * *

With none of the benevolence of his portrait Lord Button-hooke paced the office door. A fine business this had turned out to be. He was a laughing-stock. All that publicity, and then no Dyrakova. Only a sodden lavender tie.

'So you and the Prince rowed ashore,' he jeered. 'That was resourceful of you.' He turned savagely. 'And where's Dyrakova?'

The lavender tie reeled. 'Isn't she here?'

There was a knock at the door. Prince Artishok came in—every regal hair in place. Lord Buttonhooke veered on him. 'Well?'

'Good news,' said the Prince gravely. 'Dyrakova has practically consented to sell the Otchi Tchernia.'

'Oh, she has—has she?'

'She's weakening,' said the Prince. 'I think perhaps the sight of ready money. . . . Did you,' he asked, 'get that money from the bank as I suggested?'

'It's in the safe,' said Buttonhooke, 'and,' he exploded suddenly, 'it stays in the safe. Just wait till I lay hands on that woman. Making me a laughing-stock—me! Where the hell is she, anyway?'

The lavender tie shrugged. The Prince, who could have made a pretty shrewd guess, remained silent. He was reflecting what a pity it was he did not know the combination of the safe.

'I've got it,' bellowed Buttonhooke. 'She's with that thief Stroganoff. And you—the two of you—stood on that boat and let him get away with it. Pah!'

He tore out of the office. Prince Artishok, after one loving look at the safe, followed.

CHAPTER XVII

Two Giselles had been beautifully laid to rest. Two seducers had staggered their wild despair. The curtains descended and rose again upon two sets of bowing principals. Neither performance had been without its incidents.

The little Ostorojno had all the advantages of youth and endowed her Tess scenes with moving pathos.

But when it came to going mad there was nobody to touch Dyrakova. Naturally.

In the wings little round Marya had gone mad nearly as well.

A mountain of flowers staggered into the star's dressing-room at the Casino Stroganoff. It was Quill. The babble of ecstasy that escorted the ballerina to her door had unanimously picked him for the rôle of porter.

'You were marvellous,' they cooed at the ballerina.

'Superb!'

'Enchanting!'

'Almost I cried myself!'

'Always the great Dyrakova!'

'Tchort vosmi!'[1] cried the great Dyrakova. 'That conductor! He must be dismissed at once. Where's Button'ooke?' she glared.

An uneasy silence settled on the babble. They looked at each other.

A bald dome burst ecstatically into the room and flung both hands firmly round the unsuspecting ballerina.

'Dyrashka, you were superb! Marvellous! Enchanting! Almost I cried myself.'

'Not bad for your age,' observed Arenskaya, who had followed him in.

[1] 'The devil take it.' (Russian).

213

Dyrakova disentangled herself. Gallantly Stroganoff stooped to kiss her hand. It almost slapped his face.

'Vladimir!' screamed Dyrakova. 'What are you doing here?'

'I worship at your feet,' said Stroganoff glibly. 'Ah! You have made me very happy. Never since the night that Benois he nearly come, has the Ballet Stroganoff had such a success. And Button'ooke he bit the dust.'

Dyrakova swallowed. Carried away, Stroganoff shook a playful finger at her.

'Ah, my little one—did you for a moment imagine that I should permit you to dance for a newspaper? No—the *Ballet Russe* it is your home. Your Vladimir has led you back to it.'

A strangled scream tore through the ballerina's throat.

'You are tired,' said Stroganoff, kindly. 'Lie down. Relax while I tell you how clever I arrange it all.'

The ballerina opened and closed her mouth. Still no words came.

'When you step into the launch,' beamed Stroganoff, 'so tired, so ill, so swaying—it was my friends who steady your feet and guide you. And it was I, your Vladimir, who drove you to the hotel. In a beard,' he explained. 'Tiens—I have it somewhere.' He fumbled.

With a suddenness that blew away three carnations Dyrakova's voice came back.

'Aieeeeee. . . .'

A dozen pairs of hands covered a dozen pairs of ears.

'It is the last straw. It is more than too much. You plague me. You beseech me. You trick me. All this I might forgive, for you are mad—it is well known. But is it necessary that you bump me all over the road, that you twist me round corners and that you skid me into traffic lights? . . .'

'Mais soyez raisonnable,' pleaded Stroganoff. 'It is but three weeks since I have my carte rose.'

'Imbécile,' screamed Arenskaya. 'Did I not tell you not to drive? It is the miracle there was no accident.' She sat down, overcome by the shock of the narrow escape.

'Poof!' said Stroganoff, his vanity wounded. 'You excite yourself for nothing. Galybchik she tell me I am the driver superb.'

'And is it nothing,' screamed Dyrakova, 'that my reputation it is ruin? My reliability that has always been a password in the ballet. . . .'

'And our Arabesques,' screamed Marya, 'they are the password, too.'

'And was it in Yokohama that your reliability was so evident?' screamed Arenskaya. 'When you go away for two performances with the Minister of War? Or was it in Buenos Aires when? . . .'

'Aiee,' screamed Dyrakova, 'make way all of you while I scratch the eyes out of this creature.'

'And I,' promised Marya, 'scratch out the eyes of Vladimir.' She advanced relentlessly.

A furious bellow distracted her attention. It was Lord Buttonhooke—his party at his heels.

Buttonhooke glared round, found Dyrakova, and planted himself firmly in front of her.

'So there you are?' he accused. 'You false alarm! You dirty double-crosser!'

'Schwolotz,'[1] screamed Dyrakova, concentrating on this new enemy.

'Schwolotz yourself,' retorted Buttonhooke. He did not know what it meant but it sounded good.

Screaming wildly Arenskaya fell on Lord Buttonhooke and pummelled his bulging shirt into better trim.

'How dare you insult our Dyrashka? How dare you come in here and make the noise? You, bezgramotnie,[2] who do not know a brisé from a battement.'

'You flatter him,' said Dyrakova. 'I doubt if he knows a plié from a pirouette.'

Arm in arm Arenskaya and Dyrakova glared their defiance.

Arm in arm Stroganoff and Marya filled the breach.

Arm in arm Galybchik and Quill collapsed on the sofa.

Lord Buttonhooke took a deep breath.

'After this,' he said, 'you need never hope to dance at any

[1] Schwolotz—swine.
[2] Bezgramotnie—illiterate.

theatre of mine. Neither,' he remembered suddenly, 'need you hope to sell me your Otchi Tchernia diamonds.'

'Diamonds,' said Dyrakova. 'He raves of diamonds. Vladimir, my angel, call me the lunatic asylum. This man thinks I would sell him my diamonds—even if I had them. He must be mad.'

'No diamonds!' Sadie Souse made her first contribution to the conversation.

'No diamonds, my child,' said Dyrakova sadly. 'All that is left of them is a studio in Paris. No diamonds—no cars—no bankers—only a tired old woman, seasick and abused.' She burst into tears. Reaction had set in.

Everyone bustled round with handkerchiefs.

Prince Artishok sighed deeply as he edged past Quill towards the door.

'Bang goes six months build-up,' he complained.

'Hey!' said Quill. 'Wait a minute?'

'Impossible,' said the Prince courteously, and passed on.

Useless to shout when everybody was shouting already. Quill jumped up in pursuit. But the Prince had too great a start. By the time Quill had elbowed his way through the hotly disputing throng the Prince was out of sight. What was worse the doorway was blocked by Gustave. Quill grasped him urgently by the shoulder. Gustave shook him off.

'Everybody quiet,' he shouted. 'Nobody to leave the room. Sit down all.'

Quill took a fresh grip.

'Dacarpo. He's gone—after him.'

'Did you not hear me say—sit down?' asked Gustave, all formal. This was to be his big moment and no one was going to rob him of it. 'Did you not hear me order you to sit down?' he bawled at the throng.

Quill appealed to the severe figure by Gustave's side. 'Let me through, please?'

'Silence!' The Sûreté was solid for Gustave.

By this time some sort of order had been restored. Most of the *corps-de-ballet* sat on the floor—the divan had been collared by Dyrakova. Arenskaya and Stroganoff inserted themselves on either side. Buttonhooke paced up and down muttering.

'But you must listen,' Quill argued.

'Make way,' said Gustave, pushing him aside.

Kurt Kukumber strode in. Behind him, far less enthusiastic, was Vanilla. Gustave's godson brought up the rear.

Gustave ran an eagle eye round the room.

'The fat mother, she is not here.'

'She comes,' said the godson reassuringly.

She came—muttering fiercely of a daughter in hysterics and a musical director who . . .

Gallantly Stroganoff offered Madame Ostorojno his seat. Lord Buttonhooke took it.

'Bon,' said Gustave. 'Now we are all here. I commence.'

'Prince Artishok is gone,' said Quill desperately.

'Silence,' said the Sûreté, pained. How right Scotland Yard had been to get rid of this man!

'You ask yourselves,' began Gustave, 'why are we here? I tell you. It is to elucidate the assassinations of Pavlo Citrolo and the Baron de Rabinovitch. In this room there are all the persons associated with the crime.'

'Hey!' said Lord Buttonhooke.

The Sûreté quelled him with a glance.

'Among them is the guilty one. Let him tremble while I, Gustave Clemenceau, trace his guilt!'

Galybchik turned pale.

'Mais qu'est ce que c'est que ça,' screamed Dyrakova suddenly. It had just occurred to her that somebody else was pinching her floor.

The Sûreté dealt faithfully with her.

Amid a stream of interruptions Gustave began his discourse. Gradually he got more and more upset. The scene was not running at all according to script. All day he had been visualizing himself, the centre of an impressed silence, logically weighing each suspect in the balance, relentlessly sifting the evidence until at last the stark form of the murderer stood mercilessly revealed. Instead he was never allowed to complete

a sentence without some interruption. There was the Englishman fidgeting to chase some petty thief of his own. There was
this Russian dancer who seemed to think—I ask you—that she
was the only woman the late Citrolo had ever loved. There
was the man Lord Buttonhooke and the man Stroganoff,
busily conducting some quarrel of their own and paying no
attention to him at all. And there was the fair American who
appeared to have lost some diamonds. Only his murderer
maintained the proper attitude of decorum.

Tiring of his unappreciative audience Gustave decided to
blue-pencil a large chunk of his discourse.

'And so,' he said unexpectedly, 'we are left with only one
person who in each case had the motive, the means, and the
opportunity.'

Quill swore.

'One who knew the secret passage—who was blackmailed by
Citrolo. . . .'

'Not the blackmail,' objected Kurt Kukumber. 'The
collaboration.'

'Silence,' said the Sûreté.

'And,' said Gustave, 'one who had good reason to fear the
tell-tale tongue of the Baron.' With his grimmest expression he
crossed the floor. 'Dino Vanilla, I arrest you for . . .'

'It is a lie,' screamed Vanilla, leaping to his feet.

'It is a lie,' screamed Arenskaya.

'It is a lie,' agreed Quill. 'The actual murderer is by now
well on his way across the frontier.'

It seemed to the Sûreté quite time to find out once and for
all what this Englishman was babbling about.

Quill told him very quickly.

'Banco Dacarpo,' he said, 'alias Prince Alexis Artishok, left
this room just before you came in.'

Banco Dacarpo! That was different.

'Which way?' said the Sûreté and raced out of the room.

* * *

Enquiry revealed that the Prince had made for the waterfront. Further enquiry found honest Jean ruefully rubbing his head. Something had hit him on it very hard, and the launch had gone without him.

But a speed-boat, the stream-lined property of a Culture King from Kansas, bobbed invitingly at their feet.

'Dacarpo is losing his grip,' commented the Sûreté climbing in. Quill leapt after him. Stroganoff a short head behind. Gustave followed laboriously, most of his mind still on the prisoner he had left in charge of his godson. They all turned to help Buttonhooke.

'I drive,' announced Stroganoff hopefully.

The Sûreté pushed him back.

Quill started the engine. The *Pride of Pittsburg* came to life. Like a greyhound, it nosed round a few boats, brushed against a barge or so, and headed for the straight.

Outside it was still choppy.

'Le voilà!' pointed Stroganoff. In the grey dawn a black blur was riding the waves a mile or so ahead.

Quill opened the throttle. The boat shot forward. Stroganoff shot backwards—on to Buttonhooke's lap.

The *Pride of Pittsburg* ate up the distance wave by wave. The black blur solidified. Almost you could see the Union Jack.

On went the *Pride of Pittsburg*. Now you could see Prince Artishok upright at the helm, as debonair as ever and apparently not at all alarmed at his approaching fate. Easily one of the nicest murderers Quill had ever known.

Another few minutes and they would be alongside.

It seemed almost a shame to catch him.

The *Pride of Pittsburg* seemed to think so too. It spluttered, puffed, and petered out.

'Petrol tank punctured,' announced the Sûreté briefly.

The gap between the two boats was widening again. Soon the Prince would be out of sight. The figure was standing up and semaphoring. Laboriously Quill spelt out the message:

P . A . L . O . O . K . A . S .

Banco Dacarpo had not lost his grip.

CHAPTER XVIII

'I REFUSE to believe he was a card-sharper,' protested Button-hooke, 'why I played pinochle with him every night for three months and never lost.'

'Maybe we have a little game sometime?' asked Stroganoff hopefully.

With Buttonhooke and a downcast Gustave at the oars, the *Pride of Pittsburg* nosed its way slowly towards the harbour. Dacarpo would be well over the frontier before the wires could get busy.

'The capture of a lifetime,' sighed the Sûreté. 'Right through our fingers.'

'Why we chase him?' Gustave asked plaintively. He had not been told.

'It is Banco Dacarpo,' explained the Sûreté, and Gustave was impressed. Even he had heard the name.

'He disguise himself as the Prince,' said Stroganoff. 'This is clever. And Button'ooke he feed him for many months. This is funny.'

Lord Buttonhooke caught a crab.

A sudden apprehension seized Gustave. 'Is it possible that Dacarpo is our assassin?'

'Is it?' asked the Sûreté.

'There's no doubt about it,' said Quill. 'I realized it the moment I heard Dyrakova no longer possessed the Otchi Tchernia diamonds. It made everything clear.'

'Damned if it does,' muttered Buttonhooke. 'What on earth was the fellow up to trying to make me buy a necklace that wasn't there? And all this stuff about not talking to Dyrakova?'

'As pretty a swindle as ever I met,' said Quill. 'And beautifully simple—once he had won your confidence as Prince Artishok. It was easy for him to persuade Sadie she wanted the necklace. It was not difficult for Sadie to persuade you to buy it for her. Insert the story of a Dyrakova, so proud that she would only discuss money with blue blood—and there he was—the accredited intermediary. Wasn't it drummed into you that you were on no account to mention diamonds to Dyrakova—only to produce the money—ready money?'

Lord Buttonhooke groaned.

'With the vendor and the purchaser not on bartering terms, the Prince had only to wait a suitable moment to tell Buttonhooke he had clinched the deal, produce some convincing imitation from his pocket, collect the ready money, ostensibly to take to Dyrakova, and make his getaway while the ballerina danced. The Otchi Tchernia are well known and Dyrakova is above suspicion.'

Lord Buttonhooke groaned again.

'But the murders,' objected the Sûreté, 'Dacarpo has never been a killer.'

'Dacarpo,' said Quill, 'was a swindler by profession—but a murderer by accident. A man pierced his disguise. Pavlo Citrolo, the blackmailer, the man with the uncanny memory for details, recognized him. It was an unfortunate recognition for Citrolo, especially as I can prove he had no intention of blackmailing in such a dangerous quarter. His note-book tells us that he did not blackmail big shots. It says that he tried it only once and barely got away with his life. It is probable that the one attempt was on Dacarpo though we shall never know for certain.'

'But Dacarpo could not guess Citrolo's prudence. He only knew that he had been recognized by a blackmailer and he was worried. I doubt if he decided then and there to murder Citrolo. But when chance—or rather our friend Stroganoff—put him in his way, drugged in a deserted room . . .'

'It was the mistake to leave him there,' said Stroganoff gravely. 'I see now. I should have take him to the hotel.'

'But why,' demanded Gustave, reluctant to relinquish his

Vanilla, 'must it be Dacarpo who murder? There were many others in the office that night.'

'Quite,' said the Sûreté.

'The second murder proves that,' said Quill. 'The Baron was not killed until Dacarpo knew that he had been told of the impending diamond deal. As a matter of fact,' he admitted, 'I told him myself—I did not suspect him at the time. The Baron sent for him while we were all watching the ballet at the Buttonhooke Casino and demanded a show-down. Dacarpo might bluff Lord Buttonhooke that he was on the level but Rabinovitch was too much of a crook himself not to recognize another. I should think that Dacarpo probably offered him a share but the Baron's strange loyalty to Buttonhooke precluded his accepting. So Dacarpo poisoned him. Once you have committed one murder for an object, another murder comes easier.'

Lord Buttonhooke sighed heavily. He grieved for his murdered admirer, he grieved for his reputation as a shrewd business-man, but most of all he grieved because he would now have to give Sadie Souse *carte blanche* at Cartier's.

The *Pride of Pittsburg* nosed its way slowly towards anchorage.

A frustrated sun peered through the clouds. All the really interesting things seemed to happen while it was asleep.

ENVOI

'My marrows,' said Gustave proudly, 'Regardez! Nothing like this at St. Petersburg!'

It was a week since the weary row back. Quill on the point of departure had come to make his farewells.

'I trust,' said the courteous Gustave, 'that you have enjoyed your holiday.' He straightened himself wearily. 'I, too, hope to take a holiday soon. The long holiday.'

'Retiring?' asked Quill.

'Bientôt,' said Gustave. 'I tire of the life of crime. I have ma petite rente and but yesterday I bought the gold-shares that will soon add butter to my petit-pain.'

'Gold shares?' said Quill, startled.

'You have heard?' said Gustave. 'It was the good Kukumber himself who selected them for me. Now I have but to wait for the rise. . . .'

Quill left him waiting and ran back to the *Hôtel Moins-Magnifique*.

But he was too late. Kurt Kukumber had not slept in his bed at the hotel that night.

'The management wait two days,' said the clerk, 'and then we are ruthless. If his uncle do not come by then we open the box.'

* * *

The smoking-room of the S.S. *Transatlantic* displayed a notice:

> 'Passengers are warned against the menace of professional gamblers making the crossing.'

223

Feeling vaguely proud, Kurt Kukumber lit a cigar and strode off to make friends on the promenade deck.

*   *   *

'What you think!' Stroganoff pounced on Quill as he entered the office to say good-bye. 'The news stupendous. This morning I receive an offer superb from Bolivia for my ballet.'

'One night stands,' said Galybchik, not too enthusiastically.

'But the money it is good,' said Stroganoff. 'Most of it. Me and my ballet sail immediate. Already I argue with the steamship company for the credit.'

'And the Casino?' asked Quill.

'The Casino—poof!' said Stroganoff. 'For some days already it bore me. We sell—doubtless for the profit immense.'

*   *   *

The newspaper Quill bought at Dover carried an advertisement.

CASINO FOR SALE
The opportunity that tempts
Apply in haste to:
Vladimir Stroganoff
Poste-Restante
Bolivia

THE HOGARTH PRESS

This is a paperback list for today's readers – but it holds to a tradition of adventurous and original publishing set by Leonard and Virginia Woolf when they founded The Hogarth Press in 1917 and started their first paperback series in 1924.

Some of the books are light-hearted, some serious, and include Fiction, Lives and Letters, Travel, Critics, Poetry, History and Hogarth Crime and Gaslight Crime.

A list of our books already published, together with some of our forthcoming titles, follows. If you would like more information about Hogarth Press books, write to us for a catalogue:

30 Bedford Square, London WC1B 3RP

Please send a large stamped addressed envelope

HOGARTH FICTION

Behind A Mask: The Unknown Thrillers of Louisa May Alcott
Edited and Introduced by Madeleine Stern

The Amazing Test Match Crime by Adrian Alington
New Introduction by Brian Johnston

As We Are by E. F. Benson
New Introduction by T. J. Binyon
Dodo – An Omnibus by E. F. Benson
New Introduction by Prunella Scales
The Freaks of Mayfair by E. F. Benson
New Introduction by Christopher Hawtree
Mrs Ames by E. F. Benson
Paying Guests by E. F. Benson
Secret Lives by E. F. Benson
New Introductions by Stephen Pile

A Bullet in the Ballet by Caryl Brahms and S. J. Simon
No Bed for Bacon by Caryl Brahms and S. J. Simon
New Introductions by Ned Sherrin

A Day in Summer by J. L. Carr
New Introduction by D. J. Taylor

Ballantyne's Folly by Claud Cockburn
New Introduction by Andrew Cockburn
Beat the Devil by Claud Cockburn
New Introduction by Alexander Cockburn

Such is Life by Tom Collins
New Introduction by David Malouf

Extraordinary Women by Compton Mackenzie
New Introduction by Andro Linklater
Vestal Fire by Compton Mackenzie
New Introduction by Sally Beauman

Morte D'Urban by J. F. Powers
Prince of Darkness & other stories by J. F. Powers
New Introductions by Mary Gordon
The Presence of Grace by J. F. Powers
New Introduction by Paul Bailey

HOGARTH CRIME

The Beckoning Lady by Margery Allingham
Cargo of Eagles by Margery Allingham
The China Governess by Margery Allingham
Hide My Eyes by Margery Allingham

Dead Mrs Stratton by Anthony Berkeley

The Smiler with the Knife by Nicholas Blake

Words for Murder, Perhaps by Edward Candy

Inspector French's Greatest Case by Freeman Wills Crofts

Suicide Excepted by Cyril Hare

The Baffle Book: A Parlour Game of Mystery and Detection
edited by F. Tennyson Jesse

Death by Request by Romilly and Katherine John

Laurels Are Poison by Gladys Mitchell
The Rising of the Moon by Gladys Mitchell
The Saltmarsh Murders by Gladys Mitchell
When Last I Died by Gladys Mitchell

The Hand in the Glove by Rex Stout

GASLIGHT CRIME

Madame Midas by Fergus Hume
The Mystery of a Hansom Cab by Fergus Hume
New Introductions by Stephen Knight

Caryl Brahms and S. J. Simon

A Bullet in the Ballet

New Introduction by Ned Sherrin

'One of the funniest books I have ever read' –
Andrew Lloyd Webber

Never has such an incompetent ballet company taken the
stage. Most unprofessional is Petroushka, who drops
dead in the middle of the performance. Inspector Adam
Quill arrives to investigate, and discovers a cast of lunatic
suspects waiting in the wings: Vladimir Stroganoff,
impresario *extraordinaire*; Madame Arenskaya, mistress
(of the ballet); protective mothers puffing up their little
cygnets. All these (and more) could have done it.

In a gale of laughter, Brahms and Simon blow away the
pretensions of the world of dance and the staid conventions of the detective novel. – here is 'a book for anyone
who wants to roll helplessly in the aisles'
(Alan Coren, editor of *Punch*).

Caryl Brahms and S. J. Simon

No Bed for Bacon

New Introduction by Ned Sherrin

'A great joy' – John Mortimer

Five o'clock, and all's well in Merrie England. But not for long. Good Queen Bess is stirring in her four-poster and is feeling neither happy nor glorious. Down at the Globe, Will Shakespeare is chewing the end of his quill: something's amiss with *Love's Labours Wunne*. And Walter Raleigh is very hot under the collar of his latest cloak as he boils his new potato – will it achieve the perfect fluffiness for The Royal Tasting? Beautifully written, uproarious comedy, *No Bed for Bacon* is a trivial pursuit through Elizabethan England – a book for all scholars of Shakespeare, history and merriment alike.

E.F. Benson
Paying Guests

New Introduction Stephen Pile

Bolton Spa is infamous for its nauseating brine and parsimonious boarding-houses. Exceptional is the Wentworth. Every summer this luxurious establishment is full of paying guests come to sample the waters and happy family atmosphere. But life in the house is far from a rest-cure. Acrimony and arthritis are the order of the day: battles are fought with pedometer, walking stick and paintbrush, at the bridge table, the town concert and afternoon tea. The trials and tribulations of the Wentworth will be relished in drawing-rooms throughout the land for years to come.

Compton Mackenzie
Extraordinary Women

New Introduction by Andro Linklater

Rory Freemantle of the Villa Leucadia stands out even among the colourful women who have settled on enchanted Sirene. Smitten by the sight of the divine, raffish Rosalba, she throws caution to the winds and sets off in pursuit through a series of terrible parties, horrendous scenes and social disasters on the grandest of scales. *Extraordinary Women* – in which all the characters are portraits of the personalities, like Radclyffe Hall and Romaine Brooks, who haunted Capri during World War I – is Mackenzie's hilarious, affectionate celebration of the years when Lesbos floated into the Mediterranean.

'a delicious, durable book. . . a masterpiece of gentle satire, wit, and pervading unbitchiness' – Mary Renault

Adrian Alington
The Amazing Test Match Crime

New Introduction by Brian Johnston

England is agog as the final test match against Australia draws near, but no village in the land has the fate of the Ashes closer to its heart than Wattlecombe Ducis, the home of Norman Blood, captain of England. Another local hero, Joe Prestwick, just needs to be selected for the vicar's radiant daughter, Monica, to marry him: everything depends on the Test. But planning to strike a blow at the very heart of proud Albion and her Empire are The Bad Men, Europe's most wanted gang.

A wicked yet affectionate comedy of cricketing (and criminal) manners, *The Amazing Test Match Crime* demonstrates that a straight bat and a nimble spinning finger will always win through.

Anthony Berkeley
Dead Mrs Stratton

'Give Roger Sheringham his three chief interests in life, and he is perfectly happy – criminology, human nature and good beer.'

At a fancy-dress party Murderers and Victims dance beneath a mock gallows. But the revelry takes a sinister turn as a real victim is discovered, and when the local constabulary declare Sheringham their chief suspect, the case becomes by far the most dangerous of the illustrious detective's career.

Dead Mrs Stratton is one of Anthony Berkeley's most exciting and entertaining novels, and he brings to it all the wit and irony that helped establish his international reputation for original crime writing.